Wildflower

ALECIA WHITAKER

poppy

Little, Brown and Company
New York   Boston

Poppy

Hachette Book Group
237 Park Avenue, New York, NY 10017
Visit us at lb-teens.com

Poppy is an imprint of Little, Brown and Company.
The Poppy name and logo are trademarks of Hachette Book Group, Inc.

The publisher is not responsible for websites (or their content)
that are not owned by the publisher.

First Edition: July 2014

Wildflower was conceived by Kathryn Williams
and developed by Aerial Publishing LLC.

Library of Congress Cataloging-in-Publication Data

Whitaker, Alecia.
Wildflower / by Alecia Whitaker. — First edition.
pages cm
"Poppy."
Summary: "Sixteen-year-old Bird Barrett is discovered by a country music record label while playing in her family's bluegrass band. As her star rises, she must learn to stay true to her roots while navigating a brave new world of glamour and gold records in Nashville, Tennessee"— Provided by publisher.
ISBN 978-0-316-25138-9 (hardcover) — ISBN 978-0-316-25136-5 (ebook)
[1. Musicians—Fiction. 2. Country music—Fiction. 3. Family life—Fiction. 4. Dating (Social customs)—Fiction. 5. Fame—Fiction. 6. Nashville (Tenn.)—Fiction.] I. Title.
PZ7.W57684Wil 2014   [Fic]—dc23   2013023693

10 9 8 7 6 5 4 3 2 1

RRD-C

Printed in the United States of America

This one's for Mamaw and Papaw

1

"Bird!" Jacob whispers urgently over the music.

I snap out of my trance and turn toward my older brother, wondering why he's standing so close, with his upright bass practically leaning on my shoulder. All five of us are squished onto a tiny platform in some hole-in-the-wall, no-name honky-tonk, so I'd appreciate it if he could give me a little room to work. I shoot him an annoyed look.

"Take us home, Bird," my dad calls into the mic. He always says that at the end of our encore number. It's kind of our thing, but when our eyes meet, I see what he's really trying to tell me: I missed my cue.

Whoops.

My family loops back around for my entrance, and this time I'm ready. I tuck my fiddle up under my chin and raise my bow. We're playing "Will She Ever Call," a Barrett Family Band favorite. When we took to the road seven years ago, playing festivals, fairs, and honky-tonks, and joining jam sessions wherever we could, nobody had heard of the Barretts. We certainly didn't have a following. Now, it never ceases to amaze me when the crowd starts singing along.

I send my bow flying as I focus on my solo. In country music, or any kind really, the vocalist takes the melody and everyone is there to round out the sound and play accompaniment. But during a bluegrass song, every musician gets a crack at the melody—to improvise and make it his or her own. On a lightning-fast song like this one, we throw the melody back and forth between us, like playing Hot Potato.

"Yah!" my dad yells into the mic. "Yip!"

The stage shakes with our collective foot stomping. This isn't the first time I've missed a cue, and I'll probably catch flack for it later. I could blame the repetition of a musician's life on the road—when you know the set by rote, it's easy to go into autopilot. For example, this song, "Will She Ever Call": I wrote it, and could play it in my sleep.

But my real problem is people watching. Maybe a couple is having an argument in a corner booth, or maybe the bartender gets fancy and juggles bottles as he pours drinks. Or in this case, maybe a super hot and really talented boy walks into the honky-tonk, and maybe he perches himself on a stool and hangs his cowboy hat on his knee, which just happens to start pumping up and down in rhythm to a song that *I* wrote, and maybe he grins this little lopsided smile and throws us a short wave and then runs his long fingers through his dark brown hair that isn't necessarily long but could certainly use a trim, and then maybe, *maybe*, he starts to sing along even.... Well then, *seriously*! How's a girl supposed to focus?

I'll never admit it to my family, but I missed my cue today because Adam Dean is here. I've had a crush on him ever since we first saw him play a couple of years ago, and every time our paths cross, my pulse beats double time.

Meeting super talented musicians like Adam is one of the best parts about life on the road. The Barrett Family Band may never have First Family of Country Music status like the Carters, but we do okay traveling from show to show in Winnie, our RV.

My life is anything but normal, but honestly, I couldn't imagine it any other way. I'm homeschooled, so I don't have to deal with difficult teachers or mean girls, and I somehow got ahead and will "graduate" a year early. I've been to most of the continental United States, and that's not half bad, considering that I just turned sixteen. But what I love most is that this on-the-road lifestyle means my family is extra close. You have to be when you share two hundred square feet of RV living space—and when you depend on one another to keep a song on track.

"Yah!" my dad shouts, picking at his banjo as if his thumbs are on fire. I angle myself toward him on the small stage and we duel, the room ablaze. My mom is nearly laughing as she strums her mandolin, and my brothers are obviously enjoying it, too.

I love this. I love playing. I love music. I love these magical moments during a show that set my whole body on tilt. I may miss my cue from time to time, but my music means everything to me.

I stomp out the beat, shooting the bow over the strings like a maniac, the adrenaline racing through my veins as I play. Adam is here. I close my eyes and feel fused to my fiddle, breathing hard, breathing the music. I want to talk to him after the show, but I know my parents are going to want to break down and head right out. We play Nashville next, which is a pretty long drive from Kansas City, and my dad doesn't like to cut gigs too close. If I'd known Adam was going to be here, I wouldn't have been lazy on the third number and I certainly wouldn't have pulled my hair back into a sloppy bun in the greenroom while we waited to come back onstage for the encore.

"Haw!" my dad yells.

Play harder; play faster; play, Bird, play.

Ah, yeah! I fling the bow across the strings, let the fiddle fall to my side, and throw my head back. I'm exhausted. I'm exhilarated. I'm *alive.*

The small crowd applauds as we hit our last note, leaving everybody to wonder if, in fact, the girl will ever call, and I line up with my family for our final bow. Dylan gives me a strong pat on the back, and my dad reaches over and squeezes my shoulder.

"Thank you, everybody!" he calls into the mic. "We're the Barrett Family Band, and it's always great to play here. Y'all get home safe now." He waves as he leads us offstage, and I grin. My dad treats every show as if we were playing to a sold-out arena.

"You see Adam?" Jacob asks behind me as we file offstage.

"Uh-huh," I say, eager to get back to the greenroom. I want to put my fiddle away, put on lip gloss and a spray of body mist, and head back out to the bar ASAP. I don't want him to leave before I get a chance to say hi.

"He said there's a field party tonight," Jacob continues.

"You talked to him?" I ask, as nonchalantly as possible. The last thing I need is for either of my brothers to know about my crush on Adam.

"No, he e-mailed me earlier," he answers. Adam and Dylan are both nineteen. But Adam and Jacob, who's two years younger, are better friends.

In the greenroom, I plop down on the lumpy red sofa, feeling like I could pass out. The fact that the couch is about a hundred years old and patched together with duct tape doesn't make me feel good about its cleanliness, but at this point, I'm exhausted and what's one more butt? Jacob, on the other hand, is a tad OCD. He avoids touching anything in any of the "dressing rooms" that these dives provide their performers. He grabs a cloth from his gig bag and stands next to me, polishing his bass before putting it away.

I lean down, drag my own case over, and pop it open, eager to get my fiddle, Maybelle, safely back in her home. I named her after Mother Maybelle Carter, a country music legend, and even though I may not shine her up the second a show is over, I love my fiddle just as much as Jacob loves his bass. She's the most precious thing I own. About once a month, I have this recurring nightmare where I forget to put Maybelle away after a show and my dad steps on her, snapping her neck right off. I shudder just thinking about it.

"Scoot," Dylan commands, flopping down onto the couch next to me.

"Hey!" I holler, ducking. The neck of his guitar misses my head by an inch. He carelessly lays it on the carpet. Jacob shakes his head but, as usual, says nothing.

Dylan's one of those guys who can get away with anything. He's got that clean-cut, all-American-boy thing going. He has blue eyes and strawberry-blond hair, just like me. He's not quite as tall as I am—few people are— but I can objectively say that he's handsome. He can flash his big smile and get whatever he wants. And where I'm a little reserved when I first meet people, he's never known a stranger. It's hard having a perfect older brother. I mean, at least Jacob dyes his blond hair black and wants a tattoo as soon as he turns eighteen (which, for the record, drives my parents crazy). But it seems like Dylan never takes a wrong step (which, we might as well add to the record, drives Jacob and me crazy).

"A couple of guys up front were staring at you, Bird," Dylan says uneasily. "Don't make eye contact when we're breaking down, okay? And holler if you need me."

I nod, which seems to satisfy him, and then he leans back against the couch and closes his eyes. I look at Jacob and roll my own. The thing about Mr. Perfect is that he's overprotective to the point where I sometimes want to pull my hair out.

"Let's get to it, kids. Your father's going to settle with the booker, and we've got to get packed up." My mom rolls a cart over to Jacob, who arranges his bass on it first and then loads up Dad's banjo and Mom's mandolin. He even puts Dylan's guitar in its case before adding it to the stack. He knows better than to ask for Maybelle, though—I always put her away myself. Another fear I have is her falling off the cart or getting left behind. Not on my watch.

Jacob throws his backpack over one shoulder and rolls the instrument cart toward the door. He pauses at the mirror, examining his choppy new haircut and sweeping over the top section that's a little too long in my opinion, before leaving. Normally, I would give him a hard time for checking himself out, but I know I'm going to see Adam in a minute and want to assess my own appearance. I grab my purse and walk over to the mirror, thankful that my skin looks pretty good. I'm only breaking out in one tiny spot, but it's up at my hairline and as soon as I take down the god-awful bun—voilà! Bye-bye, zit. I search for a tube of pink, vanilla-flavored lip gloss and swipe some on. There. Better already.

"Who are you getting dolled up for?" Dylan asks, smirking.

I make a face at him in the mirror. "My lips are chapped. I needed some gloss...if that's okay with you." If Dylan discovered my crush on Adam, he'd never let me live it down. I toss the gloss back into my purse and grab a fresh tank top from my bag. "Close your eyes."

"Gladly."

I do a lightning-quick change, throwing my sweaty T-shirt into my purse, but before I tell Dylan he can open his eyes again, I spritz myself with body spray and hightail it out of the room. I'm not in the mood for any postshow interrogation.

I walk down the dimly lit hallway and pass through the thin curtain that lines the back of the small, low stage, purposefully keeping my eyes on my feet. My heart is racing.

It's torture trying to play it cool. I grab the mic case and pop it open center stage before finally looking up to smile at Adam.

And then my heart stops. His stool is empty. He's gone.

I stand up and put my hand over my eyes, frantically scanning the room. So much for playing it cool.

It's dark and hard for my eyes to adjust, but as the shadows give way to shapes, I see couples cuddling, a few guys at the pool table, and the regulars at the bar. The neon Budweiser and Pabst Blue Ribbon signs glare red and blue over the dartboards, and a waitress lifts a tray of greasy bar food above her head. Still, no sign of Adam. I spot my dad up front being paid by Rex, the Santa-bearded booker, and I know from the size of the rubber-banded envelope that our cut for the night will only cover us until our next stop. I see Jacob's lanky figure weaving through the bar, but he's alone, and then I feel the stage creak as Dylan joins me.

"Who are you looking for?" he asks, squinting in the direction I'm looking.

"Jacob," I lie, bending over the speakers and unplugging the mic cords.

I can't believe Adam left. Maybe he had to do something. Or maybe he just went to the bathroom. And then my heart really sinks: Maybe he left to meet up with a girl at that party.

Incredibly disappointed, I go through my nightly routine:

unplugging mics, coiling their cords, and packing them safely into the cases. Dylan hefts a speaker onto one shoulder, and Jacob follows behind him with another heavy load on the cart.

I look up just as a woman old enough to be my grandmother shuffles to the edge of the stage. "You really are something special, girl," she says in a scratchy voice. Her glassy eyes suggest she's had one too many beers tonight, but it still cheers me up.

I smile. "Thank you."

"I mean it," she continues, reaching out for my forearm. I tell myself she's squeezing me in a maternal, assuring way, but more likely she's just steadying herself. "Lordy, you make that bow fly! Just fly!"

"That's why they call her Bird," a low voice says to my right.

And from out of nowhere, a long arm falls across my shoulders and the most beautiful smile in the world is inches from my cheek. I look over at Adam and my breath catches in my throat. Here's one advantage to my being so tall: We're the same height and our faces are close enough that I can see his tiny widow's peak and the stubble on his jaw. He smells amazing, like fresh laundry.

"Our Bird just flies on the fiddle," he says, squeezing my shoulder.

My cheeks burn.

"That she does," the old woman agrees, letting go of her grip on me, her eyes twinkling. "That she does. I really enjoyed it, sweetheart."

"Thank you," I say again. She nods and shuffles away, her compliment and Adam's the best I've gotten in a long time.

"Need some help?" he asks, dropping his arm and nodding toward the stage. I already miss the warmth of his touch, but at least I feel like I can breathe again. That boy shakes me upside down and inside out.

"Yes!" I say, recovering, a little louder than I'd meant.

"Oh-kay!" Adam shouts, teasing me. I can't help but smile.

My brothers come back, and Dylan greets Adam warmly. "What's up, dude? Thanks for coming."

"Definitely," Adam says. "Nice set tonight."

"Hey, man," Jacob says enthusiastically, leaning in for a bro hug. "Sorry we can't make it to that party with you. Next time."

"For sure," Adam says.

Once the stage is clear, my brothers push the cart out toward Winnie again. Usually this is the time when Mom and I work the crowd, passing out cheesy postcards with our website, pictures, and upcoming tour information, but tonight, with Adam standing right next to me, I think I'm going to "forget."

"You still passionate about fountain Coke?" Adam asks me mock-seriously.

I faux frown. "Does Bon Jovi live on a prayer?"

He laughs out loud. "Absolutely!"

I grin, feeling pretty proud of myself. I've been saving that one up.

Adam claps his hands and says, "Let's do this." He's talking about our ongoing pursuit of the best fountain Coke in America.

He steps off the stage, and I notice that there's a little dried mud caked on the side of his cowboy boots. I love that. Adam doesn't sing about country life while wearing designer jeans and a rhinestone-encrusted belt buckle. He's legit, actually from the country, a Southern boy with *heartland* written all over him.

He surprises me by turning back to offer his hand, and I'm almost caught staring. I can't look him in the eye as I reach out and take it. His palm is rough but warm. My arm turns to jelly. Of course he drops my hand as soon as I step down, so it was more of a gentlemanly gesture than a romantic one. Still, as I follow him to the bar a gigantic smile works its way across my face.

"Don," Adam shouts, beating out a little rhythm with his hands on the bar. The skinny, middle-aged bartender turns his attention to us. "Two Coca-Cola Classics, please. Lots of ice."

"You got it."

Adam fishes out a folded piece of white paper from his wallet, along with a five-dollar bill. He slaps the money on the bar. I don't even try to pay anymore.

"So anything beat Cookeville?" I ask, peering over his arm.

Adam unfolds the tiny piece of paper with the logo from a Red Roof Inn in Decatur, Georgia, at the top and scans it. I always like to glance over his list, just to see the places he's been. "Nope. Cookeville's still the champ."

In our opinion, Coke is great from a can, still good from a bottle, yet hard to get just right from the fountain. But oh, when they do get it right, it tastes good enough to be an eighth wonder of the world. My brothers think our quest is totally lame, but I love it. It means that when we're not together, Adam thinks of me, or at least of our game, and then when we are together, he always remembers.

"Where's your list?" he asks.

I tap my temple. "All up here."

He cocks an eyebrow. "So anything top Cookeville for you?"

I want to tell him that the Coke was better in Shreveport and then even better in Chattanooga and still better in Cincinnati. I want to tell him that it was pretty great in Des Moines, which was the last time our paths crossed, and that here, in Kansas City, it will surely be the best I've ever had. Because as Don sets our ice-cold Coca-Colas on napkins in front of us, Adam looks amazing in his frayed-at-the-collar red-plaid button-down, and because every time I see him, everything around me is just a bazillion times better.

Instead, I shake my head and bite my tongue. I hold up my Coke, and Adam's hazel eyes meet mine as our glasses clink. "Here's to Kansas City," I say.

"Here's hoping."

We stare at each other in earnest, treating this moment as if it were a matter of national security, and take big swigs.

It's awful. No fizz, totally flat, watered down—basically what I'd expected from a bar soda. Adam obviously agrees with me since his face is twisted up as if he's consumed rat poison. "That," he says, pointing down at his glass, "is the worst Coke I've ever tasted."

"I'm guessing that Cookeville can breathe easy at number one, then?" I ask, grinning.

"Oh, yeah," he says, pushing his glass away. He looks over his list. "This is even worse than Allentown."

"*No*," I argue. "Allentown was pretty bad."

"Bird, *this* is pretty bad." Then, as if to prove it, he takes another swig. He immediately spits it back out. "Oh my God, why'd you let me do that again?"

I laugh until my eyes water. Who says a guy can't be smokin' hot, musically inspiring, *and* funny?

"So," Adam says, smiling at me as he leans on his forearms. "Have you written any new songs lately?"

The answer is yes, but I fib. "Nothing special," I say, shrugging. The truth is, I've written lots of songs Adam's never heard and never will because they're almost all about him.

"Bird!" Jacob hollers, coming back into the bar. Adam and I jerk away from each other instinctively. "Dad's already got Winnie fired up. He's itching to get out of here, so let's go." Then to Adam, he offers his fist and says, "Later, man."

"Later," Adam responds, bumping it with his own. "Y'all drive safe. Kentucky next?"

"Nashville."

"Sweet, sweet. I'm headed to Topeka, but I'm sure I'll catch y'all at some point," Adam says. And then he looks at me. "So can we both agree? Cookeville?"

I smile. "Cookeville."

"Oh, God," Jacob says, shaking his head. "Not the Coke thing again."

Bristling, I flick him in the biceps.

"Ow!" He grabs his arm, then looks up at Adam. "Be glad you're an only child. Little sisters are a pain."

Adam chuckles and follows us through the bar toward the front. I was on such a high only moments ago, but now, thanks to Jacob, I'm embarrassed. Every time I think Adam might like me the way I like him, I start to wonder whether he's just humoring me. Or whether he only thinks of me as a friend, or, even worse, an adopted little sister. But I can't let that be how we part ways, so once Jacob walks out the door, I take a breath and turn around to face Adam, feeling almost brave.

"That's not why they call me Bird, you know," I say, determined to give the art of flirting my best shot.

"What?"

"Earlier. With that woman. She said I fly on the fiddle, and you said that's why they call me Bird, but that's not why."

Adam grins and leans one arm against the door frame. "Okay, then. I've honestly always wanted to know. Why do they call you Bird?"

"It's after Lady Bird Johnson."

"Who?" Adam asks.

I've come to expect that question.

"President Lyndon B. Johnson's wife," I explain. "First Lady Lady Bird."

"That's a lot of 'ladies,' " he says, grinning. "And that's kind of random."

I laugh. "Well, my mom and dad met in college in Texas, and Lady Bird was from there," I say, trying not to shift awkwardly in place under Adam's gaze. "She loved wildflowers, had them planted all along the country's highways. There's even some big wildflower center named after her. It's where my dad proposed to my mom since she loves flowers. So they named me Bird."

"Huh," Adam says, nodding. "I always figured you were named after that Lynyrd Skynyrd song."

I realize that would probably be a cooler story, and I feel pretty nerdy for being named after a dead president's wife, but I like my name. Always have. So I decide to own it. I am who I am.

"Nope," I say. "Not because I'm a fast fiddler. Not because of a legendary rock song. Because of Lady Bird Johnson."

He looks wounded. "Tell me that Dylan at least is named after Bob," he teases. "I have to be able to look your dad in the eye next time I see him."

"Ha-ha," I say dryly.

A guy bumps into me, and I realize I'm blocking the door, so I step closer to Adam, letting the guy pass. "Well, name or nickname," he says, "I've always thought it was perfect for you. I mean, that old lady was right, Bird. You fly."

I blush.

"Seriously," he continues, "you kill it onstage, and your solos are the best part of every Barrett Family song." I smile broadly, feeling warm from head to toe. Then he touches my arm and leans in conspiratorially. "Don't tell your brothers I said that."

His green-flecked brown eyes twinkle, and we laugh together, easy and light. He opens the door for me, and I say good-bye, practically floating over to where my family waits in our Winnebago. And I can't tell you if my feet actually touch the ground, because at this very moment, this Bird, well, she flies.

2

CLICK.

Everything goes dark.

Annoyed with Jacob, who keeps clicking off my bed light, I sigh mightily and turn it back on. The minute we got back into the RV, I propped myself up with pillows on the bottom bunk and pulled my journal out from my pillow-case. I had to add Kansas City to my list of Best and Worst Fountain Cokes in America before I forgot a single detail. It may have tasted terrible, but Adam was there to drink it with me, which moves it straight to the top, in my opinion. Once that was done, I had to scribble out this song that's been rattling around in my head about all the sweet things I love to eat and how a boy's first kiss is even sweeter. At least,

I assume that's what it's like. And after that, I grabbed my laptop to update the Barrett Family Band's Twitter feed:

> Awesome show tonight. Thanks KC & all who came out 2 Buckle Bar! Good to see @adamdean! BFB in Nashville next. #bluegrassbarretts

Now I'm organizing my music library, searching for "Free Bird" and completely baffled that my music collection has zero Lynyrd Skynyrd. As a music buff, I pride myself on having a little bit of everything. Old bluegrass stuff: Earl Scruggs, the Stanley Brothers. Classic country: Patsy Cline, Waylon Jennings. New country: George Strait, the Dixie Chicks. Current country: Lady Antebellum, Carrie Underwood. Recently I've gotten into alt-country: Ryan Adams and the Drive-By Truckers. And, of course, I love my singer-songwriters like Alison Krauss and Emmylou Harris. Then there's my guilty-pleasure music, the pop stuff they play on the radio that Dylan, and especially Jacob, can't stand.

But no Lynyrd Skynyrd. *And you call yourself a music lover*, I chide myself, shaking my head as I download their *Complete Collection* album. It's twenty freaking bucks, but my library obviously needs it. I click BUY, thankful once again for that iTunes gift card Gramma got me for my birthday.

"Bird, you're killing me. Turn it off," Jacob grumbles from the top bunk, reaching his arm down to switch off my light again. It's after midnight and if my folks hear him, I'll definitely have to pack it up, so I relent.

"Fine," I say, exasperated. I scoot out of bed and carry my computer over to the sleeper sofa, banging into the wall as Dad hits a pothole. Dylan is still awake, the glow from his phone lighting his face in the otherwise dark RV. "Jacob's being a jerk," I whisper. "Can I sit here?"

He shrugs and moves his legs over to give me a little room. He doesn't even look up, his thumbs racing across the screen and his brow deeply creased.

"Who are you texting?" I ask nosily.

He sets his jaw as he finishes his text, tosses the phone down, and puts his hands over his face, letting out an enormous sigh.

"Whitney," he finally says, running his hands through his hair. He collapses back against the pillows and looks up at me. "She broke up with me last month, right?"

"Right," I say guardedly. *That* was not a good time to be trapped in a small space with my brother.

"And now she's sending me these random texts about the last town her family visited and where they're going next and asking if we're going to be in Nashville the same time they are."

"Are we?"

I liked Whitney and everything, but she did break my brother's heart, so she'll have to forgive me if I'm not exactly eager for the two of them to reunite.

"No," he says. "But that's not the point. The point," he says angrily, picking up his phone and gesturing dramatically with it, "is that she broke up with me. She doesn't want to be my girlfriend, so why does she send me these texts like she wants to see me again?"

"Maybe she wants to still be friends?" I answer, although it comes out more like a question.

"I don't need a friend!"

I throw my hands up defensively.

"Kids," my dad calls sternly from the driver's seat. I look up and meet his eyes in the rearview mirror. He points to the green digital-clock numbers on the radio, which clearly read 12:23 AM. "Lights out."

"Sorry, Bird," Dylan says as I close my computer and start to get up. "I didn't mean to take it out on you. This girl just drives me crazy."

"I know," I say. "But you guys used to be such good friends."

He sighs heavily. "Yeah, that's what sucks the most about all of this." He stops and looks away, so angry and sad at the same time. "I don't know. I want her back. But I don't."

I nod. I don't have much (any) relationship experience, so I know I'm probably not the best resource for my brother in the love department, but life on the road means he doesn't have many other options. And as far as that goes, neither do I. I could use some advice on the whole Adam situation. I mean, I think he might like me, but how can I know for sure? And then what if we do get together and it doesn't work out and we ruin *our* friendship? My brothers could give me the male perspective, but then Dylan would tease me endlessly or, even worse, Jacob could forbid it on the grounds that Adam's his best friend. But it's hard to make girlfriends on the road, so all I'm left with is my brothers.

"Do you ever wish you'd just stayed friends?" I ask him delicately.

"I don't know." He shrugs. "Maybe. But then, when we were together, she made me really happy, you know?"

"So you don't regret it, then."

"I guess not."

"And you guys were friends for years," I prod further. "So what changed?" He looks at me questioningly. "I mean, what made you finally ask her out?"

"It was after that bonfire at Tybee Island," he answers. "She kept looking at me with this big smile, and she kept touching my arm or back or whatever and—" He sighs. "I don't know, Bird. She was throwing out all these signals, so I went for it. A lot of good it did me," he grumbles, picking his phone up again.

"So it was something *she* did," I say.

"I guess." He squints, looking up at me closely. "Why?"

I make big innocent eyes. "No reason," I say, gathering my things and standing up. "Just talking. Better get back to bed before Dad loses it. 'Night."

"'Night," he says as his phone buzzes again.

I creep back to my bed and roll in. I'm not sleepy, but it's better than being around Dylan when he's in a bad mood. I get out my headphones and plug them into my cell phone, listening to my On the Road Again playlist and thinking about my life—how strange it is. I've been living in an RV since I was nine years old. Everything I own has to fit in my allotted space on said recreational vehicle, which isn't much. Clothes, jewelry, shoes, toiletries—ugh, *toiletries* is a word you use when you pack for vacation, not for real life.

But crazy as it sounds, this is my real life. As Winnie trundles toward Nashville, I watch the trees blur together in the darkness and wonder where I'd be right now if my younger brother, Caleb, hadn't died. Would we still be living in that two-story house in Jackson? Would my dad still be a real estate agent? Would my mom still be a health nut, obsessed with us taking our vitamins and worrying every time we got a cold? Would Jacob be the rebel? Would Dylan try so hard to be the perfect son, and would he still be Secret Service–level protective of me? Would I ever have started playing the fiddle or writing songs?

I turn up the volume on a Dolly Parton song and follow the red lights of the cars and trucks that rumble past until they fade into the night. It's often at times like these that song ideas come to me, when I'm so tired I can't tell if I'm thinking or dreaming. I start to wonder what instrument Caleb would play if he were here, whether he'd have a good voice, or what kind of gigs he'd like best.

I sigh, though, and shake my head. Sliding back the window, I let the night air whip my face and remember that, if Caleb were here, there wouldn't be a band at all. He brought us to the music, and this may not be a conventional life, but it's ours.

"Bird, you coming?" Jacob asks from the stairwell of the RV. He's holding a gigantic bag of dirty laundry while I grab both my backpack and his. Mom's halfway across the parking lot with another bag of laundry, and knowing Dylan, he's already taking his second trip around the breakfast buffet inside.

"Yeah, I just need to get my computer."

"Hurry up," he barks. "I'm starving."

I roll my eyes. "You're always starving."

Dad parked us at the Travel Centers of America truck stop in the middle of the night, and now we're taking

advantage of their facilities: laundry, food, supplies, gas…
you name it, they've got it.

"Dad, we're going!" I call back to the bedroom.

My dad coughs before answering hoarsely, "Okay, sweetie. I'll see you in there."

I look at Jacob, but he just shrugs. "Dad didn't sound too good, did he?" I ask as we walk toward the rest stop.

"No," Jacob admits, "but he drove pretty late, so maybe he's just sleepy."

"Maybe."

A little bell chimes as we open the door, and Jacob walks straight ahead, past the wall of Saint Louis souvenirs, to the back, where the laundry room is. To my left is a fast-food court with Pizza Hut, Popeyes, and Taco Bell, but I take a right and walk into the Country Pride Restaurant.

As expected, Dylan is standing at the buffet with his plate loaded up like an edible mountain. He nods toward a back booth, so I walk over and put our bags with his. I'm not looking forward to doing homework, but it will be nice to write my Spanish composition on a table that doesn't move around.

I actually caught up to Jacob in "school," so we only have one more year to get through before we graduate. My mom oversees our "classes," which I never minded before, but she's been overenthusiastic about it ever since Dylan took his ACT last year and surprised us all by scoring really (annoyingly) high. He talked about college, but decided to stay with the Barrett Family Band instead of ditching us for dormitories and frat parties. He's enrolled in an online college now because my parents insisted he continue his education, but since the course work is so easy for him, he basically watches videos on YouTube all day.

"The bacon is crazy good," he says now, placing his food on the table and glancing around the place before sitting down. Obviously he's looking for Whitney—he does that every time we stop—but I know better than to call him out on it. Steam rises from his plate, and I swipe a slice of bacon before hitting the buffet myself.

A girl about my age smiles at me when we reach the stack of hot plates at the same time. She has a round face with red cheeks, and she's wearing a necklace with her initials: VMC.

Letting her go first, I nonchalantly look around and try to guess who she's here with. Does she travel with her family singing bluegrass at small honky-tonks all over America? Doubtful. But maybe she *is* an RVer on family vacation. Or maybe her dad's a trucker and she's tagging along for the week. Or maybe she lives in this town and just comes here for the breakfast. Then a gaggle of loud ponytailed girls wearing big bows and short-shorts joins us in line, and I realize that Vanessa or Veronica or Valerie is not like me at all. She's like my cousin Daisy, in Jackson—cute and popular and on her way to cheer for something.

I frown, embarrassed by the knee-length jean skirt and *Gettin' Lucky in Kentucky* T-shirt I'm wearing. Jacob walks up to me in his ripped jeans, Converse, and a skull-covered hoodie over his messy black hair, and I want to crawl under a table.

"Mom said to hurry up," he says, totally unaware of the giggles behind him as he builds the leaning tower of pancakes on his plate. "You were right. Dad's sick. Mom thinks it might be laryngitis."

I forget everything else and nearly drop my plate. "Jacob, we play the Station Inn tomorrow night."

"Yeah, sucks, huh?" he says, flipping his black hair off his forehead. "You'll probably have to sing lead if he's not better."

"What?" I nearly shout. Two girls laugh at the french toast tray but look away when my eyes meet theirs. I blush and move down the food line feeling totally self-conscious, but when I look back, I realize that they're checking out my brother, not laughing at me. Jacob smothers his pancakes in syrup, totally oblivious.

"Jacob, I can't sing lead," I protest quietly.

"Well, Dylan screwed it up last time, and nobody wants to hear me sing."

"What about Mom?"

He shrugs noncommittally, grabbing a small plate for biscuits and gravy.

As good as the food looked a few minutes ago, I've suddenly lost my appetite. I sing, but I've never *sung*, you know? Center stage. Definitely not at the legendary Station Inn. My plate shakes a little in my hands. If I'm this nervous already, I can't imagine tomorrow night.

Jacob walks over to the table where Dylan is sitting, and I realize that the girl I first saw at the buffet is watching him as well. When she looks up and realizes that I've caught her staring, she blushes and carries her plate over to where her friends are sitting. As she goes, I can't help but wonder how my life would be different if my hair were sprayed back in a high, tight ponytail like hers. Maybe I'd be laughing my butt off in the round corner booth with all my friends. Maybe I'd be all over the high school yearbook or dating the quarterback or voted Most Popular. But then I shake my head and snap out of it. I'm not a Vanessa or a Veronica or a Valerie; I'm a Bird.

My dad *has* to get better soon.

3

"BIRD, YOU HAVE seriously got to get your own guitar," Dylan complains as he tears through the RV looking for his new strings.

"I didn't snap your stupid string!" I protest.

My dad made us practice our set twice on the drive down to prepare me for leading the band tonight, and although his heart was in the right place, three hours of rehearsing put us all on edge. Even though Dad hardly has a voice, he got on Jacob for slapping the bass too much, me for singing with my eyes closed, my mom for being flat on backup harmonies, and Dylan for "lack of enthusiasm." By the time we got to the Station Inn, everyone was tense. We set up the equipment in near silence, all of us knowing our roles, but when Dylan snapped a string while tuning before sound check, his lack of enthusiasm turned into an abundance of irritation.

"If you'd tune it right when I let you borrow it to write your dumb songs from your diary, then the strings wouldn't snap!" He rips an afghan off the sofa and jams his hands down in between the cushions. No luck.

"I'll have you know that one of my 'dumb songs' is a Barrett Family Band favorite!" I shout back, looking through our backpacks. "And it's not a 'diary,' it's a songwriting journal."

I look through the cabinets, slamming them shut when I find only crackers and soup and the gross good-for-you granola my mom likes. I really have no clue where in the heck Dylan put his extra strings, but I didn't lose them.

He plops down on the couch and hangs his head in his hands. "First Dad gets sick, and now I don't have strings. This night is jinxed," he says.

"Oh great," I say. "That's just what I need to hear before I have to sing *lead vocals* at the Station Inn, Dylan."

"Don't be so dramatic."

"I'm not the one crying into my hands."

"I'm not crying, you idiot!" he yells up at me.

I smirk and wave his pack of strings. "Yeah, I'm the idiot. You put your strings on top of the microwave, but I'm the idiot."

He stands up and grabs for them, but I pull them away too quickly. "Uh-uh-uh. What do you say?"

"I say give me those strings or I'm going to kill you."

I turn and flee down the stairs with his strings to join the rest of the gang for sound check.

"Okay, okay," he says, chasing me across the gravel parking lot to the squat stone building that is the famous Station Inn. "Give me those strings or I'm going to kill you, *please*."

"That's better," I say, handing them over. He doesn't want to, but he grins just the tiniest bit. Maybe the night's not jinxed after all.

The Station Inn is always packed, even on a Tuesday night. This venue is iconic, and as I pass the Wall of Fame, I can't help but feel intimidated. The owner, J. T. Gray, told me that last week Dierks Bentley stopped by, just got up onstage and sang with the Dusty Mountain Pickers. If that were to happen to me tonight, I'd be relieved on one hand because I could let *him* sing, but on the other hand, I'd be even more nervous because, let's be honest, he's pretty cute.

"People are already lining up," I announce to my family as I climb the stairs of the RV. Sound check went well. Now all there is to do is wait.

"Remember when I used to be worried about parking Winnie out back?" my mom muses as I join her at the mirror. She curls her auburn locks while I smooth my strawberry-blond hair, a perfect blend of my parents' hair colors. "I bet those developers are itching to plow it down and put up a spa or something," she worries as she feathers her bangs. I really wish she could snap out of the early nineties, but it's a lost cause. She reaches for her organic hair spray—her one guilty pleasure in her otherwise epic quest to minimize her carbon footprint—and that's my cue to step away. I've been shot in the eye with Chi Enviro Flex Hold one too many times.

"Bird," my dad calls hoarsely. He squeezes a lemon into the cup of hot tea on the end table next to him and pats the couch. I give myself one last look—I'm wearing a cute lacy tank top and a flirty white skirt with my favorite cowboy boots—before I join my dad, although it's nearly impossible to sit still. He puts his arm around the back of the couch, considerate not to mess up my hair, and gives me a warm smile. "You're going to be great up there tonight."

I nod. Half an hour 'til nine. *Gulp*.

"This is just like any show," he croaks. "Heck, you practically sing them all at every show anyway."

"Yeah, but backup vocals…" I start to say, but my words trail off as someone knocks on the door and a shaggy brown head bobs up the stairwell.

It's Adam.

"Oh, Judd, don't be so hard on yourself," Adam jokes.

"Folks love hearing you sing, but Bird *is* a little easier on the eyes."

My dad laughs good-naturedly and stands up to shake his hand.

"Adam!" my mom coos.

"I thought you were going to Topeka!" I blurt out, once again the very picture of playing it cool.

"They canceled the show," he explains. "I was headed to a festival in Bristol after that gig anyway, so I thought I'd stop by. Jacob told me that Judd was sick and you were filling in behind the mic and, well, I couldn't miss it." He winks, then leans in and acts like he's confessing something. "Also, I saw the BFB Facebook updates."

"All fifteen?" Dylan quips.

I feel my cheeks flame as everyone laughs. Maybe I have been a tad vocal online about singing lead tonight, but that's only because I'm so nervous. And yet, in the few minutes that Adam has been here, my jitters have cooled off somehow.

I steal a look at Adam—take him in. He's so handsome tonight, casual as usual in his dark jeans and a soft green T-shirt that brings out the green in his hazel eyes. He obviously hasn't shaved in a couple of days and he could most certainly use a haircut, and yet it totally works for him in a way that is super hot. Which is probably what I find most attractive about him: how comfortable he is in his own skin.

34

His self-assuredness puts me at ease, too. It's fifteen minutes until showtime and, surprisingly, the boy who usually makes my heart beat double time has actually calmed me.

As the laughter dies down, my dad gestures with his arms for us all to circle up. "Let's have a good show tonight, gang," he manages, his normally smooth voice like sandpaper. He grabs my hand and then Mom's, who takes Dylan's, who takes Jacob's.

"Oh, I should go," Adam says, turning for the door.

"No, it's fine, sweetie," my mom says, smiling. "You're like one of the family."

Adam smiles warmly at her, almost as if in thanks, before taking Jacob's hand and then linking his fingers through my own. I hope God doesn't strike me down, but I can't concentrate on anything other than Adam's skin against mine, even if it is just our palms. We bow our heads and close our eyes as Dad croaks out our usual prayer, asking the Big Guy Upstairs for an extra blessing on me tonight, which I second.

And then, ending it in the same way he always does, he says, "Father, let us be thankful for the few years we had with Caleb, for the sweet hugs he gave his momma and daddy and for the sweet smiles he gave his brothers and sister. The loss is great but keeps us mindful to treasure each day we have with one another."

We don't talk about Caleb a whole lot, but we still pray

for him before every gig. And we each keep him with us in different ways.

"Take good care of our boy," we all pray in unison. Adam squeezes my hand. "Amen."

When I open my eyes, I look immediately up at the clock.

"Break a leg, y'all," Adam says, giving me a wink on his way out the door.

It's showtime.

"Folks, thanks for coming out tonight," Dylan says into the microphone. "Usually it's my dad, Judd Barrett, that up-to-no-good-lookin' fella over there with the banjo on his knee, who sings lead for our group. But tonight, dear ol' Dad isn't feeling so well, so my little sister, Bird, will be filling in for him. Not sure if any of y'all follow us online"—he looks over at me and winks. I roll my eyes involuntarily, which surprisingly gets a few laughs—"but if you do, you'll know that this is a Barrett Family Band first. So won't you all give her a big, welcoming round of applause? Bird Barrett, everybody!"

The crowd applauds and one guy in the back whistles. I glance over to the side of the stage, where Adam is sitting in a folding chair, smiling broadly. I take a deep breath and step up to the center mic, flinching at the brightness of the lights and fighting the urge to cover my eyes. Everybody's faces look dark and blurry, but that might be a good thing.

"Thanks, Dylan," I say, sweat already beading at my brow even though I haven't played a lick. This is usually where my dad talks about our band and helps Dylan introduce us all. I've got his spiel down pat since he never changes it up, but at this moment, I'm frozen in place. All I see is an ocean of dark heads, waiting to bob along to the music, waiting to feel something, to be inspired. People don't come to the Station Inn for the nachos. They come to hear good music.

"Um," I say into the mic. "How's everybody doing tonight?" But my voice sounds flimsy, timid as it bounces all over the room. My pep sounds forced. The place is so still and silent, I cringe. Take a deep breath. Start over.

Dylan and my dad are the showmen in our family, not me. I am who I am: a regular girl who's filling in tonight. I have to just embrace that. And being me means changing things up. I know we agreed to start off with "Wildwood Flower," but I can't help but think how my version would pale next to the Carter Family's... which makes me think of Maybelle and how she would just hang limp in my hand through most of that song... which makes me glance over at Adam and remember how he told that lady the other night that I fly on the fiddle... which makes me think of...

The perfect song.

"Let's start off with one a few of you might already know," I say, my voice quavering just a bit. If I don't go ahead and get at least one song out of my system, I might bolt off the stage. I'm gripping Maybelle so tightly in my left hand that there are sure to be lines in my palm. I need to get out of my head and into that place where the music just flows, and the only way to do that is to play. "This is a Barrett Family Band original, one I actually wrote a long time ago, called 'Will She Ever Call.'"

I glance back at Jacob, who stands next to his upright bass, confused. I don't know what we're going to do for an encore now, but the deed is done, the words have been spoken, and my family's got to get on board. I know this song like the back of my hand, and it's the perfect way for me to fiddle just as often as I have to sing. It's always a big crowd-pleaser, and I'm hoping that once this audience gets their heads to nodding and their feet to stomping, I might relax a little.

Jacob looks over at my dad, although I don't dare, and he must nod because Jacob reluctantly counts us in. "One, two, three, four!"

I know that I panicked under pressure and that my dad might be a little peeved, but I don't really have time to contemplate my nerves besting me because this is a song that doesn't give a fiddler a minute to think. Before you can say *yip*, I'm playing Maybelle like a girl on fire, my chin down and my mind on autopilot. I feel myself relax just the teensiest bit during those fifteen glorious seconds of doing what I do best, and then, feeling better already, I sing:

> *"I close my eyes, and the movie starts to play,*
> *I see you standing there not knowing what to say,*
> *You barge on in like there ain't no other way—"*

Dylan and my mom come in with backup vocals, and I am flooded with feelings of relief and solidarity. I make it through the first verse and actually sound okay. I start to get a little confidence, find myself enjoying it up here even, but then I jumble the words and flush bright red. I doubt the audience even noticed the flub since the song is an original, but I clam up. Instinctively, I raise my fiddle, but before I really get going, I realize that it's my dad's solo. I play some soft accompaniment to keep loose, to keep the nerves at bay. Then, when I lower Maybelle to come in on the next verse, my cue passes right by me.

I gulp hard, swallowing back the stage fright. *Come on, Bird.*

"Yip!" Dylan calls into his mic, picking up the melody. I glance over at him, and his eyes are right on me, intense, as he strums, his smile kinder than I've ever seen, and as he finishes up his little impromptu lick and my cue comes back around again, he winks at me. It's not a grand gesture, but it's just what I need: a big-brother way to say, *Hey. I've got your back. You've got this.*

It works. Smiling, I turn back to the crowd and pick up where I left off, singing my heart out about a boy I met in the crowd at an outdoor music festival a few years ago. He held my hand during a slow song, and I just knew he would be the first great love of my life. He asked for my e-mail address, and I was over the moon, glued to my computer for days after that, but then he never reached out, never found me, in essence, never "called."

I was destroyed . . . and I let my diary know.

So I took the poems he inspired and combined them, my first attempt at songwriting. I changed it from "Will He Ever E-mail" to "Will She Ever Call." It had a nicer ring to it. When my dad overheard me picking it out on Dylan's guitar one night, he loved it so much that he grabbed Mom's mandolin and helped me round out the sound. He said it was catchy, and he was really excited about it. Before I knew it, he'd included it in our set, and just like that, I went from poet to songwriter, which totally blew my mind. It was insane the first time our family performed it onstage, my dad completely clueless as to what had inspired the song (he never would have approved), the crowd bobbing their heads as if it were a bluegrass standard. There is no greater feeling than hearing an original song live.

I sing it now with gusto:

"Sleep or awake, for goodness' sake,
Racking your brain, your heart in pain,
Eyes on your phone, a dog begging for a bone,
Asking, will she ever call?"

"Who-ee!" Dylan shouts into his mic, stomping his feet. It's obvious why this song is usually our closer, because the place is charged.

"Take us home, Bird," my dad says on my other side, leaning into my mic, his voice near a whisper.

The crowd is forgotten as I focus on Maybelle, the fingers on my left hand itching at the fiddle's neck and my right hand gripping the frog of my bow with the sort of anxious energy a Kentucky Derby–winning horse has at the starting gates. I count the beats into my cue, and I'm off, sawing across the strings like a demon child, pouring out every ounce of nerves bundled up inside. I close my eyes, pump my knees, and work my arm like a piston. I hear feet stomping in the crowd and smile. This is what I'm good at. This is what I live for.

When we end the number, we get raucous applause from the crowd. The audience is ours.

"Thank you!" Dylan yells, taking over the intro. "I'm Dylan Barrett, on rhythm guitar and dobro. That's my little brother, Jacob, on the upright bass—"

"Who you calling 'little'?" Jacob calls, his usual shtick. The crowd chuckles—Jacob's got a good five inches on Dylan.

"That's my dad, Judd, on banjo, and that beautiful woman over there on the mandolin is my momma," Dylan continues.

I beam at him, finally feeling relaxed.

"That was fun, wasn't it, folks?" He gets a few murmurs of agreement, and I see heads nod in the crowd. "Well, now that you know my little sister is a phenom on the fiddle, tell me what you thought about her on lead vocals." He cups his ear, and the audience responds with a smattering of applause, although someone to my left whistles. I blush, pretty sure it's Adam.

"Okay, Dylan," I say into the mic, playing along. "What do you want this time?"

"Just another song, sweet sister," he says.

"You got it. A lot of y'all might know this next one. 'Sunny Side of the Mountain.' Yip!"

Jacob counts us in, and I settle into the spotlight. I can do this. I can do this for my family, and I can do this because Adam is watching. I can do this because I am a good singer, and I can do this because I've gotten over the initial stage fright that crippled me five minutes ago. I can do this because my family loves me and the music has never let us down. And honestly, I can do this because, well, I have to.

"I mean, I started off terrified," I babble to my family excitedly as we file into the back room for intermission. "But then, I don't know, I just settled into our usual rhythm and found a groove."

My mom smiles at me. "You were terrific, baby."

"Thank God they didn't kick us out after that first flub," Dylan teases, ruffling my hair.

"Hands off, you jerk!" I yell, racing over to the mirror.

My dad stands next to me as I freshen up. "You did great, sweetie."

"Thanks, Dad," I say, smoothing my hair. "I thought you'd kill me after that first number."

He nods. "Well, that wasn't what we'd discussed—" He starts coughing, and my mom comes over with a bottle of water, which he accepts gratefully.

"Take it easy, Judd," she says. "You aren't even supposed to be playing."

He makes a face, gulps down half the bottle, then turns back to me. "But we'll end it with something else. Maybe

'Blue Moon of Kentucky-hee-hee,' " he wheezes as he walks over to the couch to lie down.

My mom nudges me as she leans in to check her own hair, enveloping us both in a mist of her hair spray. Unfazed, I stare at myself, grinning widely. Once Dylan picked up my missed cue and winked at me, it felt like everything changed. I wasn't just singing; I was storytelling. I was weaving a tale for the audience, and they were rapt, hanging on my every note. Even Adam was stomping his feet and singing along, putting both fingers in his mouth to whistle as we filed off the stage for intermission. I hate that he saw me fumble the first song, but at least I recovered, and honestly, I feel like a rock star now. A new woman, all my nerves have dissipated. Now I'm just anxious to get back out there.

"Did you guys see that creepy guy sitting at the bar?" Jacob asks, before pounding a grape-flavored Gatorade.

"Oh yeah," Dylan says. "I saw him. He was practically drooling over Bird, the perv."

"He's probably just drunk," I say.

Jacob shakes his head. "He's not drinking."

"Yeah, and he's Dad's age, but he's totally staring at you like some kind of stalker."

"Gross," I say, a little worried.

"Don't pay him any mind, Bird. Let's just get back out

there," my mom says, pointing to the clock and walking to the door.

As we head to the stage, Dylan points the guy out. "If he comes up to you after the show, just grab me, okay?" His blue eyes are icy, and his jaw is set hard.

I nod at him seriously but smile when I turn away. Dylan Barrett may hog the bathroom, drink from the milk jug, and think he's always right, but he's also the best big brother a girl could ask for.

Back onstage, I catch the eye of the man at the bar. He's older than my parents—maybe fifty—dressed in a sport coat, jeans, and expensive-looking cowboy boots. But he doesn't seem to be ogling me so much as studying me. I wish my brothers hadn't even mentioned him. Finally in a groove, I don't need some weirdo throwing me off my game, so I shift in the stage lights to get him out of my line of sight. And then I give it everything I've got, finding creative places to incorporate the fiddle while I sing.

The rest of the night goes even better than the first set. Everybody plays as well as they ever have, and by the end of the encore, I don't want to leave the stage. I could live up here. I know my dad is the lead singer of the BFB, but I think he might have to fight me for it now. I feel alive, full of purpose, inspired! I want to sing more often, I want to write more songs, and I'm thinking that I could even show my dad some stuff I've been working on in my journal and take lead on a few if we include them in our act.

But there's not a lot of time to savor the moment. As soon as we're offstage, it's business as usual, putting our instruments away and clearing out the greenroom. I freshen up my gloss in the mirror and then head back toward the stage to pack up the mics. I'm eager to get out there and talk to Adam, while my parents make it clear that they're eager to get back into Winnie and hit the sack.

"You got Maybelle, right?" Dylan asks as he pushes the instrument cart past.

"Yeah." I nod, checking that she's in her case right next to me.

But Adam is nowhere to be found. I don't get it. What is this guy's deal? I mean, he changes his schedule to come see me sing lead for the first time but doesn't look for me afterward? He's not talking to Jacob; he's not at the bar. It's like he's vanished into thin air. He's, like, freaking Batman.

As I accept compliments from a few lingering crowd members, I feel myself coming down from the performance high. Our shows are always exhausting, but it's even tougher being the front man—or front woman. And to be honest, I'm totally and completely bummed that Adam seems to have disappeared again.

Then the big guy who works the door approaches me. "You're Bird, right?" he asks.

"Um, yes," I answer hesitantly.

"Adam Dean had to get back on the road, but he told me to give these to you," he says, holding out a tiny bouquet of flowers. "He told me to be careful with them, but they're basically just a bunch of weeds." He shrugs and shakes his head as he ambles back over to the door.

Stunned, I look down at the fragile bouquet in my hands. There are tiny yellow dandelions and long white daisies. There is clover, Queen Anne's lace, and a few pale pink coneflowers. It's not something you'd get from 1-800-FLOWERS, but it's the most breathtaking assortment I have ever seen in my life. I wonder where he got them.

Wrapped around the stems is a bar napkin with the words *Lady Bird* scrawled across it in black ink. My heart races. When I unfold the napkin, I see that he's left a note:

Update your status to "Killed it."

I laugh out loud and jump off the stage, eager to get the flowers to Winnie and press a few into the pages of my journal. But my dad stops me at the back door.

"Bird, sweetie, you did it," he says hoarsely, slinging his big arm around my shoulder and leading me to the small bar. "I'm proud of you."

"Thanks, Dad," I say, beaming up at him. "I'm no Judd Barrett, but those are awfully big shoes to fill."

"Hey, are you saying I've got big feet?" He laughs. I roll my eyes. My dad's so corny.

I glance around the Station Inn and see the bare stage, the emptied room. It's as if we were never even here. It's disheartening how fleeting the truly spectacular moments in life are. But the first flowers I've ever gotten from a boy are in my hand, and that reminds me: I've got a Coca-Cola to try. Something tells me it will be the best fountain Coke in the whole world, no matter what it tastes like. I get the bartender's attention and order one.

"I can't believe that was your first time singing lead," a guy says behind us. "You were a pro."

My dad and I both swivel around. The guy who was staring at me from the bar earlier is standing there, grinning at me. He turns his gaze on my dad and sticks out his hand. "Mr. Barrett, I'm Randall Strong."

"Nice to meet you, Mr. Strong," my dad says, always polite, even when wary.

"I was awfully impressed with your girl up there tonight," the man continues, as if I'm not even sitting there. I don't get a creepy vibe now that we're face-to-face. He just seems a little flashy. Intense.

"Well, I've always thought Bird was something else," my dad agrees.

"She sure is. Listen, are y'all signed with a label?"

My dad cocks an eyebrow. "No," he answers cautiously.

"Well, I'd be interested in talking more with you,"

Mr. Strong says, smiling widely. My dad stifles a cough as best he can, but Mr. Strong quickly adds, "When you're feeling better, of course. Maybe tomorrow? I think there's something special here, and I hope that maybe we can do business together."

He pulls a card from the pocket of his sport coat and hands it to my dad. I look over his shoulder and read:

RANDALL STRONG
PRESIDENT, A&R
GREAT AMERICAN MUSIC, NASHVILLE

There's an address on Music Row, a phone number and e-mail address, and the GAM logo, a blue eighth note superimposed over two concentric circles that give the effect of an old vinyl record. I feel my jaw drop. GAM is one of the biggest labels in Music City.

I look up at Mr. Strong and consider him with new eyes. This guy's not a stalker; he's a music-industry big shot!

"Well, y'all have a good night now," he says, excusing himself. "And Bird, it really was a pleasure. Great job."

"Thanks," I say as he walks away. Once he's gone, I slowly swirl back around on my stool to face the bar. My dad's got his elbows propped up against it, studying the card in his hands.

"What's A and R stand for?" I ask.

"Artists and repertoire," he answers. He looks up at me, and my face must still look a little blank because he explains. "He's a talent scout."

I blink hard. Then my Coke appears, and I lean toward the straw, taking a giant gulp. *Mother Maybelle, have mercy, we've just been discovered.*

4

THERE IS AN odd sense of quiet in the RV today. Usually, I can't get through my shower without one of my brothers banging on the door, but today I was even able to get dressed in the tiny bathroom without protest. Most mornings, my brothers and I argue over who does which chores, but today Jacob did the dishes without being asked, and Dylan made coffee while I wiped down the foldout kitchenette. And ordinarily, my mom has to ask us a million times to turn off the TV and get started on our homework, but today we all set up camp in our regular places and hunkered down. The Barrett Family Band in Winnie as usual ... except that Winnie, who was supposed to be on her way to Knoxville, hasn't moved an inch ... and except that the leader of our band is still at the Great American Music offices talking to a talent scout who is interested in us and could possibly change our lives. Other than that, it's just your average Wednesday.

"I can't concentrate," Jacob says, exasperated. He throws his pen up in the air and puffs out his cheeks. "I can't! What the heck's a derivative and who on God's green earth cares?"

"Seriously, Mom," I complain, looking down at my calculus homework. "Have you ever needed to use a graphing calculator in your entire life?"

"Just for homework—" my mom says over the clicking of her knitting needles.

"Exactly," I interrupt.

"Which I did, as will you two," she finishes.

Jacob and I look at each other and roll our eyes. "It's been two hours," he says. "What in the world have they been talking about for two hours?"

"I'm with them," Dylan pipes up, closing his laptop and standing to stretch. "One minute, you're sitting outside your RV eating English muffins. The next minute, your dad makes a phone call that could change your life. Kind of hard to care about homework."

"You're right." Mom sighs, setting down her needles. "You're right. Y'all want to play Hold 'Em?"

"Ha!" Dylan says, pointing at her and smiling. "You're nervous, too!"

My mom smiles mischievously. "Nah, I just like beating my kids at poker."

But before she gets that chance, Winnie's door opens, and my dad appears in the stairwell. We all scramble out of the booth and charge him like a bull in a bad mood.

"Whoa, whoa, whoa!" my dad hollers, his arms up as we practically push him back out of Winnie.

"What'd they say?" Dylan asks, stomping down the steps.

"Did we get a deal?" Jacob asks, right behind him.

I follow and Mom is on my heels.

"Tell us everything," I pant. "Don't leave out a single detail."

Outside, our group has to move over for a trucker who's getting into his big rig, and I realize that right here in the parking lot of the Travel Centers of America truck stop, our lives could change forever. I laugh out loud, so giddy at all of this possibility. Traffic rumbles past us on the highway and the smells of diesel and gasoline fill my nose, but the summer sun is shining down brightly and the sky is clear. It's a beautiful day for good news.

"Well," my dad says, running his hands through his hair, looking down, and toeing a crack in the pavement. Then the semi driver fires up his engine, interrupting him. Dad can't be heard over that, especially with his weak voice, so we watch as the dude situates himself behind the wheel, checks his mirrors, and slowly pulls out. I lean against Winnie, watching the annoyance on Dylan's face, the frustration on Jacob's, and the almost childlike anticipation on my mother's. I can't see my own expression, but I'm sure it's one of joy. I don't know why, but I have a feeling. Everything was so perfect last night, like it was destined, like everything we've gone through over the past seven years has led to this very moment right off I-24. I just have a feeling.

"Okay, okay, what'd he say?" Dylan demands once the truck has moved on.

"Well, Mr. Strong is certainly interested—"

"Yeah, we know that," Dylan interrupts. "But what'd he say? Did we get a deal?"

"Let him talk," Jacob says.

"Well," my dad responds, "they didn't offer us a deal."

And then we all go silent. I hear a little girl at the gas pump begging her dad for a quarter for the gum-ball machine inside. I hear a flock of birds calling out to one another as they swoop by overhead in their perfect V. And I hear a car horn honking angrily at someone down the road. But from the Barrett family, there is nothing but silence as we let his words sink in.

"We *didn't* get a deal?" I finally ask quietly. I'm confused. Why did Randall Strong insist on the phone that my dad come to his office right away?

"Not exactly," my dad says, hands in his pockets. Finally he looks up at my mother. They exchange a look that says my dad has more to say but wants to run it by her first. She nods.

"No, no, no, no, no," Dylan says, blocking the door to Winnie as my parents move toward it. "You can't leave us all morning and go into the offices of the biggest label in country music and then come back and say it was nothing. I want to know what happened."

"Yeah, Dad," Jacob adds.

"I need to talk to your mother," my dad replies sternly.

"Okay, look," Dylan says, sighing heavily. "I get that you guys like to make family decisions in private. I understand that. And I respect that. But this isn't really a family decision; it concerns the Barrett Family Band. And we may be your kids, but we're also band members. And we deserve to know about anything concerning our group."

"He's right," Jacob says.

I nod, too. We have a right to know.

My dad sighs loudly, his face weary. I know he's got a bad cold, and I know he's tired. I'm sure he'd like nothing more than to go rest, but we want answers. What was so important that they brought him down to Music Row on such short notice if they weren't going to offer us a deal?

My dad opens the door to Winnie and sits on the bottom step. We all circle around him, trying not to hover but not willing to let him escape yet either. "That's just it," my dad says, looking up at us. "This isn't about the group. They don't want to sign the Barrett Family Band." He pauses. "They want Bird."

I gasp and step back, feeling like maybe I didn't hear him right.

"Bird?" Dylan asks, confused. "What do you mean? Just Bird? Like, just her?"

My dad nods, then looks up at me. "Strong said GAM is looking to add fresh young female talent to their roster. He loved her singing and, of course, her fiddle playing. And he said she has natural stage presence, even if she could use a little work leading a band." My dad grins wryly.

I feel my face and neck flush. I am floored. They only want me?

"What does this mean for the Barrett Family Band?" Dylan asks, his voice a tad panicky. "I put off college for this."

I look over at Dylan and feel kind of sick to my stomach. If I were to sign with GAM solo, what *would* that mean for him? For Jacob? For my parents? We got into music as a family. We need it—as a family.

When Caleb died, we all sank into a pit of grief. My mom quit her job and took to bed. I remember bringing her my Madeline books and snuggling in, but she didn't read them with the same enthusiasm as before, and usually, I ended up reading to her. She was desperate with guilt, beating herself up for not having kept a closer eye on us that afternoon. We all carried guilt, even us kids who were still so young. Dylan felt like he should've been watching Caleb and me by the pond, Jacob felt like it was his fault for distracting Dylan with his new dirt bike, and I still feel like I should've screamed for help sooner. I didn't understand that my little brother was drowning. I thought he would swim, or float, or splash around. By the time I hollered for anybody, it was too late.

When we finally started family therapy with our pastor, it felt like a last-ditch effort to keep the family together. But Brother James was super friendly, and he kept reminding us that this accident was just that—an accident, nobody's fault, and that always made me feel better. I liked being able to talk about Caleb. I liked talking to an adult whose hugs weren't so tight and whose laugh wasn't forced. And when he suggested that we get a hobby, find something that we could all do together, my dad mentioned his glory days playing in a string band in college, and Brother James jumped on it. He asked if playing music sounded like fun to the rest of us, and, well, it did.

So the next day, my dad dragged his old banjo down from the attic and brought home a bunch of well-used instruments from a music store in town. Dylan chose a steel-stringed acoustic guitar. Jacob wanted to play drums, but my dad told him that the bass was the way bluegrass groups kept beat, so he chose that. My mom quietly picked up the mandolin and clutched it to her chest, which left the fiddle for me.

That night, we said a prayer for Caleb and then strummed and plucked and basically abused our new toys. My dad picked out "Twinkle, Twinkle, Little Star" over and over and over again, showing Dylan how to move his hands and place his fingers, but it was clear right away that we'd need real lessons. The neighbors probably wanted to call the cops, but somehow that awful sound unlocked something inside my mom. When I looked over at her, still hugging her new instrument and rocking from side to side, she smiled at me for the first time in months.

We actually picked up music pretty fast, and after a few years, the Barrett Family Band was more than a back-porch way to pass the time. I won a fiddling competition, and Dylan brought the house down at our school talent show. My dad signed us up for a local festival and then another show, and before we knew it we were playing at least once a month.

I never will forget the day we came home from school and my parents asked us how we would feel about taking our band on the road. Dylan wasn't happy about quitting basketball or leaving his friends behind, but after a week of thinking about it, he agreed with the rest of us that it would certainly be a wild adventure. And the next thing you know, the house was traded in for an RV and the Barrett Family Band was on tour.

I shake my head. It's hard to believe we've been on the road for seven years—and that it's been ten since Caleb's death.

Looking at my family now, outside this noisy truck stop and this mobile home of ours, I feel my heart lurch.

"I won't do it," I say. "I want what's best for the band. Really. I won't do it."

"Oh, Bird," my mom says, reaching over and squeezing my hand. "What's good for one of us is good for all of us."

"This really is no small thing," my dad says. "I told Strong that we'd have to talk about this opportunity before diving right in, but we should all feel very excited for Bird. Just as we would for any of us if the situation were different."

Dylan looks over at me and then lets out a big breath, long and slow, almost as if he's been holding it since Dad left this morning. He shakes his head, snapping out of something, and gives me a small smile. "No, they're right. You should do it."

"Really?" I ask, hating the squeaky tone in my voice. My throat is tight, and I'm so tense that my fingernails are cutting into the palms of my hands. On the one hand, I would feel totally passed over if the roles were reversed and I can't stand the disappointment on my brothers' faces, but at the same time, I feel chosen, special, excited. This is my chance to make music of my own—on my own—but it feels wrong to leave my family behind.

"Totally. You should do it, Bird," Jacob echoes hollowly. "Congratulations." He walks over to me and drapes a long skinny arm around my shoulders. "Just don't forget the little people," he says. I smile up at him, thankful to have brothers who love me and are happy for my success even if they'd rather be sharing it with me. And then I realize I've fallen right into his trap: He hooks his arm around my neck and gives me a freaking noogie.

"Get off me, you moron!" I yell, wrestling free. Everybody laughs as I smooth my hair back into place, and although the noogie seemed maybe a tad aggressive, I guess it's better than him hating me forever.

"Well, nobody's doing anything right away," my dad says, slapping his legs and standing up. "The Barrett Family Band's got a show to play in Knoxville tonight."

"Yeah, just try not to get discovered again, Bird," Dylan teases as he walks past me.

"Ha-ha," I say dryly.

But as my family files past me into the RV, I stay put. I look around, letting his words sink in. I think I might still be in a state of mild shock. Here, in the corner of this truck-stop parking lot, I got a break. Last night, I was *discovered*. Before I can stop myself, my mind flashes forward to sold-out concerts and music videos and CDs in Walmart with my picture on the front. I think about the money I'll make and how I'll be able to buy my parents a house and my brothers fancy cars. My body buzzes with the kind of energy that sends rockets into space, but in case my brothers are watching, I keep my feet on the ground and take a few deep breaths to calm myself. I heard everything my father said, but still, it doesn't feel real.

I see a shiny black stone near the cracked pavement my dad was kicking around, and without thinking, I pick it up. This really happened. Right here in this parking lot, I got a break. I slip the small stone into my jeans pocket, rubbing its one sharp edge with my thumb, almost like pinching myself. I never want to forget the way I feel right at this very moment, right in this very place.

And then it's back to reality. "Who's ready for lunch?" my mom asks as I climb on board the Winnebago.

"I am," I say, as if my whole life hasn't just taken a wild turn.

I take shotgun, fighting like crazy not to ask my dad a thousand questions. I want to know everything—what the offices were like and what they talked about and when we'll get started with GAM. But there's no privacy on the road, and our wheels are already rolling. So, smiling like a lunatic, I kick back in the passenger seat and thumb the little black rock in my pocket as the highway opens up in front of us, full of possibility.

5

"ARE YOU READY, kiddo?" my dad asks. He and I pulled into Nashville last night from a week of shows in Knoxville and Asheville, driving the car we borrowed from Gramma while she went on with my mom and brothers to a previously scheduled family vacation in North Carolina.

It's hard to miss the GAM offices—they're in an impressive six-story building made of glass and steel that occupies more than its fair share of Music Row. We're standing in front of it now, but I pause before we actually start down the walk. This is the building some of Nashville's biggest superstars call home. I feel like I should bow or kneel or pray or offer up some sort of sacrifice before I dare set foot inside.

"Let's go, hon," my dad prods, putting his arm around

me and giving me the tiny nudge I need to get my boots going again.

Right before opening the massive GAM front door, I catch my reflection in the dark glass and smooth the front of my new sleeveless yellow sundress. I didn't have a clue what to wear today, so my mom and I hit the mall in search of the perfect sign-me-to-a-record-deal outfit. I knew I wanted to wear my cowboy boots, and when she suggested buying a new, celebratory pair, I adamantly refused. These are the boots I was discovered in, so in case they have good luck, I'm keeping them until they fall apart.

"You must be the Barretts," a sharply dressed guy in his twenties says when we approach the large front desk. His dark hair is soaked with gel, and the only thing skinnier than his jeans is his tie. He approaches us with a million-dollar smile, his hand out for a shake. "I'm Clem, Randall Strong's assistant, and we're all so very happy you're here."

We shake and exchange pleasantries, but then we're off, trying our best to keep up with the energetic Clem as he leads us through the offices. It's not that Clem's running or anything, it's that he's clearly no longer in awe of this magical place. How can he fly past all these gold and platinum records hanging on the walls as if they mean nothing? How can he not stop and gape at picture after picture of his boss posing with country music icons?

"Bird," my dad calls.

At the end of the hallway, I see my dad and Clem waiting for me outside a pair of imposing doors. That must be Strong's office. I gulp, then walk calmly yet briskly toward them.

"Bird! Judd!" Randall Strong calls, swinging the double doors open wide. He reaches out and pumps our hands enthusiastically. As Mr. Strong leads us inside toward a small table covered in bagels, cheese, and fruit, I'd wager that he has had at least three cups of coffee in the last thirty minutes. Maybe he's this friendly to everybody, but the whiteness of his large teeth is almost blinding.

The entire back wall of the room is glass, offering a breathtaking view of downtown in the distance, and Mr. Strong's office alone is much bigger than Winnie. In fact, it's all a little intimidating. I'm walking toward the massive oak desk to take a seat at one of the two chairs facing it when Clem intercepts me.

"No, you'll be over here," he says, leading me to a sitting area. Then he opens a minifridge, gets out two premium glass bottles of water, and hands them to my dad and me with a big smile before heading back to his place at the front desk.

"I'm thrilled that we could meet up again," Mr. Strong says enthusiastically, gesturing for us to take seats. Dad and I settle into two comfy leather chairs facing a beautiful antique-looking fireplace, and Strong sits on a love seat, propping one shiny black shoe on his knee and stretching his arm across the back of the sofa. His pinstriped suit and gold cuff links must have cost a small fortune.

"Thank you for having us," my dad answers politely.

"Oh, your voice sounds much better, Judd," Mr. Strong comments.

They go on to talk about the recent weather and finally the upcoming football season. I can't help but stare at all the pictures on the walls and in frames on the tables near us. I am floored by a picture on the end table next to me: It's of a young Randall Strong with his arm around Johnny Cash at the Grammys. He's, like, best friends with every country music star on earth.

"Well, I was blown away at the Station Inn," he says now.

I check back into the conversation. "Thank you, Mr. Strong," I say humbly.

"Oh, Randall, Randall. Call me Randall," he says boisterously.

"Okay, Ran—"

"So, as I was saying the last time we met," he plows ahead, interrupting me and addressing my dad, "I'd like to discuss the possibility of a development deal with Bird. That was the first time she'd sung lead for your family's band?"

My dad looks over at me quickly, but then answers,

"Yes, that was the first time, but she's been filling in this whole week while I recovered my voice."

"And how'd she do?" Randall asks, as if I'm not sitting right there.

"She was great. I think most of the stage jitters she experienced that first night have been worked out of her system."

Oh, thanks for reminding him, Dad.

"Good, good," Randall says, glancing briefly at the shiny watch on his wrist before addressing my dad again. "But, Judd, we also like that she's a little unpolished. She's got a raw edge that reads as genuine and accessible. Does she play any other instruments?"

I was so excited for this meeting. It was supposed to be about me and my potential career, but now I'm feeling a little left out. It's like I'm watching a tennis match between these two. I'm not a child. I'm sixteen, and this is *my* life we're talking about.

"I can play guitar," I say loudly. Randall looks over at me almost as if he's surprised to see me sitting there. "And I write songs."

"Oh, you write?" Randall asks, putting his leg down and leaning forward. Now that I've gotten his full attention, I sink back a little in my chair. "What kinds of songs?"

"Um, ballads mostly, I guess. Some of my stuff has a little bit of a rock feel."

"What are they about?" he asks.

I blush, thinking about Adam and how a lot of my songs have to do with him. "They're kind of personal," I say, aware of my dad sitting right beside me.

Randall claps his hands once, then rubs them together. "Good. Personal is good. They eat personal up."

They?

"Can you sing one for me right now?"

"Oh," I say, shocked. I look over at my dad, and he nods for me to go ahead, but I really feel put on the spot. I wasn't prepared to perform. "Well, I'd have to go grab my journal from the car," I tell him. "And an instrument."

"Hmmm..." Randall says, frowning.

"Bird wrote 'Will She Ever Call,' the number we usually do for our encore, and Barrett Family Band fans just love it," my dad says, sensing as I do that we're losing our hold on the meeting.

"Oh, I think I remember that one maybe."

"We could sing it for you a cappella right now," Dad presses.

"Never mind, never mind," Randall says, standing up abruptly. His forehead lines are deeply creased as he breezes by us and walks over to his desk.

My heart sinks. Why didn't I throw my journal into my purse? Why would I come to this meeting without it? And you'd think my dad would've known to bring his banjo or

Dylan's guitar, which my brother reluctantly agreed to part with while on vacation, or remind me to grab Maybelle.

"Clem," Randall says into the phone on his desk. "Get me Lorie Pierce."

I stand up and walk over, my dad right behind me. "Mr. Strong, if you just give me a minute," I say, panicked. "I can run down to the car and be right back."

"It's Randall," he says, looking up from a calendar on his desk. He flashes his bright white smile at me again, and I feel better. "And there's no need. You can sing them for me live tonight."

"Tonight?"

"At the Bluebird."

"The Bluebird Cafe?" I ask, incredulous.

"It's a local spot where singers and songwriters, some new and some established, perform their work," he explains.

"Garth Brooks was discovered there," my dad pipes up.

Randall gives him a patronizing smile. "Garth Brooks and many more."

But I don't need them to tell me about the Bluebird. Anyone who has anything to do with country music knows about the Bluebird. It's a small venue, intimate, but a performance there carries prestige. Numerous careers and megahits got their starts there. From the audience, it's magical. But me onstage? Tonight? Playing next to some of the best singers and songwriters in Nashville? That sounds terrifying.

"But today is Wednesday," I finally say. "I've never performed there. Open Mic nights are on Mondays. There's no way—"

"I'll get you a spot," Randall says, holding up a finger as he presses TALK on his desk phone. "You just bring your songs." Then he lifts the receiver and turns away, looking down on Music Row as he pulls some strings.

I look at my dad wide-eyed. "The Bluebird Cafe?" I whisper. Absentmindedly, I slip my hand into the pocket of my dress and thumb the lucky rock I found last week. It calms me, reminding me that I was good enough at the Station Inn, good enough to get Randall's attention.

My dad reaches over and squeezes my shoulder. "You'll do great."

I nod and he squeezes again. We stand there, on the other side of Strong's desk, watching the pinstripes on his suit ripple as he gestures dramatically while getting everything set for tonight. From the sound of it, he has the power to get me behind a mic onstage at the Bluebird. Which means I have eight hours to turn the stories on the pages of my journal into songs worthy of a record deal.

6

"I WROTE THIS number when I was living in Tulsa, going through my second divorce," the man sitting next to me says into his mic. He's probably in his fifties, and he sure doesn't look like a country music singer. His graying dark hair is long and shaggy, and he wears red-framed glasses. Instead of cowboy boots, he sports old tennis shoes. You'd think he was hard up, but I saw him in the parking lot getting out of an expensive-looking sports car.

I listen to Harley Duke sing a song I've heard a thousand times on the radio, but it sounds strange coming from him. I'm used to singing along with Kenny Chesney, but Harley is the guy who actually wrote it. I can't help but think how weird it would be to pour your heart out onto the page and then let some famous singer take credit for all the emotion you put behind it.

Harley and I are two of five musicians playing "in the round," which means we share the stage and take turns playing, going around in a circle. Behind Shannon Crossley, a really talented songwriter seated directly across from me, I can see Randall Strong sitting at a table next to another GAM exec. The butterflies in my stomach go crazy.

Shannon winks at me, and I turn my focus away from the crowd to smile back at her. She's maybe a little younger than my mom, wears chunky rings made from natural stones, and has jet-black hair that drapes over one shoulder. When she performed the first time tonight, I was worried that her hair would get caught in the strings of her guitar it's so long. She wrote the hit the most recent *American Idol* winner gets credit for, although when she sang it live a few minutes ago, it seemed like a different song entirely. It was devoid of that manufactured pop sound I'm used to. Shannon's voice wasn't auto-tuned or digitally altered. It cracked in places and emotion poured out. The lyrics were so much more powerful coming from her as she talked about where she came from and traveling and finding "home" outside of a traditional house. By the end, there was a huge lump in my throat and tears actually welled up in my eyes.

I look back into the audience to catch my dad's eye in

the crowd. He gives me a thumbs-up and a big smile. I can't help but wish my mom and brothers were here tonight, too. While they're hanging out with Gramma in North Carolina, I'm debuting original songs at one of country music's most iconic venues. As awesome as that is, I feel guilty that the entire BFB isn't getting this same opportunity, especially since I'm borrowing Dylan's guitar again and he would kill to play at the Bluebird.

As Harley approaches the bridge in his song, I shake my head and clear my mind of all thoughts that don't have to do with this very moment.

It's my turn next, and I look down at my journal on the music stand in front of me, trying to concentrate. I'm okay on guitar, but not as comfortable as I am with the fiddle. And the songs I'm singing tonight are super personal. I've played a few of them for my family in the past, but nobody's ever heard the one I'm going to sing next. It's about Adam, how he pops in and out of my life, and how it sometimes seems like he might like me the way I like him, although I still wonder if he only thinks of me as Jacob's kid sister. I just want him to see me, to really know me.

It's a little embarrassing singing this one in front of everybody, my dad especially, but Randall said "they like personal," so I figure this will be the perfect song for a venue like the Bluebird. It's an intimate space. Five songwriters sitting in folding chairs in the middle of a dimly lit room with the audience crowded close. It's both comforting and terrifying at the same time, which is why, just like at the Station Inn, I started with a song that I know like the back of my hand.

The crowd seemed to like "Will She Ever Call" and the little joke I opened with ("P.S. She won't") as I introduced it. That old BFB standard relaxed me and gave folks a peek into the music of Bird Barrett, but now it's time to take a risk.

Harley finishes up, and as the audience claps, I take a sip of water and double-check that my journal is secure on the music stand. I thumb my lucky rock, which is sitting there as well. My pulse is racing. As the applause dies down, I feel the roomful of eyes focus on me. My foot is tapping like wild, and it's certainly not to the music since the place is now deathly quiet. There is a strict no-talking policy here. I swallow my nerves and lean into the mic.

"Guess it's my turn again," I say nervously.

"Yep, that's how circles work, darlin'," Harley cracks next to me.

The crowd titters, and I grant him a tight-lipped smile. It's clear he wasn't crazy about a rookie like me worming my way into the round without earning my spot. I lean back and clear my throat. As much as this setup should feel like a regular jam session, I know the other songwriters aren't going to join in and the crowd won't sing along. I feel vulnerable, exposed.

"You know, I still get nervous when I play here," Shannon says into her own mic across from me. I look up at her, shocked. She gives me a warm, reassuring smile. "My songs, they're mostly autobiographical. It's nerve-racking to sing about your real life in front of a roomful of strangers." She laughs lightly.

The crowd murmurs a soft response, and I nod at her. "Exactly," I say into my mic. "That's how I feel about this next one. It's about, um—" I glance over at my dad.

"A boy?" Shannon asks, her eyes twinkling.

"Yes," I answer, blushing ferociously.

"Aren't they all?"

Muffled laughter fills the space. I smile, and my shoulders relax. I strum a little stronger and say, "I want this boy to know me better, to see the real me. That's what this song is all about."

And within the next four-count, I close my eyes, picture Adam there on a bar stool sipping a cold Coca-Cola, and sing.

"Not bad, kid," Harley says, snapping his guitar case shut. People are milling about, talking at normal level and rearranging themselves for the next show. It suddenly feels like a regular bar, instead of the intense listening room of only moments ago.

"Thank you," I say, shocked. He nods and makes his farewells to the other songwriters, and I let it sink in that I just proved myself to Harley Duke.

"Oh, Bird, you were fantastic!" My dad envelops me in a bear hug. "Outstanding. Just outstanding. Your songs were so honest and the melodies so simple and pure and—" He blinks fast and takes a deep breath. My mouth hangs open. Is my dad about to cry? "I just couldn't be prouder," he finally says, pulling a beverage napkin out of his pocket and blowing his nose.

"Allergies?" I ask, grinning.

He chuckles, then leans in conspiratorially. "Don't tell your brothers about my 'allergies' or you're grounded for a year."

We laugh and hug again.

"Bird!" Randall says, coming up to congratulate me. "You did it. That was magnificent." He slaps my dad on the back. "You've got to be proud of this one, right, Judd?"

"Oh, I am," my dad says, stepping closer to me. "I'm proud of all my kids."

"What'd I tell you?" Randall asks the other GAM exec. "She's something special, right?"

"She certainly is," the guy says, eyeing me. Something

about him seems antsy, and he looks terribly uncomfortable in his heavily starched denim shirt and creased jeans. In fact, this guy looks like he's wearing a costume, just playing the part of someone who frequents country music establishments. Maybe he's the GAM accountant or something.

"Thank you, Randall, for this sweet opportunity," I say.

"'Sweet,'" Randall repeats, chuckling. "See? Bird Barrett is fresh and young and full of talent. I think she's a perfect fit for the GAM family, don't you, Alan?" He beams at me, and his sidekick nods enthusiastically.

I gasp. "You do?"

"I do," Randall confirms. "So, what do you say, Judd?" he asks, gesturing to a now-empty table behind him. "Think you could share a piece of your family with ours? A songwriter like Bird who also has magnetic stage presence doesn't come along every day. We know that from experience." He nods at Alan, who puts his briefcase on the table and pops it open. "That's why we went ahead and brought along the papers for you to read over and sign.... That is, if working with Great American Music is what you both want. We'd like to offer Bird a deal. Tonight."

I clap my hands and squeal. My heart feels ready to burst. I can't believe this is happening to me. A development deal with the biggest label in country music? I must be dreaming.

"Wow," my dad says, running his hand through his hair. "Well, thank you. But, uh, we'd like to take the papers, talk it over, call my wife, you know, just think about it overnight, if you don't mind."

"What?" I ask, mortified.

"Just want to make sure this is what you really want, hon."

"It is, Dad," I reply urgently. And when I say it, I know it's true. I never thought I'd be a famous singer or anything, but now that I've performed my own songs, my way, for a roomful of people who genuinely seemed to like them, well, now I know it's true, and I don't want to let this chance slip through my fingers. "I want this."

"Terrific!" Randall says, beaming at me.

Alan takes out a pen, but my dad ignores him, folding the papers and stuffing them in the back pocket of his jeans. "I'd still like to sleep on it," he says again. "Thank you, Randall, for setting all of this up for us. We'll call you in the morning."

"You do that," Randall says, looking slightly perturbed. His smile hardens, but as he and Alan make their farewells, I pump their hands extra hard, trying to give them every confidence that we really do want this deal. If my dad costs me this opportunity, I'll never forgive him.

"Great set," Shannon Crossley says, catching up to us as we weave through the crowd toward the front door.

"Thanks," I say. "You too."

I follow my dad out to the parking lot, itching to get him alone so we can really talk about this. I wish I were eighteen so I could just sign the papers myself.

"What if they change their minds by the morning?" I ask the minute we walk out the front door.

"They won't."

"What if Randall discovers somebody else tonight and doesn't want me anymore?"

"He won't."

"He might."

"Bird," my dad says, stopping. He grabs both of my shoulders and looks me straight in the eye. "You were wonderful tonight. I could see the same thing they saw, an exceptionally talented and magnetic performer. Except you know what else I saw? My little girl. We didn't start playing music until the whole family agreed. We didn't sell our house and start touring the country until the whole family agreed. And I'm not about to sign my daughter to a record deal without talking to the rest of our family about it. This will put all Barrett Family Band performances on hold. We'll have to stop touring for who knows how long. Don't we owe it to our family to let them weigh in?"

His words hit me hard, and I feel my feet settle back solidly on the ground. He's right. He's absolutely right.

"And if Randall Strong is the kind of guy who would

pull his offer off the table just because he couldn't bully us into signing papers in a low-lit bar, then maybe he's not the guy we think he is."

"You're right," I admit, walking along the white lines of a parking space.

"But like I said," my dad says, draping his arm around my shoulders, "I saw what he saw, and there's no way on earth he's changing his mind. You really are something special, sweetheart."

"I'd have to agree," a man says, walking over to us from a few cars away. He's not a tall guy, but he's stout with a ruddy complexion and a receding hairline. He approaches us with a sincere smile, and although his dark eyes are intense, they are also warm. "I really enjoyed what you played in there, Miss Barrett."

"Thank you," I say. "I appreciate it."

"You were talking to Randall Strong," he states.

My dad's grip around my shoulders tightens just the tiniest bit. "Yes," he responds warily.

"If I can just give you some advice," the man says, "you don't want to sign those papers. Contracts like the one I'm sure he's offering can be a raw deal for the musician. I'm sure that as a new artist, it sounds appealing to you—and don't get me wrong, Great American Music is a powerful label—but ultimately, you'd be signing away too much."

"Well, my—my music—" I stammer.

"Will be theirs. But they won't just own the music," he continues frankly. "With a deal like that, they'll own you. Read the contract."

"And why do you care so much about my daughter's record deal?" my dad questions.

"Because I can offer her a better one," he replies bluntly, fishing in the pocket of his black button-down. He pulls out two business cards, one for my dad *and* one for me. "I'm Dan Silver."

I take the card and look down at it:

DAN SILVER

PRESIDENT

OPEN HIGHWAY RECORDS, NASHVILLE

"I was with Allied Music for twenty-two years, but it's deals like the one I'm sure Strong gave you that made me walk away in favor of starting my own label," Mr. Silver says, stuffing both hands into the pockets of his dark jeans.

"Allied's one of the biggest record companies in the country," I say.

"Yep. And Open Highway's one of the smallest," he admits with a wry smile. He takes a step back and gives me a broad, confident smile. "But you've had a long night and I'm sure you'd like to get home. Read the GAM contract, but before you sign it, do you think you could give me a chance to show you around Open Highway?"

I look up at my dad, waiting for him to respond, but instead, he looks at me expectantly. "The man's talking to you, Bird. It's your career. What do you think?"

He *is* talking to me. I look at Mr. Silver again and smile. I guess it is worth looking at all the options. "We'll see you in the morning," I say.

Mr. Silver nods and reaches out to shake our hands again. "Wonderful."

"Should we call to make an appointment?" my dad asks.

"Come in any time tomorrow morning. We'll be looking for you."

He gives us a small wave, and we watch him walk across the parking lot toward his car. Then I look down at his card again. Last week I had no offers, and tonight I got two. My stomach flips. Now, which to take? What to do? I sigh, both giddy and confused. I have so much to think about.

"Tired, sweetie?" my dad asks, his arm still across my shoulders.

I nod. As we walk toward Gramma's old car, I think about how wild life is and how it can all change in the blink of an eye. I look at the stars and send up a quick prayer for guidance. No matter what happens, I feel like I'm about to cash in a lotto ticket for the biggest jackpot of all time.

"Okay, let's call 'em," I say, tossing my cardboard food container into the trash and downing an entire bottle of water.

When we got back to the hotel, we ordered Chinese food and read over my GAM contract. Well, I skimmed it, actually. Too much legal talk made my head spin, but Dad was pretty diligent, even using the dictionary app on his phone to look up a few words.

Dad puts his phone on SPEAKER and lays it next to him on his bed as it rings.

"How was the Bluebird?" Dylan calls out in lieu of *hello*.

I grin. "Pretty awesome," I say, which clearly isn't enough because my dad launches into a play-by-play of the whole night. When he gets to the part about Dan Silver, my brothers hoot and holler in the background.

"Two offers!" Dylan shouts.

"That's crazy!" Jacob reiterates.

"Okay, boys, settle down." My dad chuckles. Then he sighs heavily, running his hand through his hair. "But seriously, Aileen. Strong set all this up for us tonight, and this Silver guy just popped out of the shadows. We told him we'd go into his office tomorrow morning, but how do we know he's not some hustler?"

"Well, it's hard to tell," my mom says. "Do you—"

Dylan interrupts her. "'Daniel (Dan) Elliott Silver,'" he calls from the background, "'born December 12, 1961, in Memphis, Tennessee, is a country music producer and former president of Allied Music. Silver left Allied in July 2013 to start his own label, Open Highway Records. He lives with his wife and two daughters in Franklin, Tennessee.' *Wikipedia* doesn't lie!"

"So then he sounds like the real deal to me," my mom says into the phone. "Have you read the GAM contract?"

"Oh, yes," my dad says, smirking up at me. "Let me tell you, Aileen, *that* was a labor of love." I give my dad a big smile, and he turns back to the phone, grinning as he gives my mom a recap of what he read in the contract. By the time he's finished, he looks stressed. "I just want to do the right thing for Bird."

I look at my dad, bent over the cell phone on his bed. His shirt is untucked, one of his brown socks has a small hole in the toe, and his reading glasses are perched on top of his messy blond hair. I'm sure my dad would love to be on vacation with the rest of my family, but he's here with me, helping me start a music career. I hop off my bed and climb onto his, sitting cross-legged across from him as we make our good-byes to my mom and brothers.

When he pushes END on the call, he looks up at me, and I see deep creases in his forehead and worry lines at the corners of his eyes. "Bird," he asks, "is this what you want?"

"What? To meet with Dan Silver?"

"No," my dad says, waving his hand over the papers next to him on the bed. "This career. This life. I just want you to know what you're getting into. This is a development deal: no promises, no guarantees. This is you starting a career at the age of sixteen when you have your whole life ahead of you. So I just want to make sure—before we talk to Silver or before we decide about Strong—is all of this what you really want?"

I nibble at a hangnail on my right pinkie finger and consider my dad's concern. Is this what I really want? I mean, a record deal and singing career wasn't really something I'd ever dreamed about, but that's only because I never thought in a million years that it'd be a possibility. But now it is. A contract with a giant music label is literally within my reach, and although I always saw my music as being just one spoke in the wheel of the Barrett Family Band, I can't help but think now that this is meant to be. I want people to hear my songs. I want to be onstage. In fact, I think I want this more than I've ever wanted anything in my whole life.

"Yes," I say, and once it's out there, I know I mean it. "Yes, Dad. I want this. My music has always been the most important thing in my life besides my family. If I have the chance to turn it into a career, then I want to take it. So yes, yes, yes, I want this."

My dad sighs and then looks at the time on his phone.

He holds it up to me and grins. "Well then, sweetie, you'd better get some sleep. 'Cause tomorrow we're getting you a record deal, one way or the other."

I launch toward my dad and give him a giant hug. My mom always says *Don't wish your life away*, but at this moment, I wish it were tomorrow already because there's no way I'll sleep a wink tonight.

7

"HMMM," I SAY, squinting into the morning sun. As predicted, neither Dad nor I could sleep last night, so we didn't waste any time getting ready this morning and making our way over to the address on Dan Silver's business card. His office is on Music Row, too, but as we stand on the sidewalk facing a small bungalow, I can't help but notice the stark difference between this place and the imposing GAM office building. "This isn't at all what I expected."

"Me neither," my dad says, looking up at the one-and-a-half-story building. "But it's kind of nice. Reminds me a little of our house on Adams Road."

"Yeah," I say, nodding. The sign on the front door is written in brightly colored lowercase letters, spaced out artistically: open highway records. We've been on the road nearly half my life, so the name feels right. I pull the lucky rock out of the front pocket of my jeans and roll it around in my hand. Yesterday I showed up at GAM full of nerves, but today, I feel more confident.

My dad leads me down the short walk and up the steps to the broad porch. He presses the doorbell, and while we wait, I picture myself writing a song in the large, white-washed porch swing. I get chills. This almost feels like home.

"Welcome, welcome," Mr. Silver says, opening the door himself and gesturing for us to come inside. The front room is open, and there is a big oak desk, but no one sits behind it. The place is oddly peaceful. "We don't have a reception-ist just yet," he explains, "so feel free to tip your doorman."

We all smile at his joke and then follow him toward the back.

"How long have you been open, Mr. Silver?" I ask, fol-lowing him to his office.

"Please, call me Dan," he says over his shoulder. "I left Allied last month and brought a few clients with me— smaller acts, but people I couldn't just walk away from," he explains, glancing back at me. "And we rep songwriters like Shannon Crossley, which is why I was at the Bluebird last night."

He stops at the door of his office and ushers us inside.

"I know this place doesn't look like much," he says with

a smile, "but Open Highway will be big one day; it just takes time. We want to make sure that the artists we scout, the new ones we sign, are the right ones to grow the label."

My dad and I nod, listening to everything he says, but our eyes are absorbing his impressive office. It's not nearly as large as Randall's, but it's filled with photos of just as many recognizable faces.

"I'm not a desperate man," Dan continues. "I left Allied because I want to accomplish something special. I want to sign artists who are willing to take chances, who care more about their music than their image. In short: quality versus quantity."

He directs us to a small sitting area. Everywhere I turn, I see Silver posing with the country music stars I grew up with. Framed pictures cover the walls and his desk: Silver with his arm around Tim McGraw, Silver squeezed between Miranda Lambert and Blake Shelton at their wedding, Silver with Jason Aldean holding up one of the many CMAs that line the mantel over the fireplace behind his desk, and on and on. The walls are covered with platinum and gold records. I marvel at how hard it must have been to walk away from all of this—to start over, to take such a big leap of faith.

Dad and I take our seats on a tan leather couch. Dan sits across from us in an old but very comfortable-looking armchair and pours everybody a glass of sweet tea. I realize then that Dan's not wearing a suit. He's in jeans and a light blue collared shirt, no jacket, no tie.

He leans back casually. "I'm not one to beat around the bush, guys," he says. "I know you have a contract from GAM, and I hope you read the papers last night—" He pauses here, looking me straight in the eye until I nod. He nods back and continues. "They're a big label and a good company. They have name recognition and represent a lot of famous artists. I'm not naive. I know that has to be appealing to you, and it may feel safe. I know because I was president of a company just as big."

He drops his leg and leans forward, his elbows on his knees and his gaze intense. "But I stand by what I said last night. They will try to package you to fit into their pop image and new-country sound."

He glances over at my dad and then turns his stare back to me.

"The reason I left Allied was because I wanted the freedom to find and develop truly unique talent again," he says. "It had started becoming all about money and just churning out the same old stuff because that's what was selling." He stops and grins. "Of course, we want your music to sell..." My dad chuckles. I return Dan's smile, his enthusiasm catching. "But we want it to be just that, *your* music."

"That's what I want, too," I say. "I loved playing my stuff at the Bluebird last night. I was nervous at first, but after we went around a couple of times, I felt like there was nowhere else on earth I'd rather be."

"And that was obvious to everybody in the crowd, right, Judd?"

"I thought she was amazing."

"Exactly, and not just because you're her father." The way Dan says things, it's as if they're facts—not questions. "Bird, you excite me as an artist more than anyone has in a long time. Your songs were full of raw emotion, and the way you played and sang from the heart, without forcing the feelings, was like a breath of fresh air. Of course GAM wants you, but we do, too. I want to operate Open Highway from here"—he knots his fist at his gut—"not from here," he says, pointing to his head.

"And where do you see Bird fitting in?" my dad asks, clearly as excited about Dan Silver's take on the industry as I am.

"We're not as big as Great American Music," he answers candidly, "but we're better. Or at least we will be with Bird on board." He turns his gaze on me. "Bird, you're what Open Highway Records is all about, and we want you to be one of our first new artists. I'm prepared to sign you to a full record deal. I think you have what it takes to turn this industry on its head, and I want to be the one helping you do it."

His pitch is impassioned. He believes I'm good enough

to jump in with both feet. I look over at my dad, meeting blue eyes just like mine, and see there exactly what I'm already thinking: Dan Silver is our man. I nod slightly.

"Okay, Dan," my dad says, looking a little relieved. "Get us some papers."

Dan grins and stands up, shaking my hand first and then my dad's before walking over to his desk.

"It's happening, Bird," my dad says.

"It really is," I answer. And although I've been on the road practically my whole life, I somehow feel like my journey is just beginning.

8

"WHAT DID THE GAM people say when you told them you were going with Open Highway?" Shannon asks, clamping a capo on her guitar.

I shrug, slightly queasy about it. "I don't know exactly. My dad called 'em."

"Good," she says with a nod. "That's what managers are for. Now, why don't we try it again in G," she suggests, flicking her long black hair over her shoulder.

The first thing Dan Silver did after I signed with Open Highway was schedule a songwriting session so I could polish my songs with a seasoned professional. He'd noticed the chemistry I had with Shannon Crossley at the Bluebird and asked if I'd like to work with her professionally. I couldn't say yes fast enough. I was a little intimidated when I first showed up at her apartment, but she's so chill that I feel like I've known her forever.

"Okay, if you think that'll work," I say, changing my fingers and starting in on the first verse again. We've decided to start with the song about Adam that I sang at the Bluebird. She's also going to help me write some new songs, but she really thinks this one could be gold.

I've never thought so hard about a song before. Usually the lyrics and melody come to me quickly, and then I move on to the next one, but today, we have worked and reworked this song to a point where I barely recognize it. With Shannon's suggestions, it feels fuller, and I get more and more excited about it as we try new things. Some changes work, like simplifying the bridge, and others don't, like changing the key.

"Stop, stop, stop," Shannon says, waving her hand in the air and laughing. "So 'G' does not stand for 'Good Idea.'"

I laugh, relieved, because I feel the same way.

Suddenly the front door opens, and a girl about my age walks in, talking on her cell phone loudly before noticing us in the living room. She instantly lowers her voice and waves, mouthing *sorry* to Shannon before dropping her backpack on the floor and hustling around the corner to the kitchen.

"That's my daughter, Stella," Shannon says, nodding toward the front door.

"Yeah, you guys look a lot alike," I say. They both have

strong jawlines and high cheekbones, and dress in a way that looks effortless and yet enviably stylish. They have the same dark, straight hair, too, although Stella wears hers with thick bangs.

"She's a senior," Shannon says.

"Cool," I say. "Me too."

"Oh? I thought you just turned sixteen."

"Well, I skipped a grade," I explain. "In homeschool. I've had the week off because my mom and brothers have been away, but they got back into town last night, so technically, I'm skipping class right now."

Shannon laughs. "Ah, just your average teen rebel, huh?"

I smile, but we both know my life has been anything but average. Looking at Stella's bag on the floor, lavender canvas that's been doodled on with a Sharpie marker, I feel a twinge of envy. It's just crazy to think about how different our days are. Like today for instance: she was at school, going from class to class, passing her friends in the hallways, and maybe holding hands with a boyfriend or something in the cafeteria—that's how I imagine it at least—while I spent the morning sitting across from my brother at an RV kitchenette doing math problems from a workbook before borrowing my other brother's guitar to work on an album for the record deal I signed last week.

"You sit tight," Shannon says, setting her guitar down on its stand. "I'll go grab us a couple of waters."

As she joins her daughter in the kitchen, I marvel once more at their place, a truly incredible loft in East Nashville. Shannon said the building used to be a warehouse, but now the units have been renovated for housing, art galleries, and studios. It's funky and fun, large and open, obviously decorated by a person with an artistic eye, and way more comfortable than Winnie. There is a Grammy statuette on one of the bookshelves and an entire room off the common living area chock-full of instruments and awards. I want to move in.

"Okay," Shannon says, coming back into the room. She straightens the tiers of her dangly turquoise earrings before picking up her guitar again. "Now, I'm still not loving the chorus. I mean, I love the song and the feel, but we need a button, you know? Something to tack it down at the end."

I frown, looking at my journal. The original lyrics were scrawled out like a poem, but now I've penciled in lots of notes and symbols in the margins and the spaces between the lines. What seemed like a simple song at first has become an intricate ballad. I like our version much better now, but right when I think we've nailed it, Shannon wants more.

"How do you know when a song is done?" I ask. I'm not frustrated; I just sincerely want to know. It feels ready to me.

She shrugs, strumming the opening notes. "When it feels whole."

I stroke the strings of Dylan's guitar and nod. I don't

really get it, but I trust her. She's the one with the Grammy, after all. We play the song about Adam again, but at the end of the chorus, Shannon stops. "What do you want from this guy?" she asks bluntly.

My hand slaps the strings quiet, and my mouth hangs open. When she puts it that way, I'm kind of at a loss for words. "I—I just—"

"She wants him to notice her," Stella interrupts, leaning against a thick wooden column with her bag over her shoulder and a peanut-butter-and-jelly sandwich in hand. Shannon and I both look up at her, surprised. I didn't even hear her come into the room. "Sorry." She shrugs, although she doesn't appear to be. "Just speaking from experience."

"No, you're totally right," I say, turning to face her. "It's like, I know him pretty well. He's really good friends with my brother." I chew on my lip and look out the window toward the Cumberland River. "But I don't know if he sees me as just a friend or as something more."

"Do you flirt?" Stella asks directly before taking another giant bite of her sandwich.

I blush. "I think so," I answer, thinking about our Coke game. But then I also think about how Jacob calls it lame, and I wonder if Adam does it just to humor me or if it really is our "thing."

"He gave me flowers," I say, perking up and thinking back to that amazing night at the Station Inn.

"He gave you flowers?" Stella asks enthusiastically, plopping down on the couch next to me. "Oh yeah, then he totally likes you."

"You really think so?" I ask eagerly. I'm so freaking pumped to finally have a girl's perspective.

Then I glance over at Shannon, worried that maybe she's annoyed that we've interrupted our songwriting session for girl talk, but she seems as engrossed in my Adam crush as her daughter. "What kind of flowers? Roses?" Shannon asks.

I grin, remembering. "It was a little bouquet."

"If a guy buys you flowers, he likes you," Stella says.

"If a guy opens his wallet for anything, he likes you," Shannon says dryly. "That's been my experience."

Stella rolls her eyes. "Yeah, because the guys you date are cheapskates."

I stare at her, unable to imagine talking to my own mother like that, but Shannon just chuckles. "True, but they make for good songs."

"Well, he didn't actually buy them," I admit. "He must have picked them. They were wildflowers."

"Oh," Stella says, drawing that one word out in a monotone way that makes me think she has more to say but won't out of politeness.

There is an awkward moment. I look down and start to strum, thinking back to the flowers and how mad I was when Dylan tossed them out. *Dad's sneezing his head off as it is,* he'd said. *Those weeds aren't helping.*

"Like in the song," Shannon says. "If you ask me, wildflowers are nice. Stella used to pick dandelions for me, and I cherished them more than a dozen roses from any man."

"I guess," I say quietly. I was excited to get flowers for the first time, but now I'm embarrassed talking to Stella and Shannon about it. It had seemed so romantic, like Adam had gone out of his way to do something sweet for me, but maybe he'd just picked them from the cracks of the parking lot as an afterthought. Maybe it wasn't romantic at all, just nice. Just like Adam.

I sigh heavily, feeling exactly the way I felt the night I originally wrote this song, months ago. Adam had said he'd loved our set and even mentioned hanging around after, but then he and my brothers just up and went bowling without me—they said it was a "guys' night"—and I was left at home with my parents and my journal.

"I just want him to *see* me, you know? Like really see me, deep down." I look up at Stella, then Shannon. "Does that make sense?"

"You want him to perceive the real you," Stella says, before shoving the last of her sandwich into her mouth.

I nod. "Exactly."

Shannon takes a sip from her water bottle and then shoos her daughter out of the room. "Go do your homework, missy. We've got to figure out this song or Dan's going to kill me."

Stella rolls her eyes and picks up her backpack. "Party pooper." Shannon returns the gesture, and I smile. Although I'm close with my mom, too, Shannon and Stella seem more like friends than mother and daughter.

As Stella slowly plods up the spiral staircase to her loft bedroom, she calls out, "Bye-bye, Birdie."

I look up and smile. "Bye, Stella."

"So…" Shannon says, reaching over and grabbing a pen. She scribbles in her own notebook and then suggests, "How about we end the chorus with 'notice me'?"

I look at my own journal, and it's like a lightbulb goes off. "It's perfect."

And just like that, the master has taught the student how a writer knows when a song is finally finished.

9

It's CRAZY HOW fast life can change. Two weeks ago, I was crammed in a tiny RV, living and touring with my family. Now, I'm standing in an equally cramped space, but it's covered wall-to-wall with spongy black foam, and the only things in here with me are a microphone and a music stand holding the pages of "Notice Me." Dan liked the demo I recorded with Shannon, and if he likes the studio recording, it will be the first song on my album.

A voice blares through the small space: "This time, hold that note in the lift a little longer." I look at the producer Dan hired for me and give him a thumbs-up through the glass that separates us. Jack Horn is supposed to be the best. He and his team of sound guys have worked with everybody from Sugarland to Willie Nelson, and although he's nice enough, he's all business. I'm used to performing for live audiences, people who stomp their feet and bob their heads, not a forty-year-old in a backward baseball cap with a constant worry line between his eyes. Every time I sing "Notice Me," Jack gives me directions on how to do it better. I thought I'd be in and out of here, but it's been all morning and we still don't have it right. I've had to pee for thirty minutes now, but I'm afraid to mention it.

"So, from the pre-chorus, then?" I ask timidly.

He nods from the control room and the music pours into my headphones. I start in on the lyrics again, leaning toward the microphone. My fingers ache for an instrument, but we laid down Maybelle's fiddling pass yesterday, and we're just doing vocals right now. I had no idea that recording a song required so many steps. The whole process is way more complicated than I ever imagined. I thought for sure my family would be my backing band, but Dan nixed the idea in favor of what he called "session veterans" who already know the sound we're going for. My dad hadn't seemed surprised, but my brothers were pretty mad when I told them.

"So we're not good enough for you anymore?" Dylan had demanded.

"You totally are," I assured him. "I'm definitely going to play that song 'Before Music' for Dan. And since you and I wrote it together, you'll get a songwriting credit if we use it on the album."

"But I'm not a good-enough musician."

"That's not what he meant," I tried to explain.

"She's even sticking up for him now," Jacob chimed in, pulling up the black hood of his sweatshirt and grabbing the car keys. "Let's get out of here."

Then they took a drive to who knows where, not coming home until after dinner. I wanted to talk to them about it again, but my dad told me they needed a little time and space. "There are a lot of changes coming that we're all going to have to get used to," he said.

Tell me about it, I think now. I love the magic of performing for live audiences, even though our shows are exhausting, but it's a whole different beast trying to keep up that same energy in the studio, take after take. And this afternoon, I'll be singing and recording every piece of harmony myself. All this for just one song.

"Stop, stop, Bird." Jack sighs into the speaker by the soundboard. He takes off his headphones and stands up. My heart sinks. I look over at my dad for some moral support, but *he's* not even paying attention anymore. He is completely engrossed in his cell phone, and honestly, I can't blame him. He's heard this song a million times by now.

"Sorry I'm messing up so much," I say into the mic.

Jack leans over the soundboard and pushes the speaker button. "Are you kidding?" he asks, seeming genuinely surprised. "You're doing great."

"Really?"

"Yeah," he explains. "I'm just a perfectionist."

"Oh my gosh," I say, letting out a breath I didn't know I was holding and clutching at the ties of my hooded sweatshirt. "I thought you wanted to pull your hair out."

"No, not at all," he assures me. "I just want it to be spot-on perfect, okay?"

"Okay."

He removes the pencil tucked behind his right ear and holds up his sheet music. "Make a note after the bridge," he instructs me. It feels so weird to be having an entire conversation through a giant pane of glass. "When you come back in, I really want you to punch it. This is the big moment, okay? And when we nail that, let's take a break."

"Cool," I say, marking it.

I readjust my headphones and take a drink of water, relief washing over me. I'm not majorly screwing up; I'm just working toward perfection. I can handle that.

"Here we go, Bird," Jack says, sitting back down and motioning to his sound team.

The music flows again, my cue in two bars. I lean nearer to the mic and focus on the feelings behind the words. I close my eyes and let my voice fill the room, bring my hand to my chest and come in stronger at the final chorus, letting loose with the vocals, pleading with this boy of mine to actually be mine.

"I never knew the words 'let's take a break' could be so powerful," I say to my dad outside the bathroom. "That was brutal."

Together, we walk down the small stairs, both of us eager to get a little fresh air before heading back into the studio.

"I thought you sounded great," Dad says. "The first few times he stopped you, I thought maybe he was hearing nerves or maybe you were flat a couple of times, but then I was just as baffled as you were. I don't know what those guys were hearing, but I guess that's why they're the professionals."

"I guess," I say, pushing open the tinted-glass door.

And then I get a wonderful surprise.

"Bird!" my mom says, walking up the sidewalk with my brothers behind her. Her arms are open wide, and I let her envelop me in a big hug. When I smell her honeysuckle body lotion, I'm instantly happier.

"Hey, Mom," I say, squeezing tightly. "Hey, guys," I say to my brothers, who seem to have forgiven me. "I didn't know y'all were coming."

"We want to see where all the magic happens," Dylan says, smiling. Jacob nods and I am so glad they are here.

"Well then, follow me," I say, feeling a much-needed burst of energy.

I lead my family inside and show them around. It's pretty exciting, giving everybody a peek into what has somehow become my whole life in just a couple of weeks. I introduce them to Jack and the rest of the crew and point out the live room, where we record.

"Speaking of," Jack says, swiveling around halfway in his chair, "we should probably get back at it."

"Could we stay and watch a while?" Jacob asks.

Jack shrugs. "Sure."

As my family squeezes onto the sofa behind the sound guys, I head back into the live room. I worry briefly that they'll figure out that this song is about Adam, but then I realize they're all going to hear it eventually, anyway. Everybody will. *Adam* will.

As I lift my headphones from the hook on the mic stand, I glance up at my family, whose faces range from surprised to amused to see me in such a professional setting. And then, when the instrumental track plays and I start to sing, I think I can see them settle into another expression, one that makes my heart feel like it might burst. Pride. I sing like I would at a Barrett Family Band performance, as if we were live, with just one shot to nail it, and I forget about being perfect for a moment. I just sing.

When I finish, I see my family clapping and smiling behind the glass before Jack presses the speaker button, and then I hear them woo-hooing loudly. "Your first fans," he says, grinning.

The door opens again, and Dan walks in with a sharply dressed woman I've never seen before. She's wearing a loose fuchsia top with a tight black pencil skirt and super high stilettos. Her brown hair is slicked back in a sleek bun, and she is carrying an iPad in her hand.

"You've got visitors," Jack says into my headphones from the control room. "Let's take five, everybody."

I take off my headphones as Dan motions through the glass for me to join them. Jack and the sound guys are milling about, and I see my dad introducing my family to Dan. By the time I try to push the control room door open, the room is crowded and pretty suffocating.

"Come get us when you're ready," Jack says to Dan, leading his sound team down the hall to the lounge.

"We're going to get out of here, too," my mom says graciously. "It was really our pleasure to finally meet you, Dan. And good job, Bird, honey. That song is just beautiful."

"Thanks, Mom," I say, giving her another quick hug before they leave.

And then it's just my dad, Dan, and the mystery woman, who is staring at me as if I am a museum exhibit instead of a live human being.

"Bird, Judd, I want you to meet Anita Handler," Dan says, introducing the woman. Her heavily painted pink lips are stretched into a closed smile and even in her four-inch heels, she still only comes up to my shoulders. She pumps our hands once, strong and efficient, as Dan continues with his hearty introduction. "She'll be your publicist and is the best in the biz. I had a heck of a time getting her down here from New York."

"I'm more of a rock and roller than a country girl," she explains frankly in a thick New York accent. "But I figure, eh, a little fresh air won't kill me."

I'm pretty sure my lower jaw hits the ground, especially if the expression on my face looks anything like the one on my dad's, but Dan just laughs and shakes his head. "You've got to know her to love her, and you will when you do," he assures us. "And she may not care for the music, but she cares for her musicians in a big way. She's responsible for the images of a lot of major chart toppers, like—"

"Oh, Dan, stop. You'll make me blush," she interrupts.

Dan smiles. "Anyway, Anita was with Allied for the last five years, working out of our New York office, but she's been in the business for almost twenty."

"Which means I got started at five years old," she says quickly. My dad and Dan laugh because she's probably more like forty-five. Still, the woman does look amazing. And when she grabs my forearm and turns the full power of her thickly made-up eyes on me, I admire the intensity there. "Bird, now that we're working together, I need you to think of me as your new best friend, your BFF," she says in total seriousness. "You will tell me everything. No surprises, no holding back. You don't know what will connect with your fans, but I do."

I've never really had a best friend before, but this doesn't sound like the way those things are supposed to go. It feels weird and, honestly, a little demanding for a stranger to expect you to just spill your guts to her.

But I trust Dan. I don't know what having a publicist entails, but if working with Anita will help me connect with my fans—or the fans I am supposedly going to have—then I'll get on board.

"I've never had a BFF," I say, smiling down at her. "I hope we don't have to get matching necklaces or something."

Anita rolls her eyes. "Oh God, I haven't worn one of those since the eighties."

"So..." I say, doing the math in my head. "When you were three years old?"

"Oh, Silver, she's cheeky." Anita looks at me appraisingly. "We're going to get along just fine."

When I look at Dan, he's beaming at the two of us, and I feel like I just passed some sort of test.

"That's a wrap," Jack says.

"Hallelujah." I sigh, peeling the headphones off my ears. I stretch big, twisting and nearly touching the ceiling, before joining Jack, my dad, and the rest of the guys in the control room. "I thought 'let's take a break' was the sweetest phrase in history, but I like the sound of 'that's a wrap' even better."

"Me too," one of the guys responds, yawning even though he's on at least his sixth cup of coffee today.

Without warning, the instrumental track starts again. Jack smiles and gestures to the sofa. I plop down next to my dad, who stretches his arm around the couch behind me, and then I hear myself. Or a version of myself about a bazillion times better than the real thing.

"That's me?"

Jack smiles softly and leans back in his chair as the music plays. He closes his eyes. I do the same and realize instantly why he pushed me so hard. That's my voice, but smoother, better. That's my poetry, spun from the pages of my journal into song. The harmonies blend like honey in warm tea. And although I was worried about the drums and electric guitar, they actually give the song a fun, effervescent sound. I am most happy about the homage to my bluegrass roots: woven through it all is the fiddle.

I open my eyes again and see that everybody in the room is smiling as widely as I am, their feet tapping along like mine. The song that I've sung into the ground today now sounds fresh as spring.

"It's still rough," Jack warns as the last notes fade away. "It still needs more mixing, but I think—"

"It's perfect!" I shout, launching myself off the couch, nearly knocking him out of his swivel chair with a giant hug. I stand up and look around at all three guys behind the soundboard. "You did it. I love it. You made me sound like a real singer," I gush. "Thank you. Thank you so much."

"Bird," Jack says, "you *are* a real singer. All we did was record what's already there."

He pushes PLAY again, which I take as the best compliment of my life. Not his words, but his actions. Seems to me that a man who's heard the same melodies over and over all week, who's recorded the same song on at least four different instruments and with at least three different harmonies, would be sick to death of this song, but he's not. As "Notice Me" fills the room one more time, I shove my hands into the pockets of my Open Highway sweatshirt and let the realization of this dream sink in.

10

"WOW, JACOB, YOUR handwriting's actually legible," I comment, looking over at the Spanish work sheet he turned in to my mom. "*Yo puedo leerlo.*"

He smirks. "*Y yo puedo* kick your butt."

My mom waves her hands between us, ever the peacemaker. "*Relájense, mijos,*" she says, smiling. Her Spanish is better than either of ours now. She says teaching us is like a refresher course for the stuff she's forgotten after all these years. I've made the case that if we're just going to forget it, anyway, why learn it at all? My brothers totally had my back, but our logic didn't fly with the folks.

"Dinner's in five," Dad says, setting a stack of bowls down in front of us.

A friend of my parents is on tour for the next few

months and has offered to let us stay at his place in Nashville while he's gone. He said it'd be sitting empty, and now he won't have to worry about somebody feeding his cat. I have to say, having my own bedroom the past couple of weeks has been awesome.

"Wow, son, your handwriting *is* a little better than I remembered," Dad adds, reading over my mom's shoulder.

"Hey!" Jacob says defensively. "It's a lot easier now that I don't have to worry about you taking a hard right turn when I'm midsentence."

"Whoa, whoa, whoa! It's all smooth sailing when Captain Judd's behind the wheel," Dad says, brushing off his shoulders. So lame. We roll our eyes and shake our heads, much to his delight.

I look back at my own work sheet and am scribbling in the future tenses of my vocab words when my dad's cell phone rings. He looks first at the screen, then quickly up at me before walking over to the kitchen, where I can see the lid of the Crock-Pot dripping with steam. Mom put her famous vegetarian chili on this morning, and the smell has been tempting us the whole day. I'd forgotten what a good cook my mom is when she's not confined to canned veggies and a minifridge in an RV galley.

"Well, Dan, she can't talk just now, actually," I overhear my dad say. "She's in the middle of a Spanish lesson with her brother." My back stiffens.

"Is that Dan?" I call, pushing back my chair. "Is that for me?"

Dad holds his hand up and turns away. "Tomorrow at ten?" he asks. He looks over at my mom, who nods her approval. "That'll be fine. We'll see you then."

He hangs up the phone and walks to the fridge. I follow him.

"Dad, was that Dan? What'd he want?"

"He wants to see you in the morning," my father answers, grabbing a gallon of milk and heading back over to the table. "Dinner's almost ready, kids," he says. "Let's wrap it up."

I stack my books and papers into a messy pile and throw it all on the couch, eager to get back to my dad so I can ask him more about what Dan said. Then Jacob's cell beeps.

"Oh, cool," he says offhandedly. "Adam might have a gig in Nashville."

I stop in my tracks, halfway between the dining room and kitchen. "What? When?" I ask, but Jacob's in another world, already texting Adam back.

"Bird, set the table, please," my mom says, getting up to check the bread in the oven. "Jacob, go tell your brother that dinner's ready."

"Ugh." I sigh, my head spinning. In the kitchen, I grab a fistful of spoons and interrogate my father. "So what'd he want, Dad? Did he like the song? What'd he say?"

"He said he wants to see you in the morning, Bird," he repeats slowly.

"You could've let me talk to him," I say, following him back into the dining room.

"Bird, he called *me*."

"Well, you didn't have to tell him I had homework," I complain, placing the spoons next to everybody's bowls. "It makes me sound like a kid instead of a professional."

"Listen," my dad says, looking me firmly in the eyes. "Record contract or no record contract, your schoolwork is still a priority."

My eyebrows arch in surprise at his hard tone. Annoyed, I take a seat at the table as my mom sets the big pot of chili on a hot pad in front of me. I know I'm only sixteen, and honestly, my dad's been a great manager so far, but you'd think I could at least take my own phone calls. It's like he and Dan and now Anita are deciding everything about my life, and I'm lucky I don't have to ask permission to go to the bathroom.

Just as my mom comes back to the table with the bread and my brothers plop into their seats, I hear my own cell phone beep down the hall. I perk up, springing to my feet.

"No phones during dinner," my dad orders, stopping me in my tracks.

"But—"

"No phones," he repeats and points to the seat of my chair.

"Oh my gosh, Dad," I grumble, sitting back down. "You know it could be important. Shannon might want to reschedule tomorrow or—"

"Then you can call her back," my dad says, folding his hands. "Bird, why don't you say grace tonight?"

I roll my eyes. That is so my dad. "Dear Lord," I begin, bowing my head.

And then a thought slips into my mind: What if it's Adam? But that's stupid because he doesn't even have my number. I shake the thought and continue, keeping it short and sweet. "Amen," we all chime, and my brothers are digging in before I've even unclasped my hands.

"You guys want to have a family jam after supper?" my dad asks during dinner. He's unaware of his dripping milk mustache.

"Oh, that sounds fun," Mom says, wiping her mouth with a napkin. "We can go out on the patio. It's a nice night."

Dylan nods.

"Definitely," Jacob says. "I'd love that."

But when everybody looks at me, I shrug. As nice as it would be to play together like we used to, I've been playing all day, every day lately, and I'm exhausted... and still a little annoyed with my dad. "I'm actually pretty beat," I say.

Jacob looks up at me, a long lock of black hair hanging over his eye. "Seriously?" he asks, midbite.

"What?"

He just stares.

"What?"

"Whatever, Bird," he says, shaking his head.

I look at Dylan for support, but he avoids eye contact and turns back to his near-empty bowl. I look at my mom, who gives me a small smile, and then to my dad, who doesn't seem to know what to say.

"What?" I ask Jacob again, feeling a little defensive. "I've been playing all day! I've been at Shannon's every morning this week, and now Dan wants to see me tomorrow for who knows what reason, probably because he hates my song. I just want to watch TV or read a magazine or something, okay?" Nobody says a word. In fact, everybody's pretty intent on their dinner. "Rain check, okay, you guys?"

"Okay," Dylan says simply, looking at me straight on. He stands up and grabs his dirty dishes. He starts to walk into the kitchen but turns back toward me, a soft but sad look on his face. "Wait, you know what? Not okay. Bird, I get it. All you do is play music, and all we do is talk about when we used to play music. You're tired. Fine. I really do get it. But as for me, I'd like my guitar back, and I'd like to play some music with my family tonight."

He doesn't seem angry, just matter-of-fact.

But his words sink in deep.

"May I be excused?" I ask my dad.

He nods, and I get up, joining my brother in the kitchen as we put our dishes in the dishwasher. I might be burned out and tired, but it would actually be nice to play some songs that aren't my own—to play for fun, without Jack or Dan watching me and scrutinizing every note—to play Maybelle again instead of a guitar. "You're right, Dylan," I say. "Let's play tonight, like we used to."

"Really?"

"Your guitar's by the front door," I call over my shoulder in response as I head down the hall to my room.

I unplug my phone from its charger and flop onto the bed, but the message I see on my phone is not from Shannon. And not from Adam. It's from a number I don't recognize:

Hey. Mom gave me ur #. Gonna check out the flea market at the fairgrounds on Sat. Wanna come? It's Stella, btw.

"Aw, that's so nice," I say to myself as I type back a reply:

Yes, def.

I stare at the phone, waiting for her response. It may not be the president of a Nashville music label, or the one boy on earth I wish would notice me, but I'm as pumped as if it were. Finally her reply comes through:

Cool. Call u.

With a smile on my face, I hop up and go to my closet, swatting a pile of dirty clothes off my fiddle case. I bring dear Maybelle out to the patio, where Dylan is setting folding chairs into a circle. The others join us, and we all sit together as the sun settles low on the horizon, tuning and prepping our instruments, just like the old days, the Barrett Family Band back together again.

11

"I BET HE hates it," I tell my dad as we walk up the sidewalk to the Open Highway offices. I toss my lucky rock back and forth between my hands nervously. My stomach has been in knots all morning.

"I doubt that," Dad answers.

"Why'd he call us in, then?" I ask for the billionth time.

"Could be for anything, Bird," he says patiently. He presses the doorbell and smiles at me confidently. "I've heard the song. Lots of times." He rubs his jaw comically and continues. "Lots and lots and lots and *lots* of times." I make a face at him. "And it's great, sweetie. It really is."

"You're my dad," I say as the door opens. "You have to say that."

A brown-haired girl in her twenties greets us and introduces herself as Steph, the new receptionist. I was kind of hoping the position would still be available in case my singing career tanked during this meeting. "Dan's been waiting for you," she says. "Y'all can go on back."

The door to his office is open, but his back is turned to us. I knock softly on the frame.

"Barretts," Dan says, turning. He covers the speaker on his cell phone and waves us in distractedly, pointing to the two chairs at his desk. "Have a seat."

No hug, no handshake, no smile.

He heard it; he hated it.

As we settle into the two chairs at his desk, he paces the sitting area and finishes his phone call. My knees bob up and down involuntarily. I'd really like to know what this meeting is about.

"Fine, tomorrow, bye," he says, ending the call. Instead of greeting us as usual, he walks behind his desk and checks something on his computer, his brow furrowed like he's got something on his mind. He looms above us but doesn't sit down, and I shift uncomfortably in my seat. "There," he says to himself, and then he looks up and points a sleek black remote toward a bookshelf to his left. "What do you hear?"

"Notice Me" starts to play in surround sound. Unsure what to say, I look at him hesitantly. "My song?"

Dan cocks his head and nods thoughtfully. "Sure," he says. "Know what I hear?"

As the song plays, I can't help but think that the quality of my voice has never sounded better, that the beat is catchy and the lyrics are perfect, and that if he doesn't like this song, then he won't like any.

I gulp hard and shake my head.

"I hear your first single," he says, grinning broadly.

"Really?" I ask, hardly able to believe it.

"Really!" he says, his eyes sparkling. He reaches out his hand to me and, letting his words sink in, I stand slowly on weak legs. He shakes my hand vigorously, then my dad's. Anita walks in wearing a black skirt suit, carrying what looks like a bottle of champagne and four glasses.

"Congratulations, Bird!" she says. She hands the bottle off to Dan and passes around the glasses. "Don't worry, Judd. It's sparkling cider."

My dad grins and puts his arm around me. In fact, he surprises me by kissing me at my hairline and whispering, "I'm proud of you, kiddo."

Dan shoots the cork across the room. We all cheer, and Anita actually winks at me. Dan deftly steps back so that the sparkling cider doesn't drench his slacks, making it clear to everyone that he's done this before, that this single isn't his first by far, and that he's making good on his promises to me. I'm really on my way.

"I still can't believe I'm a recording artist," I say, my smile wide and my eyes wet. "People will hear this song. They'll know it; they'll know me." A cold chill shakes me from head to toe.

"Bird, this will be the first toast of many," Dan declares.

While he pours, Anita turns to me. "Bird, I need to talk to you about some next steps. For one, I've put together a team of stylists." She squints and holds one hand in front of her, as if blocking out half of my face. "I met with them this week to nail down your look for your first promo shoot this Saturday."

"My look?"

Dan grins at me as he sets down the bottle. "Are you ready for your close-up?"

I start to answer, but Anita gets there first. "She will be when I'm done with her."

He smiles.

"To Bird Barrett," Dan says, lifting his glass.

"To Bird Barrett," my dad and Anita repeat, holding theirs up as well.

I face their smiles, see my future in their eyes, and laugh out loud as I toast a dream come true.

I've never been one for tennis, but as I sit in a salon chair in the stylists' area of a large studio, facing a giant mirror ringed with bright lights, I'm mesmerized by the back-and-forth between Anita and my new hairstylist, Tammy.

"So, you think red?" Anita asks.

"I think red, but you think blond?" Tammy returns, smacking her gum. These two women couldn't be more different if they tried. As usual, Anita looks chic and put-together, wearing a designer color-blocked dress, her dark brown hair shiny at shoulder length. Tammy is wearing a flowery peasant top with teal skinny jeans and wedge sandals, her blond hair pulled back in intricate braiding.

"Well, we discussed blond resonating more with Middle America," Anita says, frowning at the two color samples in her hands. One is straw yellow, and the other is coppery red. They've been talking about my hair for the past ten minutes, and truly, it's captivating. Their accents even make them sound like they're speaking two totally different languages. While Anita is snappy and her Long Island background is hard to miss, Tammy has a strong Smoky Mountains drawl. I'm surprised they don't need me to translate.

"Right, but red is more memorable," Tammy says. She runs her hands through my long hair for the hundredth time, tossing it this way and that, her touch nearly putting me to sleep. My hair is naturally strawberry blond, so I've already got the best of both worlds in my opinion, but I keep quiet. What do I know about hair? My mom trims mine.

Anita holds each hair swatch up to my cheeks once more, closing one eye as she always does when examining me.

"So you think red," she says again.

"Red," Tammy says decidedly. "I think we should go red."

Anita's phone rings, pulling away her focus. "Wilson, I do not have time for excuses," she says harshly into the phone. "Do it," she tells Tammy before click-clacking away in her pumps, like a woman on a mission.

"I would not want to be the guy on the other end of that phone call," Tammy says, grinning mischievously.

I giggle, and she winks at me in the mirror.

"So we're going red?" my makeup artist, Sam, asks as he saunters over with a couple of sponges soaked in foundation. "I'll obviously do her face once she's dyed and dried, but I need to go ahead and match her skin tone."

"No problem," Tammy says, scooting over. Fascinated, I watch her prep a small rolling table next to me with perfectly squared pieces of aluminum foil as Sam dabs the sponges at my jawline.

"Hmmm..." he says, rubbing it in and pondering the two. "Okay, this one."

I tilt my head and look in the mirror to see the side of my face he's tested with foundation and, honestly, I cannot tell the difference.

124

"I'm going to mix the color," Tammy says. She yawns as she walks across the studio. "And grab a cup of coffee from craft services."

"Grab me one, too?" Sam calls after her. Then he turns to me and starts to speak but is cut off by an enormous yawn.

I grin. "Tell me about it. It should be illegal to work before six AM."

Sam holds up his hand for a high five in agreement. I hadn't known what to expect at this promo shoot, but so far, I'm having a blast. Across the large open room, I see Anita and Dan talking to the photographer as the crew sets up a white backdrop and big lights. Tammy is hitting up craft services, which is basically a table full of food and drinks that everybody can help themselves to throughout the day. And Sam has tubes and brushes and case after case of shadows and powders lined up neatly in front of the mirror. Like a surgeon, he studies his instruments and then picks up a pair of tweezers.

"The color will take Tammy a while," he says, "so let's treat your skin while she's at it."

I hadn't expected pain to be part of the pampering, but Sam starts his treatment by plucking my eyebrows. I thought they looked okay, but he's still hard at work when Tammy comes back. I study Sam through my now-blurry eyes as he works, inches from my face. He is a pretty man, perfectly fit. He has smooth brown skin, bleached-white hair, and baby-soft hands.

But then his eyes suddenly narrow and he leans even closer to my face, so close that I can smell his tropical-fruit-scented shampoo.

"I know." I groan, closing my eyes and letting him tilt my chin up. "I know. Today of all days I get a major zit on my chin. My mom told me it's barely noticeable, but I—"

"Oh no," Sam says, cutting me off. "That sucker's noticeable, but it's nothing I can't make disappear."

Tammy snorts as she sections off my hair.

"What?" Sam challenges.

"The only thing you make disappear is eligible bachelors every time you open your mouth to speak," Tammy says. "Like last night with—"

"Okay, okay, okay," Sam says, slightly blushing as he shushes Tammy. "Don't corrupt the talent."

Tammy winks at me in the mirror again, and I laugh as I close my eyes.

"Now the other foot," my stylist, Amanda, commands. This girl is only a couple of years older than Dylan, but you wouldn't know it the way she bosses people around.

While Sam and Tammy finished my look from the neck up, Amanda unpacked more than twenty dresses from garment bags, arranging them by color on two rolling racks. Once I was passed off to her, she zipped me up and zipped me out as I modeled gown after gown for Anita, Dan, and the photographer. With my new coppery-red hair and dramatic smoky eyes, I think I would look good in a burlap sack, but finding the perfect outfit and accessories for these pictures has been like putting together an intricate puzzle. By the time lunch rolled around, the choice had been narrowed down to two dresses, and it was decided that everyone would "think it over" during break. Personally, I like Amanda's favorite, the flowy green dress I'm in now, but then again, my entire experience with fashion comes from the sale rack at T.J.Maxx.

"Is green too obvious with red hair?" Anita muses, scrunching her brows.

"Look how it pops," Amanda says. "Her skin is flawless. And this dress is conservative but flirty. It'll look great on camera."

The photographer nods slightly, then says, "Bird, give me some movement."

I feel frozen. What does that even mean? I stiffly swish my skirt, twisting my hips slightly. Sam covers his mouth to suppress a laugh, and I make a face at him.

"I like that," the photographer says. "And it will work with the fans."

"Should we do contact lenses?" Anita asks Dan. "Red hair, green eyes, green dress?"

Sam's smile drops faster than the ball on New Year's Eve. "Absolutely not," he says, stepping forward. "Too obvious, too matchy-matchy. Her blue eyes are gorgeous."

"But isn't it blue eyes, blond hair; green eyes, red hair?" Anita asks. Her question seems sincere, but Sam acts like she just insulted his grandmother.

"Yes, if you're going for boring," he snaps.

I gasp quietly, but Amanda and Tammy nod in agreement.

Anita narrows her eyes. "The whole purpose of today is to nail down her image, so these are big decisions and it's certainly worth considering all our options."

Everyone on set goes quiet. The tension is palpable.

I would never stand up to Anita or Dan about anything, but when it comes to their work, these stylists are fearless. It's almost like there are two teams on set: the stylists and the industry people. Even when we broke for lunch after hair, makeup, and wardrobe, the stylists sat together and the label folks sat together. I didn't want to choose a side, so I stuck with my dad.

"Fine. Red hair, blue eyes. Makes her even more special," Anita finally says.

"And the green dress," the photographer decides. Amanda smiles. Then the photographer turns to Anita and Dan and asks, almost as an afterthought, "Are we all in agreement? The green?"

Anita and Dan nod, then follow the photographer to set while Amanda leads me back over to wardrobe. "Of course the green," she mumbles.

"Green contact lenses," Sam says, shaking his head. "Can you imagine? She'd have to wear them all the time, nonstop, and the girl's got twenty-twenty vision." He looks at me. "Don't you?"

"I do."

He tsks. "How phony."

"Amen," Amanda grumbles. "I didn't even ask them about her boots because I didn't want to give them the chance to shoot them down, but look at these Justins." We all look down at my feet. The tall cowboy boots she's put me in are brown and trimmed with pink details up both legs and across the toes. They're rustic but feminine. I am in love with them. "Custom embroidered," she says, and we all take a moment to silently appreciate.

Amanda hands me a pair of long gold earrings, and I'm surprised that I actually get to put these on without help. She gave me a good scolding when I unzipped myself out of the first dress we tried.

But that's how it's been all morning. Sam rushed to me like he was putting out a fire when I took a can of Coke from the craft services table. "A straw!" he practically shouted, whipping one out from his waist pouch. "Your lips! Use a straw!" And I thought Tammy would have a stroke when I absentmindedly braided my hair over one shoulder. I'm wearing it down and loose for the shoot, apparently, so I didn't even realize it was "styled." I've learned a big lesson today: I'm only here to do one job and that's being "the talent." And although I'm used to setting up and breaking down the BFB equipment before and after every show and even though it feels totally lazy to not do anything for myself, I have to respect the fact that everybody else is here to do a job, too.

"We're ready when you are," the photographer calls over to us.

And now, five hours, two hair rinses, thirteen dresses, and four makeup touch-ups later, I am finally walking onto set.

"We moved her mark, James," the photographer calls.

The guy leading me nods, looks around, and then escorts me to a small X in black tape on the floor. "Do you need anything?" he asks.

"No, I'm good," I say. "Thank you."

He steps away, but before I can catch a breath, my styling team is on me again. Sam's big brush full of powder attacks my T-zone. Amanda's cold hands press the straps of my dress down flat over my shoulders, and she frees a few strands of hair from my earrings. And over us all is a foggy cloud from Tammy's enormous can of hair spray.

"Clear set," the photographer commands.

My team exits in a hurry, waiting in the wings with Dan and Anita, all of them watching a monitor. The photographer snaps a quick test shot and then consults with them. He directs a crew member to adjust a light to my right, and when I look over, I see another monitor—only this one is turned slightly toward me.

And I gasp. I was expecting to see myself: Bird Barrett, daughter, sister, fiddler extraordinaire. Who I was *not* expecting to see was a redheaded bombshell with perfect skin wearing a dress that fits like a glove around curves I didn't even realize I had. I was not expecting to see a grown woman.

This is a new Bird Barrett. I smile into the camera, letting go of all self-consciousness as I mimic any pose I've ever seen on the red carpets in *People* magazine. The studio space is flooded with a Kellie Pickler song, the camera clicks away, and the lights pop.

The photographer shouts encouraging things like: "Beautiful!"

"Yes, like that!"

"Gorgeous, Bird."

And not that bluegrass fans care much about fashion, anyway, and not that my audiences ever critiqued my look before, but I can't help but think that no one would recognize me now. I hardly recognize myself.

12

"Wow, you look incredible!" Stella shouts from the front of the Expo Center. As excited as I was for my promo shoot this morning, I've been equally looking forward to my trip to the flea market with Stella this afternoon.

"Thanks!" I say.

We've been hanging out for almost a month, but usually it's when I'm at her house to work with her mom. This is the first time it's been just the two of us.

"Red, huh?" she asks, eyeing my hair as we enter the building. "I like it."

"Me too," I say. "I think..."

"Well, the leaves are going red, so why not you?"

"It's going to take a little getting used to, but I'm glad they left it long at least."

She nods in agreement and loops her arm through mine, moving us briskly toward the market.

We are walking around booths stocked with vendors selling anything from antiques to artwork, from junk to jewelry, and although I get overwhelmed on such shopping excursions, Stella steams ahead like a woman on a mission.

"You read a lot?" I ask as she drags her fingers over the spines of several old books at one table.

"Some." She shrugs. "But I was thinking of making little shelves out of them. Putting them on brackets, like a bookshelf."

"Oh, wow."

"You think it's dumb?"

"I think it's genius."

She grins. "Yeah, I think it'll look good. I saw it online."

I help her look for thick books with pretty spines and marvel at her creativity. I never would've thought of something like that. When I find one of my mom's and my all-time favorites, a gorgeous sixtieth anniversary edition of *Gone With the Wind* in a white jacket covered with red vines, I tell her it's a must for her project. "Although maybe you should at least read the books before you doom them to a life of utility."

"Ha." She snorts. "Maybe a life of utility at Crossley palace beats a life of collecting dust at the Tennessee State

Fairgrounds." She takes the heavy book from me and wanders around the table.

I smile. "Touché."

We make a pile of books, and she expertly chooses nine from our stack. But when it comes time to haggle a price, something that always makes me extremely uncomfortable, I leave her to it and continue perusing the vendor's wares. Picking up an old book of Nashville trivia, I start thumbing through it. No, I did not know that Oprah Winfrey lived in Nashville as a teenager. Yes, I know about "the King" and those hips—who doesn't?

"You ready?" Stella asks, stuffing the last of her books into a canvas tote.

I hold the book of trivia out to her, pointing to the man staring at us from the open page. "You know that guy Adam I was telling you about?"

"The 'Notice Me' guy?" she asks.

"Yeah. He sort of looks like him." I point to a picture of Josh Turner at his Grand Ole Opry induction. "But with a little shaggier hair. And Adam's a little more...I don't know...rugged." I feel my face start to turn red.

Stella's eyes bug out of her head. "*More* rugged? Than Josh Turner?" she asks. "So then he must be, like, totally hot." I close the book and put it down, überaware that the vendor is listening to our entire conversation. "Oh my gosh, you're blushing," Stella teases, hip-checking me.

I hide my furious blushing by walking toward another booth. Her eyes are twinkling as she catches up.

"Yes, he's hot," I confirm, grinning back at her. I shoulder one of her two heavy bags, and we continue our stroll through the flea market. "But it's more than that. My family has gotten to know him pretty well—he's on the same bluegrass circuit—and he's sweet and funny and basically just a really great guy. He's also super talented. Like, the songs he writes, they're just deep, you know? He's poetic."

Stella looks amused. "You've got it bad."

I sigh. "Yeah."

"Bad enough to write a song about him."

I crinkle my nose. "Pretty bad." We both laugh.

We set our bags down at a jewelry stand and start looking through the rings. "These are like the ones your mom wears," I comment, looking at the chunky stones of opal, amethyst, and turquoise. "I love her jewelry."

"We actually make it ourselves," Stella says. "Like these earrings?" She pulls on one dangling from her ear. "I made them with my best friend, Liss." She bites her lip. "She's a year older and just went away to college, so we made matching pairs before she left."

I look at her earrings more closely as she sweeps her dark hair off her shoulder. There are two stones of tigereye dangling from her lobe, secured in place with delicate gold wire. "They're really pretty," I remark.

"Thanks."

"I bet you really miss her."

"Yeah," she says. "It sucks."

We settle into a comfortable silence as we look through rings, bracelets, and necklaces. I like that Stella isn't one of those people who have to fill every space with conversation. But when she does speak again, she takes me off guard.

"Let's text him," she says.

I look up at her, stunned. "Adam?"

"No, Josh Turner," she says sarcastically. "Yes, Adam."

"I—I can't," I stammer.

"You don't have his number?"

"I mean, I actually do have his number because I stole it out of Jacob's phone once," I admit, embarrassed. "But I've never used it."

"So what?" she says, leaning an elbow against the table. "You said you guys are like family friends, so it wouldn't be weird. Just something simple and quick, like, 'Hey, how's life on the road?'"

Reluctantly, I pull my cell phone out of my pocket, along with my lucky rock. My thumbs type as if they have a mind of their own. Stella's boldness must be rubbing off on me already. "You don't think he'll think it's weird?" I ask again.

"It's not weird. Send it."

And without overthinking it, I do:

Hey, how's life on the road? It's Bird, btw.

I press SEND, then stare at the words on the screen.

"I can't believe I just did that," I murmur, my hands shaking a little.

The next five minutes are excruciating. I tuck my phone away and try to keep shopping. I rub my lucky rock until it feels like the sharp edge could cut right through one of the calluses I have on my fingertips from playing so much guitar lately. Twice I make sure the ringer's on, and I hear phantom beeps a few times as well. Finally, a reply comes through:

Bird who?

"Oh no, he totally doesn't know who I am." I groan, showing the text to Stella.

She rolls her eyes ever so slightly. "Yeah, 'cause the guy knows a ton of people named Bird."

Oh.

"He's flirting," she says, smiling. "That's a good thing. Now write—"

But then my phone beeps again:

Just kidding, Lady Bird. How's the rising star? Been thinking about you.

138

My heart nearly leaps out of my chest. Stella, who read it over my shoulder, drapes her arm around me. "See? Flirting."

We spend the next hour walking down the aisles, shopping and sending texts back and forth with Adam. I don't buy a thing all day, but I help carry Stella's stuff, and I feel like I've downed a hundred energy drinks. Every time my phone beeps, another surge of adrenaline races through my veins and Stella helps me craft the perfect reply. She's funny, quick on her feet, and is the perfect wingwoman.

She encourages me to ask Adam when he's coming back through Nashville. I'm bummed that he says not until after New Year's because a gig he was working on fell through.

"That's, like, forever from now," I groan.

"Then it's a good thing you texted him," she says. "Y'all are talking at least. And every good relationship needs a solid foundation of texting."

I smirk. "Says Dr. Phil?"

"No, says Dr. Stel." I laugh out loud as my phone beeps again. She reads the screen along with me. "Oh! Now say . . ."

I don't know what I'm going to do if Adam texts me when she's not around.

13

"THIS LIGHT. Your hair. These flowers," Tammy gushes, securing a crown of woven daisies to my head. "It's divine."

"Thank you," I say with a huge smile. "I'm so excited, I think I'm going to bust!"

"It *is* exciting," she says in her signature drawl. "This is a big deal. You're going to be a huge star, Bird Barrett, and I'll get to say I knew you when."

I laugh, thinking about that. I mean, what if Tammy were fixing my hair right now for the Grammys? I'd walk the red carpet, wear crazy-expensive jewelry, and be so nervous sitting in the crowd as somebody like Jay Z opened the envelope for Best New Artist and announced the winner and it was me!

"Is the talent ready?" the assistant director calls. Tammy hurriedly sticks another bobby pin in my hair.

We're almost set for the very first take of my music video for "Notice Me," and I feel like I ought to pinch myself. I'm wearing a gorgeous pale pink dress, and I love the way the chiffon moves and catches in the breeze. The director told me he wants a "dreamlike, natural mood," and as the golden rays from the morning sun peek through the treetops and wash down over Maybelle and me, it looks like he's going to get just what he wants. I'm standing in a field of wildflowers, white and gold and purple and blue, and every time the autumn breeze blows, it ripples over the field as if God himself were brushing His mighty hand over it all. It's breathtaking.

"Now, one more quick spritz," Tammy says, more to herself than to me. She raises that can of hair spray, and I close my eyes quickly. I try not to cough. . . . I try not to yawn.

It was another early call. At six AM, my dad and I met Dan, Anita, my styling team, and about a dozen crew members at Open Highway, where we joined the caravan out to this sprawling "farm" in Franklin, Tennessee. Dad told me this used to be horse country, but these days it's just well-to-do people who like their homes big. One of them let Dan rent out an acre on their back lot, and that's where we are now.

The juxtaposition of the calm where I'm standing, and all the lights, generators, people, and trailers behind the cameras is almost comical. All the times I've watched music videos, I never thought about the view from this side of the lens.

"You play your fiddle on this shoulder?" Tammy asks.

I nod. She sweeps my hair back and to my other side before giving it all one last fluff.

"Okay, people," the director calls, clapping his hands. "Let's roll."

"Break a leg," Tammy whispers, winking.

I grin and watch her walk away, holding her arms out like a tightrope walker, precariously picking her way through the field. We were all given strict instructions to walk in each other's footsteps so as not to mash the flowers and "ruin the visual appeal" of the set. Watching her hips twist in her painted-on jeans as she walks off set makes me laugh, which is good because I'm wound up tight right now.

It's overwhelming, all the people standing around watching me, the cameras angled my way, the constant scrutiny. I try to find as much to think about besides this video as I can. I'm not even really singing today, just lip-synching, but the thought of mouthing the words makes me even more nervous.

"Quiet on the set!" someone yells.

I raise Maybelle to my shoulder and take a deep breath to calm my nerves. "Here we go, girl," I whisper, drawing my bow across the strings to warm up.

"Hang on!" I hear Anita call. I look up and see her picking her way through the field looking almost as comical as Tammy. Why would she wear high heels to an outdoor shoot? Although to be fair, it's the middle of October, and I'm wiggling my bare toes in cold, dewy grass, so I guess I don't have much room to talk when it comes to appropriate footwear.

"Bird," she says, getting closer. "You are a vision."

"Thank you," I say, savoring any compliment I get from Anita. If she thinks I look good, then I can relax about that part of the video, anyway.

"Listen," she says, "Dan and I wanted to run something by you." I look over her shoulder and see Dan making his way out to us, an exquisite koa guitar in hand. The three-toned wood gleams in the sunlight, and as he gets closer, I see an intricate vine inlay climbing up the neck. "We thought we'd have you play the guitar instead of the fiddle in the video."

I grip Maybelle tighter. "But I thought these shots were for the fiddling pass."

Dan stands in two foot-holes behind Anita and leans around her. "We're switching a few things around," he explains. "And I want you to have this, Bird. An exceptional artist needs an instrument of equal caliber."

The guitar he holds out to me is gorgeous. Dylan would kill for it, and I'm sure he's tired of me borrowing his all the time.

"Seriously? Thank you, Dan," I say. But I can't help think that, although I use the guitar to pick out melodies for songwriting, the fiddle is my instrument. I feel more relaxed with Maybelle, and today, of all days, I need her. Anita told me that this music video will be my introduction to the world and, more important, my first impression on potential fans. I'm already crazy nervous—I really need my fiddle.

Anita can obviously sense my reluctance. "Listen, Bird, you are a true talent. Your fiddling is perfection. But Dan and I just feel that the guitar will be more accessible to your fans. More people play the guitar. It makes you one of them." She squeezes my arm. "And besides that, the fiddle tends to cover up that beautiful face of yours, which is the last thing we want when the label is forking over big bucks to make a music video."

Although I'm not happy about abandoning Maybelle, I look at Dan and think about how much he's already put into my career, about how much industry gold he's made, about how everything I know about the country music scene could fit into the palm of his hand. I chose to work with Open Highway because I trusted them to help me make it as a recording artist. As much as I hate to change instruments, I know I need to trust them now.

"Can you ask my dad to bring me my case?" I finally ask.

Anita takes the guitar from Dan, and he backtracks through the field for my dad. I might trust them with my career, but I don't trust anybody in the world with Maybelle.

My song plays loudly from the speakers for the gazillionth time, and it all feels so weird. I don't like lip-synching and tried to sing for real at first, but that got old fast. And as Dan reminded me on a quick break, I still have to have a voice for recording more songs.

Maybe you like me, or do you like me not, I mouth along with the track, swaying from a tire swing under a gigantic bendy old tree.

"Loosen up, Bird!" the director calls, watching his monitor. "Tuck your elbows in. You look like you're trying to fly away."

Embarrassed, I grasp the rope a little tighter and pull my arms in, which forces me to lean back some.

"Oh, love that," he calls. "Yes, toss your hair back as you swing. Look up at the sky. No, don't squint, Bird, keep your eyes open. Keep singing." The director is nice, but I can feel his patience wearing thin with me. He's great at coaching me through the shots, but it seems like all my natural instincts are wrong. And to tell you the truth, it feels corny walking back and forth through a patch of flowers, swinging from a swing, and singing longingly into a blank, lifeless lens with twenty people standing around staring. "Cut!" he calls. "Moving on."

"Halle-freakin'-lujah," I whisper to myself, jumping out

of the swing before the crew guy can help me. "Sorry," I mumble, passing him quickly and making a beeline for my trailer.

As I open the door, Amanda turns away from a white dress she's steaming. "From what I saw earlier, it looks like things are going well," she says with a smile. Yes, a smile. Chilly, perfectionist Amanda actually smiled at me.

I must be blowing it.

She unzips me from the pink dress, and I slip into a robe. Then as I take the seat behind a big, brightly lit mirror, she taps twice on the trailer door, and before she can back away, Sam and Tammy are bounding up the stairs, nearly knocking her over.

"You're a natural!" Tammy squeals enthusiastically.

"I wouldn't go that far," Sam says bluntly. "But you're getting better, Bird, and you *look* fabulous."

As Tammy chastises Sam for his tactlessness, which Sam defends as honesty, I grab my cell phone and text Adam.

My shoot's in a field of wildflowers. The original Lady Bird would be proud ☺

I set my phone in my lap and close my eyes so my stylists can work. I zone out as Tammy removes the daisies from my hair and Sam brushes powder over my face. Instead of brooding over my performance so far, I think about that little bouquet of flowers Adam gave me at the Station Inn and try to relax. Ever since the day at the flea market with Stella, Adam and I have been texting back and forth, mainly about his tour and my deal, but at least we're texting. I wouldn't say we're really flirting hard-core or anything, but I finally feel confident in our friendship separate from his with Jacob. That's a big step in my book.

My phone buzzes in my lap, and I sneak a peek while Sam grabs more gloss:

We're all proud, Lady Bird. Send a pic!

The door of the tiny trailer swings open. "Knock, knock!" Anita calls in an unusually cheery voice. She steps in looking flustered, which actually worries me a little but then makes perfect sense a moment later when a tall, gorgeous guy walks up the stairs behind her. He looks like he could be a Hollister model. Unconsciously, I sit up straighter. So do Sam and Tammy.

"Bird," Anita says breathlessly. "I want you to meet McKay Evans. He'll be playing the guy you want to notice you in the video."

McKay holds his hand out, and I can't help but notice the bulging muscles in his strong, tanned arms. I know I'm

147

beet red, but I shake his hand as indifferently as possible and smile. "It's nice to meet you, McKay."

"Glad to be here," he responds sincerely, giving me a small grin that exposes a deep dimple.

Dimples, too? *Seriously?*

"McKay, some powder," Sam commands, turning McKay's chin from my direction and brushing over his face.

"And just one little flyaway," Tammy says, dabbing her pinkie finger into some pomade.

I glance at Amanda, who rolls her eyes, and then over at Anita, who is almost drooling, and try to suppress a laugh. I may need noticing, but that's certainly not McKay's problem.

"I need to change her for her next look," Amanda announces, ever the party pooper. Although, in her defense, it is starting to feel a little claustrophobic in here, and everybody's waiting on me.

"Yes, yes, we're going," Anita replies, turning away. "Just wanted to introduce you quickly before you're thrown together on set."

McKay briefly touches my shoulder and looks at me in the mirror. "See you out there."

I can only nod.

As he walks toward the door, Amanda stops him briefly and rolls a lint brush over a pristine spot on his white V-neck. Sam smirks at Tammy behind me.

"Couldn't keep your hands off, could you?" he teases Amanda as McKay exits.

She shoots him a murderous look, but I also notice that her face flames red.

"Can I have her in ten?" a production assistant calls from the doorway.

"You can have her in five," Amanda answers, unzipping my dress from its hanger. "But you can have these two right now." She turns toward Sam and Tammy and points to the door. "Out."

Before getting up to change, I think about another person I know who would die over McKay: Stella. I pick up my cell phone again. The shooting script calls for a fantasy scene where I walk around the love interest, look at him with yearning, and even "caress" his arms and blow in his ear. I was nervous about it before, but after meeting McKay, I'm terrified. I need backup, so I fire off a quick text to my new bestie.

U still coming?

And the true wingwoman that she is, her reply is immediate:

On our way.

"Imagine he's the guy you wrote the song about!" the director calls over the music.

As if I weren't tense enough already.

I glance down nervously at male model McKay, who's gazing up at me from where he's perched on a bale of hay. His face is uncomfortably close, since I'm bent over with my arms wrapped around his neck. He smells like bronzing lotion.

"Okay, you don't have to sing now, Bird," the director calls, completely throwing me off. "Just interact with your guy." I blush.

"You wrote this?" McKay asks quietly.

"Um, yeah," I say, trying to stay in character while we talk. Tentatively, I run my fingers over his shoulders. They're, like, rock hard.

"Yes, good, Bird!" the director calls.

"Wow," McKay says. "I'm impressed."

"Pretend he just said something funny!" the director calls.

I throw my head back and laugh, releasing the giddy feeling inside. McKay's not really my type (while they adjusted the lighting for these shots, he gave me a detailed rundown of his favorite protein shakes), but that doesn't mean that when he smiles up at me with perfect teeth and big brown eyes, I don't swoon a little.

150

"It's still not there," I overhear the director say. He twists around in his chair and beckons to Dan and Anita. "We need to feel like she's really into him."

Dan frowns and strokes his jowls, but Anita, as always, doesn't hesitate to express herself. "Look at her," my publicist responds, gesturing emphatically at the monitor with her red fingernails. "She's about to throw up, she's so nervous around this boy. *That's* how girls feel around guys they're into."

I cringe and walk behind McKay again, keeping beat with the song and trying to ignore them. It's totally quiet on set, except for my song, and if I can hear them talking, then so can McKay, and this is hard enough already.

"It just feels a little...awkward," the director says, crossing his arms.

"Awkward," Anita repeats, hands on hips. "Like girls are around boys they like. I think this is wonderful. It feels much more real this way than some overly flirty take on it; otherwise, she wouldn't have to beg to be noticed." I take stock of myself, trying to figure out what they're seeing.

Dan mumbles something that I can't make out, and the director considers it. Then he calls, "Bird! Can we try you sitting with your head on his shoulder?"

I glance over at McKay's face quickly and then look away again. He scoots over a tiny bit on the hay, and I squeeze next to him, doing what the director asks. My hair

151

cascades down McKay's chest, and with my head cocked, I stare into the camera lens as my voice on the track pleads with him to "notice me" already.

"Oh, I love that," the director calls, leaning forward. "Now look at each other." We are so close that our noses nearly touch. I gulp hard. "That's great, guys. McKay, could you gently push her hair back from her cheek?"

When I feel his fingers on my face, I close my eyes involuntarily and get an enormous cold chill.

"Oh. There's your moment," Anita says softly.

"Cut it!" the director calls. "That was beautiful, you two."

"Moving on!" his assistant calls, and the entire set comes to life again.

I politely extricate myself from McKay and find my dad grazing at the craft services area. "Is Stella here yet?" I ask, swiping an apple slice from his plate.

He shakes his head and pulls my cell phone from his shirt pocket. No messages. No missed calls. "Oh," he says, pointing behind me. "Speak of the devil."

Spinning around, I see Stella and Shannon walking around my trailer, and can't be more relieved. "I'm so glad you're here," I say, throwing my arms around Stella. I pull back and grab her shoulders, looking at her seriously. "We have an emergency."

"Oh no," she says worriedly. "What's wrong?"

With one arm still around her, I turn and point toward

the set, where Amanda has taken off McKay's shirt and is rubbing baby oil on his very chiseled chest. "*That's* the emergency."

Her eyes pop as her face registers what I already knew. "Whoa."

"Exactly," I say, grinning. "How am I supposed to concentrate like a professional when I have *that* going on?"

My dad glances at us, obviously flustered by our ogling, and shakes his head as he engages Shannon in conversation. He hasn't been crazy about these "fantasy" scenes, either.

Stella lifts her enormous sunglasses from her eyes. "Are they giving him a pitchfork?" she asks, confused.

"Yes. The script says he's supposed to wipe sweat from his brow while I circle around him longingly."

"You're blushing." She smirks, clearly enjoying this.

"I'm dying," I say.

"Well, okay," Stella says, eyeing McKay boldly. "Pretend like he's one of your brothers."

I screw up my face. "How am I supposed to act romantic with one of my brothers?"

"Well..." she starts. But she can't take her eyes off McKay as he flexes so that Amanda can examine her work. Finally Stella sighs dramatically, completely at a loss. "Yeah, I don't know, Bird." Then she wiggles her eyebrows. "But it's not a bad problem to have."

"Ha!"

"At least he doesn't look anything like Adam. You don't have to worry about revealing the identity of your muse."

"True," I say, appreciating that new insight.

McKay looks up at that moment and flashes us his million-dollar dimpled smile.

"Hey, ladies," Stella says, imitating a deep guy voice. I laugh out loud. "Who's your friend? She's hot." She's talking out the side of her mouth like a ventriloquist, which makes me laugh even harder. "Think *she'd* care for a roll in the hay?" She turns to me, her eyes full of mischief. "Because Bird," she says in her normal voice, hilariously intense, gripping my arm like it's life or death. "I would. If he asked, I totally would."

"Stop," I say, laughing so hard that my eyes are watering. And now she's dropped the bit and joins in. We're falling against each other, laughing like hyenas and gasping for air. The crew is starting to take notice, but I don't care.

"Is the talent ready?" an assistant producer calls.

"Oh, fancy," Stella teases.

I shake my head and grab a mint from the food table, still giggling as I walk toward my mark. I dab under my eyes, knowing that Sam is going to murder me if I've smudged my makeup, but as I walk toward him and McKay on set, I also know that the last five minutes were worth the scolding I'll get. I feel better than I've felt all day.

With Stella in the wings, I finally relax. As the music plays and the cameras roll, I circle McKay playfully, still a

154

little self-conscious, but at least no one is cringing at the monitor anymore. I glance over at Stella when he seductively wipes "sweat" from his brow and barely keep my composure when she dramatically fans herself. Before I know it, I'm having the time of my life.

"That's a wrap!" the director calls as I kill yet another daisy, plucking it bare and hoping that he loves me.

"Phew," I say, stretching before I stand up from where I was sitting cross-legged in the field of wildflowers. "What a day."

The crew member helping me up smiles, and everyone claps. I see lighting guys shaking hands with props people and assistants helping themselves to snack food. It seems like everybody relaxes just a touch before getting to the hard work of packing up.

As I walk past the monitors and lighting equipment toward my trailer, the director calls out to me. "Hey, Bird. Take a look."

He has the director of photography rewind some of the footage to the scenes where I'm interacting with McKay. Stella is at my side right away, and then my dad steps up, too. "There," the director says. "Play back."

I'm a little anxious about what I might see, but when

the film rolls, my chin nearly hits the ground. "It looks like a real music video," Stella comments, taking the words right out of my mouth. Anita, Dan, and Shannon join us, and I can feel the crowd ever so slightly pressing in behind me as the footage rolls.

The whole thing is surreal. I'm looking at my real-life story playing out on the small screen. I mean, it's a little more polished than me pining over Adam in the Winnebago, but even with all the wardrobe changes and the hair and makeup and McKay's oiled-up chest, the scenes feel easy and light and not overworked. I watch breathlessly, amazed that I somehow come across as confident and sure instead of awkward and uncertain.

"It's perfect," I whisper, watching as our two figures pass each other by, the sun setting behind us, the gold and purple flowers grazing our thighs. "It's just perfect."

I fell asleep in the car ride home from Franklin and basically sleepwalked to my room. I did not pass Go; I did not collect two hundred dollars. I didn't brush my teeth or wash my face or brush my hair. I didn't even change clothes.

And yet, for the past ten minutes, I have tossed and turned, tugging my blankets this way and that. I have counted the stars outside my window, spotted both Dippers and Orion's belt, and wondered at the man in the moon. I even prayed, thanking the Big Man for today.

But I have been completely unable to turn off my brain and just sleep. Something is nagging at me, but I can't figure out what.

And then I turn my head away from the window and it hits me: Maybelle. I feel a pang of guilt.

"I'm sorry," I whisper to her case on my dresser, thinking how excited I was last night as I practiced for the shoot. "I won't forget you. I promise."

But when I close my eyes, sleep still won't come. It's not until I pull the covers back and set my feet on the cool hardwood floor, not until I take Maybelle out of her case and tuck her under my chin, not until I play the fiddling pass from "Notice Me," quietly so I don't wake anybody up, that I finally settle, finally feel whole. It's not until then that my day is complete.

When I finish the song, I bow to the imaginary audience in my vanity mirror. Smiling, I tuck Maybelle back into her bed and then crawl into my own. And before I know it, I'm out cold, dreaming about Adam standing in the tall flowers, his hazel eyes twinkling and his deep voice sexy as he whispers in my ear, pushing me on a tire swing as if there's nowhere else he'd rather be.

14

"So you played a honky-tonk waitress today?" my mom asks, chopping vegetables for a stir-fry while I set the table.

"Yeah, in some hole-in-the-wall on Lower Broadway," I reply, grabbing silverware for five out of the drawer.

"Was it like yesterday's shoot?"

"Not really," I answer. We had our second day of shooting for my video today, and my mom wants the full play-by-play. "Actually, the owner's name is Dylan, and I told him I have a brother with the same name." I pause and look over at my brother, who's staring at his computer screen, in a world of his own. "Except this guy had a really great personality," I say. Grinning, I wait for him to react. He just ignores me.

But Jacob looks up from his homework and smiles. "Burn."

I nod, and we bump fists. "Anyway, the director thought it would be an interesting role reversal if the guy I want to notice me is the singer and I'm just a fan in the crowd."

"Hmmm," my mom murmurs as she checks the rice cooker.

"And the extras were all really nice," I say, coming back into the kitchen for the plates and bowls. "This one guy—" I begin, but Dylan startles me by clearing his throat so loudly I'm worried he might've hurt himself.

Mom and I look over at him, but he keeps his eyes glued to his computer as if it was nothing. I glance at my mom, who shrugs her shoulders, and then at Jacob, but he's got his head down finishing up his homework. *Wonder if he'll let me copy his later,* I think as I take the dishes into the dining room.

"So anyway," I start again when I come back to the kitchen for a pitcher of water. Then Dylan starts tapping his pen against the counter, something he knows I absolutely abhor. It doesn't seem to be on purpose, since he's totally absorbed in his work, so I try to ignore it.

"This one guy actually said he's seen the Barrett Family Band play before," I tell her, but Dylan starts tapping louder. "I think it was a few years ago before I'd hit my growth spurt, because he said I was only 'yay big,' which, what does that even—" I can't take it. "Dylan! Do you mind?"

"What?" he asks, looking up innocently as his pen *tap, tap, tap*s against the countertop.

I make a face, gesturing toward his pen.

"Oh, this?" he asks, tapping away.

"Yes, you know I hate that," I say. "I can hardly keep my thoughts straight."

"Imagine trying to do your homework while your kid sister babbles on and on about her music video starring the boyfriend she's never had," he says, closing his laptop.

I'm taken aback. "If my talking is bothering you, you can ask me to stop," I say.

"Okay. Stop."

"Hey, hey," my mom says, trying to diffuse the situation. "Dinner's ready."

She hands Dylan some hot pads and Jacob the napkins, and I follow them into the dining room, setting down the pitcher a little more firmly than usual. My dad walks in, kisses my mom on the cheek, and as everybody sits, I fill our glasses. I can't help but think about the video shoot again . . . and about how much more fun waiting tables at a honky-tonk is than doing it at home.

"Dylan, will you say grace tonight?" my dad asks as I take my seat. I think he has some kind of sixth sense, always picking whichever one of us is in the worst mood.

We all fold our hands, and Dylan says his usual prayer for football season. When he ends with, "And, Lord, if you're watching football..." we all know to join in with, "Please take the Titans to the Super Bowl. Amen."

That usually makes me smile, but I'm still pretty ticked off about what he said in the kitchen.

"Did Bird tell you all about the shoot today?" my dad asks before shoveling a forkful of veggies into his mouth.

"Yep," Dylan says, nodding emphatically. "Oh yeah. We heard all about it."

I bristle.

My dad seems mildly confused by his antagonistic response. "It was a fun day. We—"

"When are we going back on tour?" Dylan cuts in, putting his fork down midbite. "Seriously, it's been a month and a half of sitting around this apartment doing jack squat. I want to get back on the road."

My parents glance at each other, exchanging one of those looks that say they've discussed the issue but were putting off talking to the rest of us about it. "Well," my dad begins.

"We can't just leave Bird," my mom explains.

"And we can't tour without her," my dad continues. "I'd say we'll be here for a couple more months at least. We'll wait and see how her record goes and then make plans from there."

"So what are we supposed to do?" Dylan asks impatiently, gesturing toward himself and Jacob. "Just sit around Nashville watching the world revolve around Bird?"

Nobody says anything.

"Seriously," he continues. "What about the Barrett Family Band? What about our careers? Our music?"

"Maybe Adam knows somebody who needs musicians," I offer.

"Our own sister doesn't want us as her backup," Jacob pipes up, not unkindly, but matter-of-fact. "Why would somebody else?"

I suck in air, feeling punched in the gut. "That's not—"

"I'm not hungry," Dylan says, throwing his napkin down in frustration. He picks up his plate and stands. "It was good, Mom, but I'm not hungry. May I be excused?"

My mother looks slightly pained but nods, and he carries his plate to the kitchen, slamming it down a little louder than necessary. Jacob stands and follows suit. I sit, stunned by how quickly a perfectly wonderful day turned sour.

"Bird," my mom says, reaching her hand out to cover mine. But I pull away, feeling a lump in my throat.

"I'm not hungry, either," I say, and before she can stop me, I get up and go to my room.

"So do you like it?" Stella asks on our video call, aiming her laptop toward the mirror she picked up at the flea market the other day.

"I wouldn't even know it was the same mirror," I say, once again in awe of her artistic eye. "It was so dirty and cracked before."

She turns the computer back to herself and grins. "I got this frosted spray paint and treated the entire glass with it. And I found these twigs out in the field while I was at your music-video shoot. I'm going to give it to my mom for Christmas."

"That's so cool," I say. My phone beeps. "Oh my gosh, Adam just texted me."

"*Ooh*, tell me."

"Okay," I say, opening the message. " 'Late night, no crowd. Miss the BFB.' " I look up at her and pout. "Aw, poor Adam."

"You going to write that?"

"No way," I say, but then a knock at my door turns my attention from the video call. "One sec," I tell her, getting up from my bed and opening the door. I'm surprised to see Dylan standing there.

"Can I come in?" he asks quietly. He holds up both hands. "I come in peace."

I shrug and open the door all the way before heading back to my computer where Stella waits.

"I'll call you back," I tell her, reaching for my laptop. "Cool."

I close the computer and take a seat at my desk. Dylan sits on the bed and looks down at his sneakers, obviously thinking about what he wants to say and how he wants to say it. I'm still hurt from his outburst at dinner, but I give him a minute to gather his thoughts. He doesn't seem to want a fight.

Finally, he sighs heavily. "Bird, I guess first off, I need to say I'm sorry. I didn't mean to snap at you earlier."

I nod. "Thank you. And I'm sorry I was distracting you and Jacob while you were doing your homework. That was rude."

He shakes his head. "Nah, we've worked through a lot more distractions than that in the RV." He runs his hand through his strawberry-blond hair and then pats it back down again absentmindedly. "The truth is…I guess I'm jealous. I mean, I'm happy for you. I really am. You're a talented musician, and if all this were happening to me, I'd be just as excited as you are." He looks at me and smiles sadly. "But it's not. It's not happening for me, and now we're here and I feel stuck. Now nothing's happening for me."

I sigh heavily. I know he wouldn't want me to, but I feel guilty. I wish this *were* happening for him, for the entire Barrett Family Band. As happy as I am that I'm getting all these opportunities, it's moments like these that make it bittersweet.

"I love music," he says quietly. "You know I love making music. I passed on college to keep touring with you all. I loved picking out songs together and playing dive bars and honky-tonks. I loved it, Bird. And I want to be there for you, and I really am happy for you. But I'm unhappy for me. And I hate it. But I am. And I'm a little angry, I guess. And it's not fair. And..." He stops and gulps back a frog in his throat, which breaks my heart. "I don't know what to do about it. I just..." He exhales loudly. "Yeah, I feel stuck."

I nod, feeling awful for my big brother. It's so strange to hear him say that he'd want to trade places with me. I've always been the one who wanted whatever he wanted, had to do whatever he did. I've always looked up to him: Dylan the charismatic one, the confident one, the charming one. Dylan, for whom all things seem to come easy.

"I'm sorry," I say quietly.

"No, Bird," he says, scooting over so that he's closer to me. "That's not what I want. You shouldn't have to apologize. I just have to grow up and realize that your success doesn't cancel out the possibility of my own." He sets his mouth into a firm line and nods his head decisively. "I just have to work harder."

I grin. "You been talking to Dad?"

He looks up at me sheepishly. "He's old, but wise."

I laugh softly. "Dylan, you know you're really talented,

too, right? I mean, you have an incredible ear, and you pick up songs and harmonies faster than anyone I know."

"No, I know," he says, nodding. "I guess I just feel a little left behind." He rolls his eyes. "It's so stupid. It's actually kind of embarrassing."

I sigh. This stinks.

As we sit, I try to think about ways I can make this up to him—to everybody. I can hear the whir of the ceiling fan, a car horn outside, the TV on low in the living room. And then I hear the hum of a small white lie forming in my brain. Words that may not be true tumble out of my mouth, but I can't stop them.

"You know, I played our song 'Before Music' for Dan, and he really likes it."

Dylan looks up at me, surprised.

I forge ahead, knowing I shouldn't. "Since the song is pretty personal, you know, being about Caleb and all, I think maybe Dan might want the whole family on that one."

"Really?" Dylan asks, brightening a bit.

I nod, wringing my hands and hoping to God that I can make this happen.

"Oh, Bird, that's awesome!" he says, pumping his arm in the air. "Aw, man, why didn't you tell me?"

I bite my lip. "Um, I don't know for sure that we're recording it for this album, and I didn't want to get everybody's hopes up," I say, realizing the magnitude of what

I'm promising when I see how excited he is. If I can't make this happen, he will be completely devastated. "So don't tell the others," I add quickly. "But yeah. I think it'll be pretty cool."

"It'll be amazing," he says, his smile wide and relaxed.

His blue eyes sparkle and he looks like my big brother again—the one who led impromptu jam sessions at RV parks when he was thirteen. The one who convinced our parents to let him drive Winnie over the Golden Gate Bridge when he was sixteen and had just gotten his license. The one who has my back at all times, who loves his family, who loves his music.

When he leaves my room, I turn around to my desk and open my laptop. Stella is still online, so I video call her again. On the third ring, she answers, her friendly face filling my screen.

"Oh no," she says, immediately seeing the worry on my own. "What's wrong?"

"Have you ever made a promise you're not sure you can keep?"

She sighs. "Tell me everything."

15

"Long night, huh, baby?" my mom says, running her hands through my hair.

"Uh-huh," I mumble. I'm lying sideways on our little couch in the RV with my head on my mom's lap as we drive the two hours down to Jackson for Christmas at my granddad's. I'm exhausted from the release party last night for my single, and the rocking of the Winnebago along with my mom's fingers in my hair has me on the border of unconsciousness. And yet the perma-grin that attached itself to my lips last night is still stuck on my face.

"I know you're tired," Mom says softly. "Dan was yanking you around that party like a rag doll." She makes a tsking sound. "Somebody ought to remind that man that you're sixteen years old and a party 'til two in the morning is unacceptable."

I would roll my eyes at her, but seeing as they're closed it would be a wasted gesture.

"It was only one party," Jacob says from the kitchenette. "And it was in her honor."

"That's true, Aileen," my dad pipes up from the driver's seat. "It was for work. And it was fun."

My mother harrumphs, but I love it. Yes, it's been a long four months—I practically lived in the studio or at the Crossleys' all of November and a lot of December, even missing Thanksgiving at Gramma's to record over the long weekend—but last night's big party for my single made the crazy hours worth it.

The whole celebration was an out-of-body experience. I wore an honest-to-God designer gown and my mom let me wear the teardrop diamond necklace my dad got her for their twentieth wedding anniversary. We were picked up in a black stretch limo, and when we got to the club, Dan greeted me on a red carpet. Inside, photographers were waiting and the entire place was decked out with giant pictures from my promo shoot.

I finally got to sing "Notice Me" live, and it was ah mazing. The minute I walked onstage and slipped my guitar over my head, I looked out at the crowd and felt that old familiar sensation of both delight and fear. Singing live again after all those months was like dropping down that first big plummet on a roller coaster, thrilling and exhilarating, and even though I did feel a slight pang of guilt having a fiddler in the band play all of Maybelle's parts, I wouldn't have changed a thing.

After the performance, I wove my way through the crowd toward my family. My mom had her arms out to hug me, but as I walked toward her, Anita expertly cut me off. "Bird," she said, steering me toward Dan, where he stood talking with a couple of guys in suits. "Come with me. You should be working the room."

"But—"

"Bird!" Dan called as he motioned me over.

"Charm them," Anita instructed, her huge smile never wavering as she ushered me over to the group. My own smile, however, flipped upside down the minute I saw a familiar GAM exec with ice in his eyes. I froze.

"Bird," Dan said, as if this weren't going to be totally awkward, "I'd like you to meet a few people. This is Robby Ellis and Jesse Goldman, from Sony and Universal respectively." I pasted on a smile and shook their hands. "And I believe you know Randall Strong, from GAM."

I nodded. "Hi, Randall."

"Hello again, Bird," he replied, sipping a whiskey as if amused. "I enjoyed your song. It's come a long way since the last time I heard it."

His big teeth gleamed in a fake smile that made me feel incredibly uneasy.

"Little-known fact," Randall said, turning toward the other two execs, "*I* actually discovered Bird Barrett before Dan here swept in and stole her away." He chuckled, but it was obviously forced humor.

"Really?" Robby remarked.

"Yeah. Thanks for that, by the way," Dan replied. "Although if I remember correctly, Bird was still a free agent when I signed her. Perhaps your offer just wasn't appealing enough."

"Perhaps." Randall smirked. "I think I came out on top, though. I just signed a new talent. I think she'll give your little Birdie here a run on the charts." Then he turned his intense gaze on me. "As soon as we release her album, you can expect a little friendly competition, Miss Barrett."

Dan actually laughed out loud. For me, though, it was all I could do not to cry. What if Randall was right? What if he had dodged a bullet by signing somebody else?

"Well, I certainly look forward to hearing her stuff," Dan said, clapping Randall strongly on the back. "Y'all have a good night and thanks for coming out."

Dan grabbed my hand and led me away, rescuing me from the cold and calculating Randall, and making me 100 percent certain that I had made the right choice a few months ago, even if Randall had been the one who got me the opportunity at the Bluebird.

"Breathe," Dan said when we were out of earshot. "He's still a little sore, and I'm sure watching you perform what will obviously be a giant hit was like salt in the wound."

I nodded and inhaled deeply, wanting to believe him—wanting more than ever before to make it in this business, to prove myself, to be the star everyone told me I would be—desperately hoping that I wouldn't let Dan down.

"Did you see the look on his face when you walked up to us?" Dan said with glee in his eyes. "Priceless."

I couldn't help but return his smile. The president of my label had every confidence in me, so I wasn't going to sweat Randall Strong or his "competition" for even one more minute. It was *my* night.

I sigh contentedly now. "Last night was so awesome," I murmur, happy nevertheless to be spending today in my flannel pajamas as we cruise down the highway.

"How many views does your video have?" Jacob asks me. I refresh YouTube on my phone.

"Two thousand forty-three," I answer, "and forty-one 'likes.'"

"And it hasn't even been twelve hours," Jacob says, stretching.

As brutal as my alarm clock was this morning, I wouldn't want to miss Christmas in Jackson. Even if I am a walking zombie, I'm excited to see my granddad, cousins, aunts, and uncles again. This will be the only thing in the past few months that hasn't changed, that bears some resemblance to my life before the Station Inn.

"I'm looking forward to—" I begin, but my words are swallowed by a giant yawn.

"Why don't you try to get a little sleep in your bunk?" my mom suggests.

"Hmph," I grunt as she rubs my back. "With Dylan snoring like a bear?"

Suddenly Jacob shouts, making an unintelligible noise before crying, "Turn that up!" He slides his skinny frame out from behind the table and lurches toward the front of the RV. "Dad!" he shouts again. "Turn it up!"

My eyes widen like saucers as my normally quiet brother spazzes out. Jacob slips down into the passenger seat, immediately cranking up the volume on the radio, and then I bolt upright, cold chills all over my body.

"That's my song," I whisper.

"That's my song!" I shout.

"Woo-hoo!" my mom yells, clapping. She stands up and clasps my hands, and we start to jump up and down, nearly toppling over as we rock the RV.

"Whoa, whoa, whoa!" my dad calls, trying to keep control of the swaying vehicle as we speed down the highway.

"If I'm a wildflower, then you're the blowin' breeze,"

Dylan sings, hopping down from the top bunk, his eyes still sleepy and his face lined from the pillow. *"I could get swept away, don't know where you'd take me."* He grabs my hands and sings loudly, *"And maybe we could shine so bright in the sunlight."* I laugh hysterically as he dances me through the small space and dips me down so that my head is between my dad and Jacob.

"Is it real? Do you see? Say—you notice me!" they shout, looking down at me dangling there.

Dylan pulls me back up and then grabs my mom's hands, dancing along to my song on the radio and acting like a total fool. I can't stop laughing.

Just then, my phone rings on the couch. I figure it's Stella, or maybe Dan calling to congratulate me. Excitedly, I grab it and flop down on the cushions, trying to catch my breath as I check the phone. But it's not Stella. And it's not Dan.

It's Adam.

Quickly, I stand up and make my way to the back of the RV, staring at his name on the screen, my pulse off the charts. As soon as I'm alone, sliding the small accordion-like door firmly into place behind me, I plop down onto my parents' bed and answer.

"Hello?" I wait. "Hello?"

But it's too late. The line is dead. I lie back against the pillows and listen to my family singing along wildly to my song on the radio. I stare at the screen of my cell phone, willing a voice-mail alert to appear. When it does, my heart nearly stops.

I wonder if he's just heard my song.

Well, our song.

The song about him.

Nervously, I press PLAY and hold the phone up to my ear:

"Hey there, Lady Bird," Adam says. *"I'm standing in the middle of the Comfort Inn continental-breakfast area when your song comes over the speakers, and I just about spit my coffee across the room, everybody looking at me like I'm a crazy person. I was like, 'I know that voice! I know that girl!'"*

I hear him laugh to himself.

"You should see the looks I'm getting. Anyway, just wanted to say congratulations. That's awesome. Merry Christmas and give my best to your family. Hope to see y'all again real soon. Bye."

I can't wait to tell Stella. My thumbs move across the screen, texting at supersonic speed:

My song's on the radio! Adam called!

And it's as if her phone is in her hands, she responds so quickly:

OMG! Call him back!!!

But I can't, not in the middle of all this cramped chaos. I'll have to wait until we get to Jackson.

Grinning like a fool, I hold the cell phone to my chest and take a huge breath. I hear the fiddle pass blaring from Winnie's speakers and open the door, rejoining my family and playing air fiddle while Dylan rocks the air guitar. We all sing the last chorus together in the tiny cabin, and then the music fades and my song comes to an end. Dylan picks me up and spins me around, knocking Mom onto the couch in the process.

"That's my little sister!" he shouts.

I laugh as he spins me, even though I nearly whack my head against the cabinets.

"Shh! Shh! Shh!" Jacob hushes us frantically. Dylan sets me on my feet again.

"And that there was Bird Barrett with her new single, 'Notice Me,'" the DJ says. "Bird is only sixteen years old, and she actually wrote that song, so I'd say she's an act to watch. We look forward to hearing more from that gal. Next up this hour, we have—"

"'An act to watch,'" Jacob repeats, turning the volume down and twisting around in his seat. "Bird, you're 'an act to watch.' That's crazy."

"It is crazy," I agree, nodding slowly.

And everybody goes from wildly excited to quietly reflective. Dylan sits down next to my mom and Jacob faces forward again, each with a smile and a look of wonder on his face. I look out the windshield, and my dad winks at me in the rearview mirror.

As the highway opens up in front of us, the yellow lines lead the Barretts back to Jackson, to what used to be, to life before I had a song on the radio. *What's good for one of us is good for all of us,* my mom had said when Randall Strong first approached my dad. Looking around at my former bandmates and my forever family, I think how lucky I am that that is so true. I really hope this single does well, for all of us.

16

"So it's not a nickname?" asks Richard, the blogger sitting across the table from me.

"Nope, just Bird," I answer. "On my birth certificate and everything."

"Huh," he muses. "That's charming. I hate nicknames. It's, like, name your kid what you're going to call your kid, you know?"

I scrunch up my nose. "I don't know. Seems a little harsh."

"Maybe," he says, clearly not caring what I think, anyway. "So how does it feel being on the cusp of country music stardom?"

"Well, if you'd asked me a year ago where I'd be right now, I'd have said touring the country in an RV with my family, being homeschooled by day and playing music by night. The—"

"But that's what's so incredible, isn't it?" he interrupts with a big smile. "I wouldn't have asked you anything a year ago. Nobody knew you then, but now you're the next big thing. Now you're on your way. How does that feel?"

I squint my eyes, slightly offended. I've been sitting at a table at a diner called Noshville with this guy for the past ten minutes, but I'm still not comfortable and we definitely don't gel. Richard looks like he's in his thirties or forties. He has a bushy hipster 'stache and acts like he knew every hot band before they were hot. He smiles and nods at everything I say as if we are the best of friends, but his enthusiasm all feels immensely fake to me. I'm supposed to be at a local radio station in half an hour, but Anita owed this music blogger a favor so here I am, whether I want to be or not.

"Well, I wouldn't say *nobody* knew me," I reply with a tight-lipped smile.

"Oh, no, no, no," he rushes in. "I didn't mean—well, you know what I meant, right?"

"Did I expect to have a song on the *Billboard* charts, climbing up there pretty quickly? No, Rich, I did not."

"Richard," he corrects, dropping his fake smile.

"Oh yeah, my bad," I say, hiding a grin as I squeeze lemon into my hot tea with honey.

Anita and Dan keep telling me that "Notice Me" is bound for the top twenty, that I'm going to be huge this time next year, but although Dan acts confident, what if they're wrong? What if I put everything on hold, especially my family, all for nothing? I've never wanted anything in my life as much as I want this single to do well—as much as I want to make it—and what if I don't?

Instinctively, I put my hand in my pocket, but the emptiness there reminds me that I lost my lucky rock over Christmas vacation, which only makes me more worried.

"You know," I say, focusing on the task at hand and trying to be pleasant, "I'm glad you chose this restaurant. My family and I used to stop here when we played Nashville."

He nods absentmindedly, turning to a fresh page on his yellow legal pad. Guess that tidbit wasn't article worthy. I wrap my hands around my mug, warming them as I lift my tea for another sip.

"Speaking of your family," Richard says, tapping his pen on his pad, "you had a brother who died, right?"

I'm so shocked that I nearly spill my drink. I set the mug down on the table quickly. Blink hard. Blink again. "I'm sorry?"

"You had a brother who died," he repeats, looking at me as if I don't know who he's talking about. He thumbs back through a couple of pages. "Caleb, that's it. Caleb died when you were little, is that right?"

When he makes eye contact again, he must see the astonishment on my face, because he plasters a sympathetic smile on his own, an obvious afterthought.

"Yes," I answer. "He did."

The man has no tact, no thoughtfulness, almost seems inspired by the fact that my hands are shaking just the tee-niest bit now and that my breath is caught at the back of my throat.

"That must have been sad," Richard states, his pen poised over the fresh page.

What do you think?

I look out the restaurant window, studying the parked cars and icy windshields while I collect myself. I know Anita included my family's history in the official bio in my press packet—"a tragic story with a fairy-tale ending" is how I think she spun it. In fact, allowing her to share the fact that I had a brother who passed away, which is what ultimately got me into music, was how I was able to get my family on my album and make good on my promise to Dylan.

Both Anita and Dan loved "Before Music," a song Dylan and I wrote about life before we lost Caleb, which is bittersweet because it was also our life before music. They wanted it on the album, but when Anita went on and on about the "hook," she wasn't talking about the chorus; she was talking about the press angle. It was Anita who convinced Dan to let Dylan play on that track and sing backup vocals as well. She said it was "sweet and sorrow-ful," which was nice of her, but then I also heard her say, "The fans will love her even more." And although Dan had been adamant about using session veterans, her powers of persuasion worked again because he let my entire fam-ily play on our song "Yellow Lines," a number we wrote together after Christmas. It's about our life on the road, but Anita had said, "It's a terrific marketing angle." I didn't really care how she spun it as long as my family got some recognition on the album.

But sitting here now, across from a man who is either callous or clueless, I don't know if trusting Anita with my past was the right decision. "Yes, it is sad," I answer simply.

"And how does that affect your music?" he asks. "If at all."

"It affects my music in every way," I answer hotly. I don't know how this interview got so off course. I was prepared to talk about what it was like to record my first album, who my musical influences are, even what or who inspired "Notice Me." But I was not prepared to talk about the drowning of my five-year-old brother. I write what's in my heart and I want to be known for my emotional honesty, but this stuff about Caleb is so personal, so painful, so *big*.

I take a deep breath, remind myself to stay professional. "Caleb is the reason we first turned to music," I share. Rich-ard scribbles furiously, practically salivating. I really don't care for this creep, but I continue. "After everything that happened—"

At that moment, Richard's iPhone beeps next to him. "I'm so sorry, Bird," he says, deeply conflicted as he looks back and forth between his phone and his legal pad. "You were saying?"

I open my mouth to speak, but then his phone beeps again, and this time he holds up a finger and checks the screen, literally putting me on hold after asking me about the death of a family member. I've had it.

"I think I have to go now," I say, standing up and grabbing my coat. "Thanks for the interview, Richie."

"It's *Richard*," he corrects again, narrowing his eyes as he pockets his cell phone and gets up to follow me. "And I have a couple more questions—"

But what he wasn't banking on was my dad sitting at the table behind us. His lean frame looks bigger in his tan Carhartt jacket, and he towers above Richard, blocking his path. "Thanks again for the interview," my dad says, his eyes hard, his smile tight. He clutches the blogger's hand in what appears to be quite a firm handshake. "We hope you'll like the album."

Once we step outside, I feel like I can breathe again. "Thanks, Dad," I say quietly as I duck my face into my scarf and we walk to the car.

He nods and puts his arm around me. "This will get

easier," he promises me. "With time, we've learned that everything gets a little easier."

I hope he's right.

"What a jerk," Stella agrees later. "He's lucky you even *gave* him an interview. Does he know your video has, like, a hundred thousand views?"

"Three hundred thousand," I correct.

"Oh, ho-ho!" she says. "Pardon *moi*."

I blush. "Sorry, I've been a little addicted to the 'refresh' button on YouTube."

She grabs my hand and pulls me off her couch. "Come on, don't let a stupid blogger get in your head. At least it went better at the radio station."

"True," I say, following her up the winding staircase to her loft.

Stella pauses at one of her new little shelves bracketed on the wall. It's made from the copy of *Gone With the Wind* that I picked out at the flea market. A photo of the two of us sits on top. "You think Margaret Mitchell is rolling in her grave?"

"Just don't have any librarians over," I say.

She laughs and hurries up the steps, taking them by twos as she winds around. "Okay, so forget the song and forget the video or anything to do with work, and get ready for presents!"

"I'm sorry we couldn't exchange earlier," I say again, climbing onto her bed. My life in the weeks leading up to the release of "Notice Me" was chaotic, so Stella and I are only now exchanging Christmas presents.

I pull a box from my bag and hand it to her. She raises her eyebrows inquisitively. "Oh, such fancy wrapping," she jokes about the newspaper I used.

"Ha-ha," I say, but I feel a little self-conscious. I pull my knees into my chest and cross my arms around them as she peels off the paper and peeks inside the box.

"Oh my God, when did you get these?" she squeals, carefully pulling out three ceramic bowls. They are very delicate, oval and shallow, the inside of each a hand-painted abstract fish.

"Remember when we left that gallery and then when we got to your car I said I had to run back in to pee?" I ask, grinning. She nods. "Well, I actually went back to put these on reserve."

"You little sneak," she says, setting them carefully back into the tissue paper before throwing her arms around me. "I can't believe you did that. Seriously, Bird, thank you. These bowls are one of a kind, you know."

"Yeah, I know, I know," I say, returning her hug. "But so are you."

She makes a face. "Wah-wah," she says drolly.

"Oh my gosh, that was so cheesy, right?"

Stella tosses her head back and laughs. "Totally," she admits. "But that's the songwriter in you. Don't worry, I'm used to it."

She opens the top drawer of her dresser and hands me a small box, beautifully wrapped in shimmery cream-colored paper with a thick wire-rimmed red ribbon. "Okay, now yours," Stella says.

I pull at the ribbon slowly, and as it falls away from the paper, she reaches over and starts tearing. "Hey!" I shout, shielding my gift.

"Well, hurry up," she complains. "The suspense is killing me."

"You know what it is!" I laugh. "And the wrapping is so pretty, I don't want to ruin it."

"Oh man," she says, rolling her eyes as I carefully lift the ends so the tape doesn't tear the paper. "I'm wrapping your birthday present in a grocery sack, then."

I make a face. Finally, I expose a green box and set it on my lap. When I lift the lid, I gasp. "My lucky rock!"

I look up at her, and she beams back at me. "Do you like it?"

I lift it out of the box carefully, speechless. The black rock flecked with tiny silver slivers is now encased in brushed-silver wire and attached to a delicate silver chain. "It's incredible."

"You're always touching it, pulling it in and out of

your pockets, and I was afraid you were going to lose it," she explains. "So I texted Dylan while you were in Jackson and told him to swipe it from your jeans when you weren't around."

"Dylan was in on this? I'm going to kill him! He helped me turn the RV upside down looking for it."

"Yeah, he told me."

I look at her inquisitively. "How did you have his number?"

She shrugs. "We exchanged them at your release party."

"Oh," I say slowly. The release party was such a blur, but now that I think about it, I did see them talking pretty intently at one point. "Wait, are you guys, like, *talking* or something?"

"No!" Stella says quickly. "I mean, yeah, we've texted a few times but not like that. We're just friends. That's okay, right?"

"What do I care if you're friends with my brother?" I ask, fastening my new lucky necklace behind my neck. "You've only known him since the release party. You'll realize how annoying he is soon enough."

We both laugh.

"But seriously," I say, "if you guys do, I don't know, *like* each other, you don't need to hide it from me or anything, okay? Just tell me."

Really, though, I'm relieved that she doesn't like Dylan

as more than a friend. If they ever got together and it didn't work out, my relationship with at least one of them would suffer. And I know I have a huge crush on Jacob's best friend, so maybe I don't have room to talk, but somehow that seems different.

"I would"—she nods—"but really, there's nothing to tell. Dylan is nice and everything, but he seems so ... I don't know ... normal."

I laugh out loud. "Right, 'cause growing up in an RV is totally normal."

"You know what I mean."

"Yeah, I guess," I say, shrugging. "If you *had* to go after one of my brothers, I'd say Jacob's probably more your type. The rebel-without-a-cause kind."

She rolls her eyes. "My type hasn't really worked out for me so far. The last guy I dated was a skater in my art class and a complete flake."

"Well, maybe it's good if you're friends with Dylan. You can get some insider information on Adam for me."

She arches her eyebrows. "Aren't you guys texting a lot now?"

"Yeah," I say, fingering the rock at my sternum, running the pendant back and forth across the delicate chain. "But it's nothing deep. I've told him about recording and work stuff, but I mean, when we first started texting, I was pumped that maybe we'd start flirting more and maybe talk on the phone some nights. But the one time he called, I missed it, and by the time I could call him back, it felt weird, so I didn't. And we haven't even seen each other since, like, the end of the summer, when he left me those flowers at the Station Inn." I throw myself back on Stella's bed and look up at the ceiling. "At this point, I don't know what he's thinking. For all I know, he's met someone else."

"And is still texting you?" Stella asks skeptically.

"I guess it feels like we've sort of plateaued. Just 'Hey, how's Birmingham?' or whatever city he's in, and 'Great, how's the record?' Stuff like that."

"Well, that's more than before."

"True," I say, standing up. I gaze at my new necklace in her full-length mirror. Then I slip the pendant under my shirt. "I like that I can still tuck it away."

She nods. "I put it on a long chain on purpose."

"I can't believe you turned a piece of pavement into something this beautiful, Stella."

"It's beautiful because you treat it that way," she replies.

"'It's beautiful because you treat it that way,'" I repeat quietly, thoughtfully. I turn around and grab my bag, rummaging around in it until I find my journal and a pen.

"What are you doing?" Stella asks.

I grin. "Songwriting."

I open the book to a fresh page and scribble *Treat Me Beautiful* across the top. I frown, bite my lip, cross out *treat*, and scrawl *see* in its place. "See Me Beautiful," I mumble. That still doesn't really work, but I'll come back to it. I think there's something to the idea at least. If I've learned anything from Shannon, it's that there's lots of time to polish. The most important thing to do when inspiration strikes is to get the main idea on paper. I jot down a few phrases, just so I don't forget later:

"Look at this stick-straight frame,
For that I've got Momma to blame.
My mouth is small,
I'm way too tall,
But through your eyes I became,
Beautiful."

"Hmmm," I muse, chewing on the pen cap. The melody I hear in my head is slow and almost melancholy, but reading back over it now, it sounds like a limerick. Still, I know that once I have my guitar, I can alter the melody or rhyme scheme to find what feels best. I look over at Stella. "It's the little imperfections that make us beautiful, don't you think? Like—oh!" I start writing again, my hair falling onto the page.

"I'll go get one of my mom's guitars." Stella sighs, heading toward the spiral staircase.

"No," I say, snapping out of my trance. I close my journal, feeling guilty. This isn't supposed to be a work night. I'm over here as a friend, not as a collaborator with her mom. Walking over to the rail of her loft, I call down after her, "You don't have to, Stella. I'm done. I'll just—"

"My mom's a songwriter, Bird," she calls back, already halfway down the steps. "I know how these things work. You've got to write the song when it wants to be written."

17

"Pizza," I say to my mom, loading up our grocery cart with frozen four-cheese pies, "should be one of the major food groups."

She snorts, riffling through the pile I've already contributed to the cart. "Along with bite-size Snickers and ice cream?"

"Hey! The pizza's whole wheat and the ice cream's organic."

My mom shoots me a look. "This is why I still do the shopping for our family."

My phone rings just then, and I dig for it in my purse. Anita's name flashes on the screen, and I start to wander away, but not before I catch my mom putting my pizzas back in the freezer.

"Hello?"

"Bird, I have *Billboard* news," she says, getting right to the point. "Your debut single is number three on the Hot Country chart, and you've broken the top twenty on the Hot 100."

"Really?" I ask breathlessly. "Oh my gosh, I can't believe it."

"We're all very excited," she says, her nasal accent and deep voice making her sound anything but, which makes me laugh out loud.

"Oh, Anita, that's the best news," I say, nearly skipping down the aisle to help a short lady who can't reach a can of soup on a high shelf. She smiles her thanks, and does a double take as if she recognizes me, but I wander over to the next aisle before I know for sure.

"And that gorgeous music video we shot?" she continues, pausing for effect. "It just hit one million views on YouTube."

"Shut the front door!" I shout into the phone.

But then the screen goes black, and a message appears: *Call Failed*.

"Grrr..." I try calling her back right away but get a busy signal. She's obviously trying to call me back, too.

"What's all the fuss?" my mom calls, pushing the cart toward me.

"Mom, it's crazy! My video just broke one million views, and my song—"

The phone rings again, and Mom waves her hand, telling me to go ahead. "Anita, I'm so sorry," I say excitedly.

"Um…" A low voice comes over the line. One I know, but one I'm shocked to hear. "It's Adam."

My mouth falls open, and I turn away. I feel my stomach flip over like a flapjack. I walk quickly down the aisle and out of Mom's earshot.

"Hello?" he asks.

"Adam," I finally say, ducking into the cereal aisle. "Hi. I thought you were my publicist. Anyway, hi."

"Hi," he says. I can tell he's smiling, which makes me smile even bigger. "It's good to hear your voice live. Lately I've only been hearing it on the radio."

"Oh my gosh, I know," I say with a shiver. He is so sweet. "I've been crazy busy."

"Well, I think the work's paying off," he says. "I hear your song everywhere."

I feel myself blush as I trace the letters F-R-O-S-T-E-D F-L-A-K-E-S over and over again nervously. "Yeah, Anita was actually just telling me that my single made it into the top twenty on the charts." I pause, moving on to the Froot Loops and tracing those letters. "I can't believe it."

"Wow," he says. "Well then, we've got to celebrate."

OMG! OMG! I am screaming in my head.

"That'd be awesome," I say calmly instead.

"I'm playing Nashville next week but coming up today to spend some time with friends. Would you want to grab a bite to eat tonight? I mean, if you don't already have plans or anything."

I chew on my lip, frowning. I'm pretty sure Adam Dean just asked me on a date, and now I have to freaking say no. "I can't. We're behind on my album and working around the clock. I have to go to the studio in an hour and every day and night 'til it's done."

"Well then, how about breakfast? Can you let me take you out for the best pancakes east of the Mississippi?" he asks.

"My mom's?"

He chuckles. "Okay, the second-best pancakes, then. Can you meet tomorrow morning?"

"Yeah, that'd be awesome," I say. "But, Adam, it'd have to be crazy early."

"Well, I'm not a morning person," he admits, "but I'd like to think I've always been a Bird person. And for you, I will set an alarm."

I get goose bumps.

"Okay, sounds great," I say, trying to play it cool while my heart is racing a mile a minute and I feel like I might burst out of my own skin. "So six thirty won't kill you?"

"Ouch."

"Yeah, I know," I say, disappointed. "If it's too early—"

"Bird, I'm joking," he says. "Six thirty, bright and early, no problem. It's actually perfect because we might miss the line that's always wrapped around the block."

"Oh, look at you, Mister Silver Linings," I tease.

"I try," he says. "So six thirty—wow—tomorrow morning. It's a date."

"It's a date," I confirm, grinning from ear to ear. I doubt I've ever looked so forward to breakfast.

"Who was that?" my mom asks from behind me as I end the call.

"Mom!" I shout, spinning around. "You scared me half to death."

"Sorry," she says. "I thought you knew I was here."

"No, I did, I just—" I stop, totally flustered. "You surprised me, that's all."

I flip my hair back and push the shopping cart, scanning the aisle with great focus. I need to get it together so I can ask my mom about this thing with Adam in a casual, no-big-deal kind of way. I've never been on a date before, and I'm sure my dad would go berserk under normal circumstances, but since it's Adam and since it's breakfast, I think I can get the green light from my mom without even bothering dear old Dad.

"So what else did Anita have to say?" she asks.

After the conversation with Adam, I'd nearly forgotten. "She said my song is number three on the Hot Country chart and broke the top twenty on the Hot 100!"

"Oh, honey, that's wonderful!" she cries, hugging me right there in the canned-goods aisle. "I am *so* proud of you."

"Thanks," I say, letting her hug me once again.

"Is that why Adam called, too?" she asks, raising her eyebrows suggestively.

I blush and push the cart again. "Yeah. Actually he wants to take me out to breakfast to celebrate. That's cool, right?"

"Sure," she says. "Maybe Jacob would want to join you guys."

My eyes bulge, but I play it cool. "Maybe," I murmur indifferently.

I glance over at her and notice she's suppressing a grin as she double-checks her grocery list. I think we both know that I'll accidentally forget to invite him.

"Are y'all ready to order?" the waitress asks, yawning. That, of course, starts a chain reaction, and we all laugh through wide-stretched mouths. Any other day, I would've snoozed at least three times if my alarm had had the audacity to go off at five o'clock in the morning, but today I sprang out of bed, having barely slept at all.

After I left the studio last night, Stella came over and helped me pick out a first-date outfit. I needed something that would look nice, without making it look like I was trying too hard. At the same time, we had to keep in mind that after breakfast I would be in the studio for at least twelve hours, so I needed to be comfortable. We ended up choosing straight-leg dark jeans, a soft blue fitted T-shirt from the Bluebird Cafe, and a slouchy ivory sweater I borrowed from Stella. Dressing for breakfast was a lot more complicated than I could ever have imagined.

But part of me, a tiny silly part, wonders if maybe Adam didn't put the same amount of effort into our date. I mean, I know he didn't call his best friend over and take pictures of himself in ten different outfits and then scroll through them until he'd found the perfect combination, but his normally shaggy hair has been trimmed, and it looks like he nicked his neck shaving. Who shaves for breakfast at dawn? Unless you really care how you look to your dining companion. And this dining companion thinks the one sitting across the table from her looks good enough to eat.

The thought makes me blush, and I snap back to the moment, ordering chocolate-chip pancakes and then gawking at Adam after he orders sugar-cured ham and eggs.

"What?" he asks.

"You can't seriously come to the Pancake Pantry and

198

not get pancakes," I reprimand him as he passes the menu to the waitress. She hurries away, her tables filling up quickly.

"It comes with buttermilk pancakes," he assures me, his sleepy hazel eyes still the most gorgeous on the planet. "And hash browns. I'm a growing boy."

"Where do you guys put it all?" I ask, shaking my head. "Jacob eats like a monster, and he's still as skinny as a rail."

Adam shrugs. "Powerful genetics, I guess."

I grin. "You're ridiculous."

He leans forward. "What's ridiculous is that you have a song out on the freaking radio," he says, pounding the table with both hands. The couple at the table next to us glances over at the sound of our silverware clattering.

"I know," I say. "It's insane. It's—it's unbelievable, really."

"It is insane," he concurs, "but it's most certainly not unbelievable." He pauses for a second. "You know, you've always had this quality, Bird. You just pull people in, and I think it's because you don't even realize you're doing it."

I blush. "Thank you."

He nods, starts to say something, then closes his mouth again and breaks eye contact. He grabs the sugar bowl and focuses on arranging all the sugar packets by color while I look around the restaurant, taking in the exposed wood beams and the signs on the wall. I'm always a little keyed up around Adam, but being here with him one-on-one takes the nerves to a whole new level. As the silence between us grows, I start to worry that, off the road, we won't have anything in common. Suddenly, I want to order a Coke.

"How do you like your label?" he finally asks, setting the sugar bowl aside.

"I like them a lot," I answer, carefully removing one packet of Splenda and pouring it into my steaming cup of tea. "Dan's great and—"

"He's the one who set up the Bluebird for you?" Adam interjects.

I twist my mouth into a frown. "No, actually that was this other guy from GAM."

"Great American Music wanted you, too?" he asks, incredulous. "That's the biggest label in country music."

"Yeah," I say, "but he was really flashy, and the big label was overwhelming. With Open Highway, it feels more laid-back. And Dan is really focused on making my music honest and not, I don't know, sell-outty."

Adam cocks an eyebrow and grins. " 'Sell-outty'?"

I smile crookedly. "You know what I mean."

"So you get a lot of say with things, then," he says, nodding. "Like, nobody's taking your sound and twisting it or changing you to fit their mold. That's cool."

I nod. "Yeah, it is cool," I say, although I don't mention that Dan and Anita didn't want me playing Maybelle in the music video. Nor do I tell him that it was pretty hard to convince my label to let my own family play on the record.

The waitress arrives with our food and lays the spread out on the table between us, my chocolate-chip pancakes stacked all the way up to the heavenly place from which they came.

"There's this new country singer, Kayelee Ford. Have you heard of her?" Adam asks. I shake my head. "She just signed with GAM, and they're fast-tracking her, pulling out all the stops."

"Oh?" I reply casually, though I immediately think of what Randall said at my release party and wonder if this is his new mystery artist.

"Anyway," Adam continues, pouring ketchup all over his hash browns, "she's doing this single release party in a couple of weeks, and I got a gig to play in her band." He grins up at me.

"Wow," I say, shocked. I nod and fake a smile. "That's great, Adam."

"Thanks. I'm pretty pumped."

I concentrate on my pancakes again, really pouring on the syrup. I know I shouldn't be jealous—I don't even know this girl—but I am. "So, just curious, why would you want to play in her band? You're a solo act."

He shrugs. "Yeah, I want to do my own music," he

agrees. "But life on the road is tough, and, I don't know, it'd be nice to put down roots."

"Really?" I ask, surprised. If Adam were in Nashville, we could see each other all the time. We could play together, maybe write together. We could, I don't know, have more breakfast dates. Or regular dates.

"Yeah," he says, nodding. "I guess I'm kind of tired of living out of my truck, being on the road all the time, just playing covers and not really making a name for myself." He looks up at me and smiles. "You inspire me, Bird. You make me want to write more, maybe try to put together my own album. I have a friend who's thinking of renting a place in East Nashville. I thought I might stick around."

"That would be great," I say enthusiastically.

"Yeah, so if I play with Kayelee, I could get a steady paycheck while I network," he goes on. He points his fork at me before shoving another bite in his mouth. "You guys have a similar sound, actually. And she's tall like you, but blond."

"Interesting," I remark, feigning casual interest when really all I want to do is look up this girl on the Internet. I'd bet my boots this is Randall's new girl.

"Yeah," he says, his mouth full. He swallows before finishing. "But way different backgrounds. I think her family's pretty rich."

"Must be nice."

"Tell me about it."

I take a bite of pancakes and consider this girl Kaye-lee...and Adam...making music together. I watch him eat, take him in. Of course she'll have a crush on Adam. He's gorgeous. His eyelashes are long enough that they nearly touch his eyebrows, and his lips are full and pink. He has that baseball-player build where he's not too skinny but not too bulky, either.

He glances up at me between bites and smiles as he chews. Caught staring, I look down and take another bite of my own food, my face flaming.

"Want to try the ham?" he asks, tilting his plate toward me.

I shake my head, take a drink of water, and gather my thoughts. "You know," I say, "we still have a couple of songs to lay down on my album. Maybe you could play on one."

As soon as the words come out, anxiety takes hold.

Adam looks floored. "Seriously? I hope you don't think I was fishing—"

"No, of course not! It would be fun. I'd love to have you on the album." I fork another bite, realizing I've gone and done it again, just like when I promised Dylan. I remind myself that it eventually worked out with my brother. I know that once Dan hears Adam's music, he'll totally be on board.

"Um, it'd be awesome," Adam finally says. "I mean, if

that's what you want. But Jacob told me your producer is only using session veterans for your debut."

I know this is my out, my chance to take back the offer until I've cleared it with Dan, but the thought of Adam making music with a girl who looks and sounds like me is enough to spur me forward. "You're a veteran," I remind him. "I think we'd sound great together. And besides, it's my album."

What am I doing? I pop another huge forkful of pancake into my mouth to shut myself up.

Adam nods, thinking it over. "Okay," he finally says. "Cool. Thanks, Bird."

"Y'all doing okay over here?" our waitress cuts in, splashing water into our glasses as she scans the rest of her section.

We both nod and she's gone again in a flash, completely unaware of the water pooling on the table and heading toward my lap. I scoot my plate away with one hand and reach for a napkin with the other, my eyes on the ice-cold water that has already drenched my place mat. But instead of grabbing a napkin, my hand lands on Adam's as he leans forward in an attempt to help clean up the mess.

And it's as if I've touched a live wire. I look up at him quickly. His eyes meet mine. Our hands freeze in place, both of us clearly feeling the electric pulse. Adam snaps out of it first, blinking and sliding his hand under mine for a couple of napkins. I break the mini-trance as well, breathe again, and scoot over in the booth as he sops the water up just in time.

"Thank you," I say, reorganizing everything on my side of the table so I don't have to make eye contact right away.

He clears his throat. "No problem."

And then a flash goes off in my face.

"Hi," comes a small voice to my right. A chubby young girl is standing at our table holding an iPhone, looking equal parts nervous and thrilled. "Are you Bird Barrett?"

I blink, look at Adam, then turn toward her again. "Yes," I say slowly.

She gives me a shy smile. "Could you please take a picture with me?"

It's an "aw" moment. It's the stuff dreams are made of. This little girl is, well, my first fan.

"I'd love to," I say, shifting over in the booth and patting it so that she can sit next to me.

She turns around toward her mother, who's been waiting a few steps behind, and we pose for the camera. The mother checks the snapshot and nods, indicating that it's great, but Adam stops her.

"Wait, want me to take one of all three of you?" he asks.

"Oh," the mother says, suddenly conscious of how she looks as she fluffs her hair and straightens her scarf. "Well, if you don't mind."

She crouches next to her daughter for the picture, and then they ask me to sign their complimentary Pancake Pantry matchbooks. Before I know it, a few other folks wander over from their tables, asking me to sign their napkins and place mats, all of them saying really nice things about "Notice Me." I can't help but think, *Boy, have they ever.*

"I'm sorry," I whisper to Adam at one point when he shovels in a bite full of eggs and ham before taking the next camera phone.

He shakes his head. "Are you kidding? I'm perfecting my fallback career as photographer to the stars!"

I giggle and pose with the next little girl and her brother, who looks like he'd rather be anywhere else. Their mother, who hovers to the side like all the moms have at first, joins us for the second shot.

But as much fun as I'm having, I want to get back to being alone with Adam. Besides that, my phone says it's seven thirty and I have to be at the studio by eight.

"Check?" the waitress asks, appearing out of nowhere with to-go boxes.

"That'd be great," Adam says, reaching for the bill at the same time I do. He waves me off. "This one's on me, Bird."

"Fine," I say, "but you have to let me buy next time."

He grins. "Next time, huh?" I look away, take a drink

of water, and don't even try to stop the nervous tapping of my foot under the table. He laughs softly. "It's a deal."

As Adam thumbs through the cash in his wallet, I channel all my giddiness into one more picture with another fan. Walking out, I see flashes in my peripheral vision. It is in this moment, ducking out of a restaurant as unassuming as the Pancake Pantry, that I realize that recording artist Bird Barrett may end up being just as big as Dan and Anita promised.

"Wow," I remark to Adam. We walk briskly up the street on an adrenaline high. "That was something else, huh?"

"Yeah," he says, fumbling in his jeans pocket for his keys as we shiver outside his truck. "I'd say things are about to change a whole lot for you, Lady Bird." He opens the squeaky passenger door and gestures for me to get inside, ever the gentleman. "In fact, pretty soon, you won't want to be seen in this old camper-top pickup. I'll have to rent a limo next time."

I make a face as he shuts the door. "Yeah, right!"

I reach over the seat, unlock his door for him as he walks around the front, and pray that the heater warms us up quicker than it did on the way over here.

"A limo," I scoff, blowing air into my cupped hands as he pulls out of the parking space. "Please."

"Jacob and Dylan said y'all had one for the release party,"

Adam comments. I look at him, his profile so handsome as he leans over the steering wheel to wipe at the windshield.

"Yeah, but that was for a big event," I say. "And anyway, the label sent it."

"Ah," he says, nodding. "Where to?"

I give him directions to the recording studio, and he drives, granting me control of the radio. He immediately recognizes an overplayed Luke Bryan song, but then when I change the channel, he surprises me by naming a Katy Perry hit after just a few beats. "Impressive," I say. "But how good *are* you?"

He smirks. "Try me."

We scan the stations, seeing who can name each song and artist first. He completely throws me off when he names a hip-hop song I've never heard by a rapper who seems pretty angry at the world.

"You win." I laugh. "The studio is just there, on the corner."

"Cool," he says, pulling up to the curb. The sun has made its way from behind the sleepy clouds, and it looks like it will actually be a gorgeous January day.

"Thanks again, Adam," I say, reaching down for my to-go box of pancakes. I place my other hand on the door handle but don't open it. I don't know. Maybe it's because I have five more minutes until I have to be inside. Or maybe it's because the heat is finally really blasting, and I don't want to face the cold again. Or maybe it's because I'm with Adam, and I don't want breakfast to be over yet.

"You know, Bird," he says quietly, the cab very cozy and the radio low, "I remember the first time I met you. We were playing some barbecue joint in Louisville, and it was only my second gig ever, so you can imagine how nervous I was. And I looked out into the crowd and saw you sitting in a corner booth with your family." He shakes his head and grins. "But while all of them were clapping or bobbing their heads or whatever, there you were hunched over the table writing like a maniac in that notebook of yours."

I try to think back. "I was probably writing a song."

"Well, whatever it was, I was convinced the whole time that you were telling your diary how god-awful I sounded."

"What?" I exclaim.

He laughs. "I know! It's crazy, I know. But, you know, nerves."

"Yeah, I do know."

Nerves. Twitching, pulsing, tingling, lighting every part of me on fire. Like in this very moment when all I can think about is Adam's hand accidentally touching mine at breakfast, how he left it there for a second before pulling away, and how close he is right now. Nerves that notice the windows fogged up and nerves that can't hide themselves as they set my legs bouncing. Nerves that usually lead me to say something stupid.

"I should go," I say, checking the time on my phone. "I can't be late."

"Yeah," he says. "Thanks for meeting me this morning."

"Thank *you* for breakfast," I say, reaching in to give him a hug.

But as he moves toward me, he doesn't lean to the side like I do. He lifts a hand to my face, briefly, stopping all time and action, and then he tilts his head and brings his lips toward mine. And it's happening. My first kiss. My first kiss *with Adam.*

His full, soft lips meet mine, and he holds them there, gently, for just a moment. Nothing crazy. No tongue or smacking or anything other than a sweet, perfect first kiss. Not anything other than sweet, perfect bliss. My heart is writing songs.

When he pulls away, I open my eyes and sink into his, the dark green-and-brown swirls there pouring over me and melting me to my core. He doesn't say anything, nor do I. He just brushes a thumb across my cheek, and I try with all my might to keep leaning toward him as if the seat buckle weren't digging into my hip.

My phone rings. The clock starts to tick again. The world turns once more.

"Probably Dan," I whisper without checking my phone. I lean back over to my seat, take a breath, and slow my spinning mind. "I'd better get in there."

He nods. "Cool, yeah, of course," he says.

"Thanks again for breakfast," I say, holding up my pancakes.

He grins. "My pleasure."

I reach for the handle again, and this time pop the door open. Adam leans across the seat as I get out. "Hey, Bird?" he calls. I bend down to look back in, pushing my long red locks out of my face. "I play the 5 Spot on the twenty-third if you want to come," he says hopefully, almost bashfully. "I mean, I'd really love it if you were there."

I nod furiously. "Yeah," I promise. "Yes, totally. I wouldn't miss it."

"Sweet," he says, looking adorably relieved. "It's not for a couple of weeks, but I'll text you." I smile, stand back up and shut the door, then give him a little wave as I walk up the sidewalk toward the studio.

And like a total cheese ball from a dumb romantic comedy, I cup my hand to that spot on my face, the place his thumb caressed while we finally kissed, and I hold his warmth there, wishing I had time for just one more.

"I think we got it," Jack says into my headphones. "Take five, and we're moving on."

I nod and give the guys in the booth a thumbs-up. It

hasn't really felt like work today. Ever since Adam dropped me off, I've had the energy to do take after take. Jack even commented that my voice sounds better than ever. I guess that's what happens to a girl when the guy she writes songs about finally does notice her.

Then Dan shows up, pushing the door open and motioning for me to leave the booth and join him in the hall. Surprised, I take my headphones off.

"Hey, Dan," I say timidly, hoping that he's in a good mood.

"Bird! You sound terrific. Just checking in. Everything okay?"

"Good," I answer, wringing my hands nervously. "Everything's good."

"Good," he echoes. "I'll let you get back to it, then."

"Actually," I say, stopping him as he turns to go. "I wonder if I can talk to you about something real quick?"

"Sure," he says. "Shoot."

"Well," I start, not knowing exactly how to word my request. But Adam was right: I went with Dan because he's all about the music, *my* music, and I'm more like a collaborator here than a puppet. Armed with that confidence, I pitch my idea to Dan. "It's just—I have this idea for the song we're doing next week. It's got a rock feel, but it's bluegrass, too, and I think I know the perfect guy to play lead guitar on it."

Dan's eyebrows arch up so high that McDonald's would be jealous. "Oh?"

"Yeah," I say, surging ahead. "My friend, Adam Dean? He's this really talented musician who's played the same circuit as my family's band for the past couple of years, and his own music is, well, amazing, and he would kill the guitar solo, not to mention that I'm comfortable with him already, and he could even do the backup harmonies, which, since I already know him so well, will probably sound really amazing and—"

"Bird," Dan says, shaking his head as I take a big breath. "We talked about this. We want seasoned guys on this album. We want the quality to be the highest caliber there is."

"Me too," I say, nodding. "That's why I think, if you'd just give him a chance—"

"Bird," Dan interrupts.

But I push on. "Just hear him play—he has tracks on his website—you'd see that he'd be—"

"Bird," Dan says again.

But I can't stop now. "The people at GAM think he's good enough to play for *their* new artist and—"

"Bird!" Dan says, raising his voice and stopping me in my tracks. "We've already got your family on two tracks. I told you from the start that I wanted pros, and this guy, I've never heard of him."

"Well, you'd never heard of me before that night at the Bluebird," I say quietly.

Dan takes a deep breath and runs his hand over his balding head. "Bird, I'm sorry, but listen. I'm under a lot of pressure. I want Open Highway to be big. I want people to take notice. And I want that for you, too. I want Bird Barrett to be the next big thing. I want people to know you. I want you to sell out arenas, to land talk shows and tours. I want you to make it, Bird. Can you understand that?"

I swallow the lump in my throat and nod.

"I know this has all taken some getting used to," he says, gesturing around the studio, "but really, you've got to trust me here. Okay?"

I nod again. "Okay," I whisper, looking past his shoulder.

When he nods, I take that as my cue to head back into the recording booth. I need some space. I need a minute.

I grab my purse from the couch and plop down in its place. I dig through its contents, hunting for my phone so I can text Stella. Ever since getting a deal, I've actually found myself feeling a little lonely, and music was never like that before. For me, music was always about people coming together—that's why the BFB was formed in the first place—and it's killing me now that I can't share any of this with the people closest to me.

I sigh heavily. I'm tired, I'm mad, and the cloud I was

floating on when Adam kissed me this morning is evaporating. I unlock my phone and see a text waiting for me from Adam:

I can't stop thinking about... pancakes.

I lie back on the couch and stare at the ceiling as tears spring up without warning. How am I going to tell Adam that my label doesn't want him? Why did I open my big mouth again, anyway?

And then I remember why: Kayelee Ford. I do a quick Web search of her name on my phone. When a Barbie in cowboy boots pops up on-screen, my height but curvier, my age but prettier, I think about Adam playing music with her instead of me and let the tears fall.

18

STELLA, WHO IS waiting for me in the lobby of the discount movie theater, throws the glass door open as I approach. "I cannot believe…" she states dramatically. "You just met"— she pauses, then drags his name out—"Jason Samuels! *The* Jason Samuels. Hot as hell, sexy as sin, you can play tic-tac-toe on his abs Jason Samuels."

I've spent more time in the studio this week than I have at my own house, so I'm excited about a night off to hang with Stella. I didn't record today, but I was still working. Anita pulled some strings, and we visited the set of a major motion picture, our goal to meet the director and some of the cast in the hope that one of my songs will make its way onto the sound track. Yes, it was insane being on set. Yes, it was unbelievable to be at arm's length from the stunning

Hollywood faces I usually only see in the tabloids. And yes, I cried after the first three takes of Jason Samuels's death scene (spoiler alert). But while hanging out with movie stars is fun and all, nothing beats a Friday night out with your bestie.

"Well, I hate to disappoint you, but I didn't actually meet him," I confess.

"What?" Her face falls.

"Yeah, Anita was livid," I say as we walk through the crowded lobby and join the concessions line. "It's a historical romance set in the 1800s or something. So when we walked over during a break to introduce ourselves, his publicist cut us off and said he never drops character and meeting me would be like 'stepping back into an alternate world.'" I raise one eyebrow. "That's a direct quote. I think your celebrity boyfriend is crazy town."

"Not crazy—dedicated," she defends him, starry-eyed. She links an elbow through mine as we consider the menu. "Do you remember him from that vampire show where he fell in love with every girl he was about to kill, so he couldn't bring himself to drink their blood and finally had to suck only the blood of dudes so he wouldn't starve to death? I loved that show. Brilliant. He's so freaking hot. I can't believe you almost met him."

"I slipped his makeup artist your number," I joke, unwrapping my scarf. "Of course, the only way Jason

Samuels can have hair and makeup people around him is if they pretend to be nurses checking on him between takes."

She looks at me skeptically.

I raise both palms in defense. "I can't make this stuff up."

"Okay, so my future husband may have a few quirks. What about yours? Have you talked to Adam lately?" she asks.

"We've texted. He had rehearsal yesterday for that gig with Kayelee Ford." I sigh heavily.

"Yuck."

"Exactly."

"So you haven't seen him since last Friday's . . . breakfast?" she asks, wiggling her eyebrows suggestively.

"No," I respond, blushing.

Stella grabs my phone, pulling up the camera. "Okay, so get your gloss and use the phone as a mirror," she commands, aiming the screen toward me so that I see my own reflection. I look okay, thanks to Amanda sending over an outfit and Anita touching up my makeup in her car right before we went onto the movie set today, but Stella clearly has something up her sleeve.

"Why?" I ask slowly, while following directions. I grab my lip gloss from my purse and smear it on, totally nervous about the mischievous gleam in her eyes. "What?" I ask. "What is it?"

"I got you a present," she says mysteriously.

"Stella!" I hear a familiar voice call. Dylan is across the theater, walking toward us with her big purse in his hands.

"My brother is here?" I ask, completely surprised.

"Brothers," she corrects. "But that's not the present."

I frown. "I hope not."

"But when Dylan texted me earlier to ask if I'd heard about the James Bond marathon here," she says, "and to ask if I wanted to come along tonight with him and Jacob and their 'good buddy from the road,'" she continues, making air quotes, "I suggested that we go to the one that started after you got off work." Her eyes gleam, and my own go wide as saucers. "So," she says, clearly satisfied, "the gang's all here. They're saving seats for us inside."

Stupefied, I stare at her. Then I have a tiny freak-out, squealing as I throw both arms around her. "Oh my gosh, oh my gosh, oh my gosh! I cannot freaking believe this." I spin us both around as Dylan approaches.

"Tell me you're not as hung up on that tool Jason Samuels as Stella is," he moans, totally misinterpreting my excitement. "If I have to hear about his *gorgeous eyes* one more time..."

Stella hip-checks him. "Don't be jealous, Dylan. If you'd rather, I could talk about his butt. It's a masterpiece, like it was carved out of stone."

"Ha!" I laugh out loud at the same time as my brother covers his ears.

"This is exactly what I was talking about," he says, shaking his head. "That dude needs to get an action flick on lockdown stat or he might as well turn in his man card."

Stella rolls her eyes, but after being on set today, I kind of agree with Dylan.

"Hey," Dylan says, uncomfortably holding out her orange purse like it might bite him. "You missed a phone call and I didn't want to go through your bag so … here."

"Oh, it was probably just me," I say.

"Probably, but thank you, anyway," Stella says, taking her bag from him and fishing through its contents. Then she looks up at my brother as if inspiration has just struck. "Actually, now that you're here, why don't you help me carry all the popcorn and drinks? Sorry, Bird, but he's stronger. Go save our seats?"

"Yep, totally," I say, itching to see Adam again. I slap my brother on the back. "Butter on mine? Please and thank you."

And oh so quickly, I'm walking across the lobby toward the theater, my mind racing and my pulse beating just as fast. Adam is here. Ever since the Pancake Pantry, I've been on a roller coaster of feelings, on a total high when I think about our kiss and on a complete low when I think about having to tell him that he can't play on my album after all. And even right now, as I open the door to the dark theater, I'm equal parts apprehensive and eager to see him.

As my eyes adjust, I scan the shadows and pull out my cell phone to find the guys, but then I hear my name.

"Bird!" Adam calls, standing up awkwardly and waving one arm.

I flash a big smile and wave in return as I carefully make my way up to where he and Jacob are saving seats. For a brief second, I worry about where I'm expected to sit, but Adam moves Stella's coat over, freeing up the seat next to him, and I'm relieved. I get a cold chill as I head toward them.

"So basically, the next time we play Black Ops, you need to get a better headset, man," Jacob continues, obviously talking about their new gaming obsession as I slide past him. "Hey, Bird."

"Hey, guys," I say, trying to play it cool as I step over Adam's legs and settle in.

"You got here just in time," Adam says, turning toward me, his face just inches from my own. "The previews haven't even started."

"Oh, good," I say. I swing my hair over one shoulder and nervously finger-comb it, trying to distract myself from his full pink lips and what it would feel like to kiss them again. My pulse is racing. "I love the previews."

"Me too," he says, smiling.

I can't believe I'm on another date with Adam.

"Did you see Dylan?" Jacob asks, leaning forward.

Okay, a date with Adam and my brothers.

"He's got it so bad for your friend Stella," Jacob continues. Adam shakes his head and chuckles, which spurs Jacob on. "Seriously, he was carrying her purse. Did you see him? It's ten times worse than with Whitney."

I look at him in disbelief. "I think they're just friends, Jacob."

"They are," he says, "because she's not into him. I mean, she's got this artsy, cool vibe, and he's like, I don't know, square. It'd never work."

"What he means is," Adam translates, "he thinks she ought to go out with *him* instead."

Jacob looks at Adam like he's wounded, starts to protest, but then cracks up instead, his neck reddening the slightest bit. He shrugs, owning it. "She's hot."

They laugh together, so I join in, but from this exchange, I can't tell what's real and what's them joking around. Does Dylan actually like Stella, or is Jacob just giving him a hard time about carrying her purse? And does Jacob really like her, or is Adam just teasing him, too?

The theater is full by the time Stella and Dylan show up. They file down the row and get situated as the opening scene rolls, James Bond in a tuxedo and in what seems to be an impossible escape situation. They pass everybody their snacks, and I watch them both closely to see if there are any signs of a budding relationship, but Dylan acts normal, checking that the ringer is off on his phone before putting it in his pocket, and Stella, who, thankfully, sat next to me and kicked Dylan to the end, seems more excited about my quasi-date with Adam than about either of my brothers being here.

"You didn't get a drink?" Adam whispers on my other side, taking a sip of his gigantic beverage.

"Guess not," I answer, frowning. "I told Dylan about the popcorn and forgot all about the Coke."

Adam's expression is pained. "How could you forget?"

I laugh. "Well, I didn't know you were going to be here," I say. "And it's not technically after a gig, so..."

"You're right." He nods. "This isn't business; it's pleasure." He is definitely flirting. I am definitely in heaven. "If you give me a few bites of that popcorn, though, I'll let you have a few sips of my Coke. Deal?"

I envision our fingertips brushing in the cardboard tub, imagine his lips on the same straw that I'll be using, wish more than anything that my brother wasn't sitting on the other side of him. I haven't stopped thinking about that first kiss since it happened, and sitting next to him in a dark theater isn't helping matters. I focus, flash Adam my warmest smile, and agree. "Deal."

By the time M has given Bond his mission, my forearm

is touching Adam's as we share the armrest. He glances over at me with a sideways smile when I laugh at Bond's cheeky banter with a statuesque beauty. After about an hour, Adam shifts his body so that he's leaning my way, and I, as nonchalantly as possible, lean toward him. He's so close I can smell that fresh-laundry scent of his that I love—I can actually feel heat coming off his body—and this closeness is all I can think about as James Bond runs across buildings and smashes sports cars. When the credits finally roll, I can't even tell you what Bond's mission was. I was too focused on the few moments when Adam chanced brushing his pinkie against mine.

The lights come up, and we join the rest of the crowd, slowly filing out of the theater, stepping on popcorn kernels and sticky mystery liquid. In the packed lobby, Dylan breaks away from the group to use the bathroom.

"I need to go, too," Jacob says, joining him.

"Oh! Me too," Stella adds, clearly spotting a golden opportunity for me. "Bird, hold my coat?"

And just like that, Adam and I are alone—finally.

My stomach flips.

"Oh, I love these things," he says, gesturing toward a photo booth behind me. I hadn't even noticed it. "Here," he says, reaching for his wallet. "Let's do it."

"Fun," I say, trying to play it cool, when in reality I'm ecstatic.

Adam holds the red curtain back, and I duck inside, with him right behind me. I toss my coat and Stella's at our feet as he feeds money into the machine, and then we don't have much time to get situated before we see the countdown.

"Okay, funny face," he commands, crossing his eyes. I don't have time to pose before the flash goes off because I'm laughing so hard at how goofy he looks.

"Serious!" he calls, scrunching his eyebrows together. I follow suit, my mouth pursed tightly but unable to completely erase my smile.

"Ummm..." he says, searching for a fun idea.

"Hair mustache!" I offer, holding up a long red lock. He nods enthusiastically and presses the side of his face against mine as we drape my hair over our puckered lips. I fight the urge to turn mine toward his. Surely he's going to kiss me again. *Please kiss me again.*

"Normal one," he says this time, pulling his face away and throwing his arm around my shoulders. We lean our foreheads close and smile into the camera.

My heart feels so full it could spill over. I know I'm not, but I feel like Adam's girlfriend.

After the last flash pops, he doesn't hurry to leave the photo booth, and he doesn't move his arm. He faces me, and I gulp hard. His lips are inches away. His eyes look back and forth at each of mine. He's going to kiss me again.

"Where'd they go?" I hear Dylan ask.

Adam and I both flinch just the tiniest bit, and the moment is gone.

"I don't know," Stella says, her voice abnormally loud. "Maybe they went out to the car," she suggests.

"Wait, isn't that your coat?"

I break eye contact and look out the bottom of the curtain where Dylan's sneakers appear next to Stella's coat, the arm of which is peeking out. Adam drops his arm and takes a deep breath before exiting the photo booth.

"Oh, hey, guys," he says. "You want to go next?"

I grab the coats and slide out of the booth behind Adam, handing Stella hers as we wait for the pictures to process. *Sorry*, she mouths when I catch her eye. I shrug. I don't want her to feel bad—it was still an amazing night—but we were so close. He wanted to kiss me. He totally wanted to kiss me. I mean, I *think* he wanted to kiss me.

Adam turns to me as the photo strips print out. "I thought we'd have to fight over who gets which pics, but it prints two sets, so we both get one."

He hands a photo strip to me gingerly, and I look at the images, as does the rest of our crew hovering around. We all laugh, pointing out our favorites.

"Dude, sweet 'stache," Jacob teases Adam, pointing to the third pic.

"Okay, I need food," Dylan announces, clapping his hands once. "Who's with me?"

I open my purse as the group meanders toward the front doors. Before we go out into the cold, I slip my strip of pictures into my songwriting journal, not wanting them to get bent or torn. Adam tucks his into his shirt pocket and then zips up his fleece.

"Um, are you Bird Barrett?" a girl about my age asks as she approaches.

"I am," I say, smiling, slightly embarrassed still when I'm recognized in public.

"Can I have your autograph?" she asks, holding out her ticket stub and a pen. Her friends whip out their camera phones behind her.

"Wow, a whole two and a half hours before getting spotted," Dylan cracks once the girls have left. "That's a record these days."

Stella swats him. "Come on, boys," she says, linking her arms through my brothers'. "Let's go get the car."

Adam stays behind. I notice more people glancing our way, trying to decide whether they should come over to me. I love my fans, but Stella has just given me another opportunity to be alone with Adam, so I pop my hat on my head and duck my chin under my scarf, making a beeline for the doors and the parking lot. Adam follows me out.

"That was fun," he says as I lead him away from the box-office window and the crowd under the marquee.

"Yeah, it really was," I agree, zipping up my coat. I smile. "And now, we eat."

"Ugh," he says, hanging his head. "I wish. The movie went a little longer than I'd expected, and the band backing me for my show on Thursday is probably already showing up for practice."

"Oh," I say, bummed.

"Yeah," he says, seemingly just as bummed.

I don't want to add to the disappointment, but I also know I need to tell him about my conversation with Dan. I feel a knot in the pit of my stomach.

"Um, so I talked to my label about you playing on the album with me," I say, hating myself as the words come out. I don't flat-out lie, but I certainly don't tell him that we recorded the song I'd wanted him on this past week. I just deliver the blow as softly as possible. "Apparently they've already booked all the musicians we'll need for this album."

"Oh yeah?" Adam comments, running his hand through his hair. "That's too bad, but I kind of figured. I mean, it was cool of you to ask, but I knew it was a long shot."

"Yeah," I say, shifting my weight. "I should've asked Dan before even bringing it up."

He shrugs. "I mean, it would've been awesome, Bird, don't get me wrong. But I know that I still have to prove myself. That's what's great about landing this gig with Kayelee. She likes my sound and—"

"*I* love your sound," I cut in.

He puts a hand on my shoulder, looking me right in the eyes. "Please don't stress about me not being on your album, Bird. Okay?"

I bite my lip and nod. "Well, for what it's worth, I totally wish it were you."

He smiles sweetly and steps closer. My pulse picks up.

But then his phone beeps, and he pulls it from his jeans pocket, one more moment gone. "Speak of the..." He trails off, texting back a quick reply. "That's Kayelee's people now," he says, holding up the phone. "Details about her release party next weekend. Things are happening for me, Bird. They just take time."

I nod, force a supportive smile.

"And speaking of time, I really do have to go. It was good to see you again, Lady Bird," he says, his eyes twinkling in the streetlights as he leans in for a hug.

"Yeah, you too, Adam," I say over his shoulder. He holds the embrace just a fraction of a second longer than normal, even gives me a small squeeze, but then he pulls away and is waving his good-byes to Stella and my brothers as they pull up to the curb. He jogs to his truck in the parking lot.

I watch him for a few seconds before a young girl notices me and asks me to sign her pack of Milk Duds. I do, grateful for fans like her, but even her enthusiasm about my single can't brighten my mood. Although Adam seemed cool about it, I made a stupid promise that I couldn't keep, and as I get in the car, I can't help but think that maybe I ruined a perfect night.

19

STELLA YAWNS, STRETCHING from head to toe before sitting up and grabbing us both another muffin from the plate Shannon brought us this morning. "I'm so bummed that Adam didn't kiss you."

"Join the club," I say dryly. Dylan dropped us off at Stella's house on the way home last night and we stayed up late talking about Adam. And even though we've only been awake a little while, we're already overanalyzing every part of the night all over again. "I could swear he was going to, but I don't know. Maybe not. I mean, my brothers were right there. Maybe he was just going to—"

"He was going to kiss you," Stella says, cutting me off. "Don't overthink it."

I sigh. "But then I had to tell him about not being on the

album after all. I know a break like that would really boost his career, and I know that if Dan would just listen to his stuff he would love it. Ending the whole 'almost date' like that was the worst."

Stella seems confused. "I thought you said it didn't even faze him?"

"Yeah," I say, chewing. "But still."

My cell phone rings, and I sit straight up, hoping like crazy that it's Adam. But then I slouch again when I see the caller ID. "Anita," I say, holding the phone up to Stella.

"Take it," she says, waving me off as she grabs her own phone and leans back against her pile of pillows.

"Hello?" I answer.

"Bird, you'll never believe it," Anita says by way of greeting.

"What?"

I hear her fingernails clacking away on a keyboard, which means that at nine thirty on a Saturday morning, Anita is already working.

"Jason Samuels's publicist just called me and felt terrible that you two didn't actually get to talk on set, what with his dedication to his craft," she says wryly. "Anyway, they want to set up an outing: the two of them and the two of us. I really think this will be a wonderful step toward getting your song into the movie, don't you?"

"Sure," I say, rolling my eyes.

Stella raises her eyebrows questioningly.

"From what his publicist told me," Anita continues, "Jason was quite taken with you."

"Taken with me?" I ask. "He didn't even talk to me."

Who? Stella mouths.

I cover the speaker. "Your celebrity boyfriend." Her eyes nearly pop out of her head, and I suppress a laugh.

"He's an odd one, to be sure," Anita says candidly, "but an outing like this will be great networking for you, Bird. A friendship with a power player like Jason Samuels could do a lot for your image, much more than that boy from the Pancake Pantry."

My jaw drops. "What are you talking about?"

Anita sighs. "Bird, don't be coy. It's my job to know these things. And I'm not the only one. Someone posted a picture on your fan forum of the two of you having breakfast together."

"I haven't seen the photo," I reply, thinking back to that morning. I glance up at Stella, who is trying desperately to piece together the conversation. "Why would anybody care who I eat pancakes with?"

"Your *fans* care," Anita explains. "And it's my *job* to care, I might add. And listen, Bird, although I ought to be hearing these things from you, it's a *good* thing that you've got a fan forum. People are starting to know you."

I pull my lucky rock pendant out from under my T-shirt

and run it back and forth along its silver chain. So much has changed so fast.

"Anyway," Anita continues, "the director is on the fence about using your song on the sound track, so if Jason's people are reaching out, then meeting them is what we're going to do."

I sigh. "Of course. You're right. Let's meet 'em," I say. "But should I call him Jason or General Whitfield?"

Anita actually laughs out loud, the first time I've ever heard her do that, and I finally catch a glimpse of the person behind the machine.

"We'll be in the neighborhood," my dad grumbles as he pulls up and double-parks in front of a coffee shop. He wasn't crazy about this meet up, insisting that Anita was playing matchmaker for a boy who's ten years older than me, but my mom reminded him that it's business and that both of our publicists would be there. He relented, although not happily. "Just call us if you need anything, you hear?"

"Yes, Dad, I'll be fine," I say, exasperated.

As Mom and Dad drive off, I enter the coffee shop, a bustling neighborhood place called Fido, and look around for everybody. This place is much bigger than I expected, actually. The bar is backed up even though three baristas are attending to people's orders, and as I wander slowly through the packed rooms, where people sit by the windows with their laptops and others chat around tables of four, I'm hoping Anita got here early and grabbed us a table.

I've just started to call her when I hear my name.

"Bird?"

I look up to see Jason standing right in front of me, his thick brown hair pulled back in a low ponytail. And I know that it's silly, but I suck in air, fast. I mean, this is legit surreal. I'm about to have brunch with super famous heartthrob Jason Samuels. *How is this my life?*

"Oh, hey," I say, holding out my hand to shake his. "Should I call you...Jason?" I ask hesitantly.

He smiles. "Yeah, sorry about that yesterday. I don't ever break character when I'm on set. I totally commit."

"Of course," I say. "No worries."

"Like, for example," he goes on, "this movie starts in the hospital where my character wakes up and discovers he lost an arm in his last battle." He squeezes my shoulder, almost in a reassuring way. "It's sad, I know." Once he realizes that I'm emotionally stable after hearing this news, he continues, "So even on lunch or dinner breaks, I make sure to eat with my left arm only. Or I have someone feed me."

I laugh out loud before I realize he's not kidding.

He drops his hand and looks away. "Wow," I say, clearing my throat. "That's serious dedication."

"Well, people have come to expect a certain level of craft from Jason Samuels," Jason Samuels says. I cringe when he refers to himself in the third person, but I congratulate myself for not rolling my eyes. I don't know what Anita expects from me, but I really am doing the best I can here.

"Well," I say, "whatever you're doing, it works. I can't wait to see the movie." At least that's honest.

"Thank you, Bird," he replies. "And I'm a big fan of your music."

I cock my head, taken aback. "You know my song?"

"I'm kind of a music connoisseur," he says quite seriously. "Plus, it's on the radio, like, every other second."

Jason freaking Samuels knows my song.

"I guess," I say sheepishly. "I'm still getting used to that, actually."

"Yeah," he says dramatically, staring off into the distance. "The limelight is a tricky place to live."

There is a small lull in the conversation, and I check my phone. Still no word from Anita. I watch the front door, starting to get worried.

"Should we get in line?" Jason asks.

"Sure," I say. "Let me just text my publicist. It's really not like her to be late."

Jason smirks. "Do you actually think she's coming?"

I whip my head up. "Of course she's coming."

He shrugs. "Mine isn't."

"What?" I ask, incredulous.

"I'm guessing it's a setup," he says matter-of-factly.

"No way." I fire off a quick text to Anita. Now I'm really worried:

Hello? Jason is here. We r waiting 4 u.

"Let's at least get in line," Jason says, yawning. "We shot until three in the morning, and I could really use some caffeine."

"Oh my gosh, that's brutal."

"The cost of the craft," he says.

We join the line and stand next to each other, both studying the menu and neither with much to say. I remind myself of the reason for all of this: getting my song in his movie. So I take a deep breath, force a smile, and get down to the business of making Jason Samuels like me enough to influence his director.

"It's crazy how crowded it is in here, right?" I ask, trying to make conversation. Jason yawns again, and I cringe overdramatically. "Yeah, I know. My small talk needs work."

This actually makes him laugh out loud. "No! Oh my

God, no." He slaps his face with his hands and shakes his head, trying to wake up. "It's this movie schedule. It's killing me."

"Uh-huh," I say sarcastically. "That Bird Barrett. *Yawn*."

He laughs out loud again, really looking at me for the first time today, almost as if pleasantly surprised. I grin—now we're getting somewhere.

"Okay, seriously, let me try again." He straightens an imaginary tie and puts on a stuffy British accent. "Why yes, Bird. It is quite crowded in here. I believe it is the overflow of people who thought they were die-hard enough to wait in that Pancake Pantry line, but forty-one degrees is colder than they realized, and alas, they were not."

I laugh. "Those pancakes are pretty good," I say. Then I blush, thinking about what's even better *after* said pancakes.

"Yeah, they rock." He nods, putting his hands in the pocket of his hoodie and stepping forward with the line. "But Fido has great food. I'm going to get a burger—I mean, if you have time."

"Oh yeah, sure," I say, checking the time on my phone. Still no word from Anita, who is now twenty minutes late.

Just then a woman about my mom's age approaches Jason. "I loved you in *Cupid on Earth*," she says in a thick Spanish accent.

"Oh, thank you," he says, joining his hands like a yogi and bowing a little.

"Would you sign my coffee cup?" she asks, the tray of to-go coffees in her hand shaking. Bless her heart, she's so nervous that I'm afraid the whole thing's going to spill. But Jason is gracious. He takes the pen from her and autographs her coffee-cup sleeve with a flourish. Her eyes shine.

But before he gives it back to her, he passes the pen to me and asks, "Do you know my friend Bird Barrett? She's a big star, too."

I blanch, completely uncomfortable. The lady studies me but is totally thrown for a loop. That's the moment when I realize that the only thing more humbling than being approached by fans is *not* being approached by fans. Still, the lovely woman wants to be polite in front of Jason Samuels, so she flashes me a big smile. "Hi," she says.

"Hi," I reply, totally awkward.

"So you don't know her?" he asks. The woman shakes her head. "Oh, well, Bird is visiting Nashville from her native country of Russia, where she is an enormous success," Jason says seriously. "You've heard of Cher? Bird is the Cher of Russia."

The lady's eyes widen and she gasps. I turn toward nutcase Jason Samuels, worried that he might be losing his mind right here in front of me, but when I see the mischief in his no-longer-sleepy eyes, I realize he's just having a little fun with this lady. I'm so stunned that I nearly laugh out loud.

"Bird," he says, raising his voice and overenunciating each word as if I'm deaf, "how are you lik-ing A-mer-i-ca?"

I certainly did not peg Jason Samuels as a jokester, but looking at him now, I consider him with new eyes. Slowly, I turn toward his fan, happy to play along. "Rrrrreally verrrry much," I say, nodding energetically.

In my peripheral vision, I see Jason swallow what would've been a hearty laugh, and I can barely keep a straight face myself. He hands me her cup, and I sign my name next to his, hoping the giggle that escapes won't blow my cover.

"It was really nice meeting you," Jason says as he hands the coffee cup back to her, quite clearly concluding our interaction. She nods and gives him her biggest smile one last time before walking to the front door, where her husband and teenage sons wait.

"Nice accent," Jason says as we move forward a little more in line.

"You're crazy," I say, finally able to let out a good laugh. "But you probably just made her entire vacation."

Jason shrugs. "What can I say? Cougars love me."

I nearly lose it.

We get our food (a burger and a triple-shot soy latte for him and a jasmine tea and coconut muffin for me) and find seats. Now that the ice has been broken, we actually settle into a surprisingly comfortable conversation. Considering what a weirdo he was on set the other day, I was completely convinced that we'd have absolutely nothing to talk about, so Stella and I had role-played questions before I came, although every scenario ended with her asking if she could be the mother of my children. But even though all the characters Jason plays in movies make him seem like just a pretty face, now that we're two regular people hanging out in a coffee shop, I realize there's a little more depth to him than I'd figured. He's really a nice, if slightly quirky, guy.

My phone beeps in my pocket.

"That better be my publicist," I say. Jason shakes his head, and as I check the text from Anita—Something came up. Can't make it. Call me after.—I get the sinking feeling that he was right all along. "She can't make it," I say sheepishly.

He grins. "Shocker," he says, before taking another big bite of his burger.

I feel so stupid, so naive. I thought this whole thing was about getting one of my songs in a blockbuster movie, but apparently Anita had a secret agenda. This woman expects me to trust her and then does something shady like this. I'm fuming.

"You okay?" Jason asks.

"Oh, yeah," I lie. I take a deep breath and force a small smile. After all, it's not Jason's fault, and in all honesty, I'm having an okay time.

As we eat, it becomes obvious that everyone in the entire building knows Jason Samuels is here. I thought he would be the kind of guy to milk all the attention he could get, but he chose to sit facing the wall and keeps his eyes on our table, even though there are more than a few people who would like to get his autograph or take a picture with him. I'm about to ask him how he got into acting when two tweens walk by our table, singing my song and breaking into a fit of giggles the minute they are past us.

"So," Jason says, leaning in low and jerking his head back toward them, "how are you handling all the fame?"

I consider it. "Well, it's really new, you know? My song's only been out for a few weeks. I'm not at the level you are or anything, so it's fine."

"You will be," he says confidently, taking a small sip of his latte. "And listen, the spotlight can be so strong, it blinds. You almost become, like, two people. The famous version of yourself and then the one only your friends and family know."

I nod vigorously. "Oh my gosh, you're totally right. I mean, I've already felt that a little."

"You'll find a balance," he says, "but it's tough at first. The best advice I can give you is to carve out a little space each week for Me Time."

"I wish," I say. "I practically live in the studio."

"You'll burn out," he says, shaking his head. "Trust me.

That's why I kite surf every weekend. I love the beach, even if not much else about LA."

"You don't like Los Angeles?"

Jason shrugs. "I like it okay, I guess. It's just that the business can beat you down. Hollywood is so fake."

I take another drink, not really sure what to say. Only a half hour ago I thought Jason Samuels was the phoniest guy I'd ever met, so I just nod.

"Sorry," he says. "I found out yesterday that I got passed over for this action movie, and honestly, I really wanted it."

"But you play a general in this movie," I say. "So there must be some fierce war scenes or something."

He grins ruefully. "Nah, the whole thing takes place *after* I've been injured. It's more a love story between a wounded soldier and an unhappily married nurse, but I'm sick of doing chick flick after chick flick. No offense."

"None taken."

"I want to drive a getaway car or blow up a prison or do something totally badass." He sighs, picking up his burger again. "But hey, it's work. At least this time we get to shoot on location. Nashville is a great town."

"Oh, yeah," I agree. "I love it."

We finish up our food and I feel myself relax as we get to know each other. When he tells me that he took his grandmother as his date to his first awards show, I realize that there's a heart of gold under all those muscles. I'm completely astonished, but I feel like Jason Samuels is someone I could actually be friends with.

"Should we go?"

"Yeah," I say, standing up and slipping on my coat.

"Oh, you've got an eyelash," Jason says, shocking me by leaning in close. His thumb is an inch from my eyeball before I even register what's happening, so I close my eyes instinctively. His thumb brushes under my lashes and then the touch is gone.

"Make a wish." He grins, holding up a lash thickly coated in mascara.

"I wish there was more time in the day." I sigh.

"Amen, sister," he says, offering a high five. We walk through the coffee shop, him smiling and nodding to the people he catches ogling him on the way out but walking with purpose to minimize the chances of getting stopped.

"You need a ride?" he asks at the glass doors.

"My folks are waiting," I admit self-consciously. "My dad wasn't happy about me getting brunch with an older guy, especially one who happens to have been voted Sexiest Man Alive."

Jason smiles, holding the door open for me. "You worry about bringing guys home to your dad. I worry about bringing girls home to my publicist."

I laugh.

"Sad but true," he says, and I can tell he really means it.

When we step out onto the sidewalk, though, my happy-shiny feeling disappears. From out of nowhere, flashbulbs go off, and three men with big cameras start shouting my name. "Bird! Over here! Jason, is this your new girlfriend? Bird! Bird!"

Unfazed, Jason puts on his sunglasses and pulls up his hood. The flashes keep going off, and without even realizing it, I've got my arm up shielding my eyes. Jason takes charge, slipping a strong arm around my waist and leading me toward a black SUV with tinted windows parked nearby. I just want to get out of here, so when Jason holds the passenger door open for me, I get in.

"What the heck?" I ask when he gets behind the wheel after pushing past some guys taking my picture through the windshield. "How'd they know you were here?"

"We," Jason corrects.

The three paparazzi are standing outside the car, still snapping away when Jason starts to slowly pull out of his parking space. I'm on edge, worried we might run over someone, but Jason is totally calm. Like dogs who bark at cars, the photographers manage to walk away in one piece.

"I'll go around the block," he says, glancing over at me. "We'll circle back, if you want to tell your parents."

"Thanks," I say, pulling out my phone and texting

them. "This is insane." I shake my head and put on my seat belt, totally flustered, while Jason is the picture of peace. "I still don't get how they just showed up like that," I say.

"Bird," he replies patiently, "I'm sure your publicist called them. Or mine. Who knows?"

"Anita?" I say, surprised. "I don't think she would do that."

He looks amused. "She's the one who set up the meeting in the first place."

I gawk at him. The first thought that comes to my mind is her saying that Jason was "taken" with me. Fuming, I feel my face burn. I can't believe she lied to me. I can't believe I believed her.

"Classic setup," he says. "But don't sweat it. I'm glad she did. That was a pretty good burger . . . and the company was *okay*."

"Ha-ha," I say dryly.

He pulls up in front of a bookstore and double-parks behind my parents, switching on his emergency lights. "It was nice to meet you, Bird Barrett," Jason says, offering his hand and shaking mine exaggeratedly.

I grin. "Eet woz rrrreally my plez-ure," I reply in my bad Russian accent.

He laughs pretty hard as I open my door. When I step out, he calls, "Hey, I really do hope we use your song in the movie."

I lean down before closing the door. "Me too. See ya later, alligator."

"Oh," he says, wincing. "Now I know I have met the real Bird Barrett. After a while, crocodile," he says mockingly.

I stick my tongue out and slam the door. Within seconds, hip-hop music booms from his pimped-out ride and he joins the flow of traffic on Twenty-First Avenue. Hurrying the few steps to where my parents wait, I get in the backseat, grateful for the warmth and for the normalcy of Gramma's old sedan.

"How was it?" my mom asks, turning around in her seat as I buckle up.

I catch my dad's eye in the rearview mirror and know better than to tell the truth. My beef is with Anita, and I can handle it myself.

"Fine," I say, plastering on a smile for them both. "It was just fine."

20

"Bird!" Stella calls, pounding on my bedroom door.

The beating is intense, as is the high-pitched tone of her voice, so I throw off the covers and fly out of bed, terrified. "What is it?" I say, swinging open my bedroom door. "What's wrong?"

"OMG, have you read the new *Us Weekly*?" she asks, holding up a copy of the gossip magazine as she barges into my room.

My pulse slows down a little and I rub the sleep from my eyes, but I'm still confused. I look over at the clock on my bookshelf; it reads 9:00 AM. "Um, no." She throws her lavender messenger bag onto my bed and opens it with purpose. "It's Thursday. Shouldn't you be at school?" I ask.

"I *was* there," she says hurriedly, pulling out her phone

and a bunch of other magazines before sitting down and facing me. She looks really anxious. "But then I found out about all of this and ditched."

"Found out about what?" I ask slowly, an inexplicable feeling of dread coming over me.

"Have you been online?"

"No, but—"

She holds up her cell phone and explains: "*TMZ* says Jason Samuels is your 'muse' and that you guys are a hot and heavy couple who've secretly been involved this whole month. You met him at a party over the holidays in Nashville and have been, quote, 'the song in his heart' while he shoots his new drama."

"Oh my God!" I exclaim, shutting the door quickly and grabbing my laptop off my desk.

"So you haven't read *Star*," she guesses correctly. "Or *InTouch* or *OK!*?"

"No," I say, feeling queasy. "I just woke up."

I climb onto my bed and grab a magazine, completely mortified.

"'Jason Samuels gets cozy with his new Song Bird'?" I read, my voice getting higher with each word. Under the headline is a blurry shot of Jason with his arm around me on the sidewalk in front of Fido.

"We weren't 'getting cozy,'" I snap at the magazine. I hold it up to Stella. "These idiots were waiting for us outside, and Jason was just leading me through. When all those cameras got up in my face and the paparazzi were yelling, I froze."

She bites her lip. "You do *look* cozy," she concedes, fanning out all the articles and pointing to a pic in another magazine.

I feel sick. According to *Us Weekly*, I've been into Jason for a long time and now that my single is number ten on the *Billboard* Hot 100 chart, I'm over the moon that he's "Noticed Me." There are a couple of pictures of Jason touching me, once when he put his hand on my shoulder at the beginning of our "date" and once when he brushed away that eyelash. And in *Star*, there is a picture of us laughing at our table in Fido with a headline asking, WILL JASON MOVE TO NASHVILLE FOR LOVE? And then, to top it all off, *OK!* magazine has eyewitness statements of how we were sharing a burger and making out in his car, complete with a series of photos of him ushering me into the front seat.

"This is completely made-up!" I shriek, trying to remain calm and failing miserably. I look at her, my eyes a little wet. "What if Adam sees this stuff?"

She bites her lip.

"Stella?"

She exhales loudly. "Yeah. I think that would be bad."

I throw myself back against my pillows and bury my head under my comforter. "No, no, no, no, no."

"I'm sorry," she says, kicking off her shoes and moving up on the bed to where I'm hiding.

"This isn't happening," I moan.

"You could text him," Stella suggests.

I pull the covers off my face. "And say what? 'Oh, hey, Adam. I know we're not technically dating and I don't know what that kiss was or if we'll ever kiss again or if you even want to since it's been, like, two weeks, anyway, but just in case you do—'cause I really do—I'm definitely not dating Jason Samuels even though it totally looks like it, okay?'" I look at Stella and she twists her mouth, thinking. "And then what if he says, 'What are you talking about? You went out with Jason Samuels?' Like, he may not even know. He doesn't read this stuff." Even as I say it, I can hear how pathetic that hope is.

"Okay, so it's presumptuous to text Adam since y'all aren't technically a thing, but I definitely think you need to talk to Anita," Stella says. She leafs through one of the magazines again. "She obviously set you up. You need to ask her WTF."

I groan. "I already called her when I was really ticked off the day I met Jason, but she turned it back on me. She got mad, saying that she was hurt I'd question her motives and that she couldn't really remember whose people called whose. But then she called again yesterday and said my song is definitely being used in the movie now, so it was 'all for the best.' I don't see the point in calling her again. I mean, it's done."

Stella frowns. "In other words, 'all publicity is good publicity'?"

I sigh, looking down at a small picture of Jason and me laughing in the corner of the cover of *InTouch*.

"I wonder what your fans think," Stella ponders aloud. She grabs my laptop and types in the URL to my fan forum. "Oh no," she says.

"What?" I ask, sitting up and tilting the screen my way. To my horror, there are two thumbnails side by side, one of Adam and me at the Pancake Pantry and one of Jason and me at Fido. The article is all about comparing my body language in each picture and what it says about my interest in each of the guys ... *that I'm dating*.

"This is a nightmare," I grumble, shutting the laptop firmly.

"You want to see a nightmare?" Stella asks. She picks up a tabloid and flips through the pages expertly. "Then look at the bedazzled midriff-baring shirt Kim Kardashian is sporting on page twenty-two of *Us Weekly*. Stars are *so* not like us."

And despite everything, I smile.

"I really think we've got it," Shannon says, setting down her guitar after what's already been a long day.

"You're sure?" I ask, looking at the lyrics in front of me. "We hardly changed anything on this one."

Shannon smiles warmly at me. "Sometimes it happens that way. The hook is catchy, the lyrics are smart, and now that we've upped the tempo, I think it will really complement the rest of the songs on your album."

"If you're sure..."

"I'm sure," she says. "Let's take a break and then lay down the demo. I'll e-mail it over to Dan later tonight, but I'm positive he's going to green-light it. This actually might be one of my favorites."

I smile, feeling the same way. After the crappy "personal life" morning I had, it was nice to have a productive workday. I set down my own guitar and stretch my arms up over my head as her phone rings.

"This is Shannon," she answers brightly.

But then she bolts up, standing still as a statue, her face suddenly tense with worry.

I feel my own stomach twist. "Is it Stella?" I ask.

Shannon glances over at me and curtly shakes her head before leaving the room. I get that it's totally uncool to spy, but I walk closer to the kitchen, anyway. I've never seen Shannon so freaked out and I'm concerned.

"Tell me you're joking," I hear her say.

I take a breath and waltz into the kitchen as nonchalantly as I can, my hand to my throat to exhibit the pretense that I am suddenly so parched that I can't possibly wait another second for a glass of water. Shannon barely takes notice. She is sitting on a bar stool at the counter going through pages in an open binder and talking to the person on the other end of the line about "filling a hole." From the bits and pieces I overhear, I start to relax. Nobody's sick. Nobody's hurt. It's just something to do with a show.

"No, no, no," Shannon says, barely audible. She shuffles through the pages again and pulls out what looks like a set list. Then she flips her long black hair over one shoulder and pinches the bridge of her nose. "She was our opener, Kevin." A pause. Then a curt reply. "Yes, I understand it's just a high school showcase, but I happen to have a daughter who attends said high school."

"Can I help?" I ask quietly. I hate to see her so stressed out.

"No, Bird," she says, waving me off. Then she looks up at me, locks her eyes on mine, almost as if she's just registered what I said. "Kevin, let me call you back."

She ends the call and takes a deep breath. "Bird, I know you've got a lot on your plate right now. And I know this is a lot to ask. But yes. You actually can help. But only if you really want to."

"Anything," I say.

"It's two thirty now," Shannon starts, checking her phone. I've never seen her so worked up. "I am putting on a big fund-raiser at Stella's school tonight to raise money for the arts program, since the state cut the budget—again."

"Oh, that's terrible," I say.

"Yes." She nods. "It is. That's why we're throwing the fund-raiser. This is Nashville, Tennessee. You would think that Music City of all places would get it. Anyway, the show starts at seven thirty tonight, and I've just lost my opener to the flu. I can make some calls, but..."

I volunteer readily. "No, I'll do it," I say. "Let me help. I can do 'Notice Me.'"

Shannon exhales loudly, her shoulders relaxing. "Oh, Bird, you're a lifesaver," she says, putting her hand to her heart. "Let me just call Dan."

"No!" I say, reaching out a hand. I think about the advice Jason gave me, about finding balance, about differentiating Me Time from Work Time. "I want to do this for you, Shannon, because you've done so much for me. But I don't want Amanda to send over an outfit or Anita to put out a press release. I don't want it to be a 'work thing.' It's my song and I want to sing it at my best friend's school." I frown. "I don't know why you guys didn't mention it to me in the first place."

"You've been so busy in the studio," Shannon says. "I know firsthand what it's like to put out an album on a *normal* schedule, and Open Highway has you on the express track. I honestly don't know how you haven't had a nervous breakdown—I would be fried. I just didn't want to add anything else to your plate."

"Oh, no, I *miss* live performances. I used to be onstage every night with my family, but now I only sing in the studio." I feel myself getting preshow jitters already, feel the old adrenaline kicking in. I smile. "I'm even going to bring Maybelle. This will be fun!"

"What will be fun?" Stella asks as she walks in the door.

Shannon looks up at her daughter. "Bird is going to open at the fund-raiser tonight."

Stella looks up at me, surprised. "Seriously?"

I nod.

"OMG, that's so exciting!" she says, stomping her foot. "Let's go pick out something to wear. You can borrow that cute purple dress I just got. My friends are going to love you." She grabs my hand and drags me out of the kitchen.

"I have to stop by my house on the way to grab my fiddle," I tell her.

Stella stops dead in her tracks. "Wait, what about Adam's show? It's tonight, right?"

My mouth falls open. I'd totally forgotten. "Oh."

"Yeah." She shrugs. "No biggie. Just tell my mom you have plans already. We can still get ready together, and I can drop you at the 5 Spot on my way to the school and then meet up with you later."

I contemplate the situation, wondering if I can possibly do both things. I promised Adam that I'd be there tonight, but I also really want to help Shannon. Without her, I wouldn't have had the courage to sing from my heart at the Bluebird, and I definitely wouldn't have been able to turn the songs in my journal into singles for the radio. And if I'd never met Shannon, then I'd never have met Stella.

"No," I say, not wanting to let them down. "I'll open for your show and book it out right after. I can make both, even if I show up a little late at the 5 Spot. Adam will totally understand."

"Are you sure?" she asks.

"One hundred percent," I say.

And even though I'll be cutting it close, when she throws her arms around my neck and gives me a big hug, I know that it's the right thing to do.

21

THE GYMNASIUM IS pretty full. The bleachers are packed, as are the folding chairs lined up on the floor. And a bunch of kids have crashed right in front of the stage, their jackets and purses in piles around them as they sit in clumps waiting for the show to begin.

Shannon finally walks toward a mic stand set up in the center of a small stage. Black curtains are draped on either side of the risers, and I wait behind them with the band that Shannon hired to accompany all the solo acts like myself. The makeshift stage takes me back to life on the road, relieving some of my anxiety about this intimidating audience. It's not like I'm playing a sold-out arena or anything, but I've never performed for this many people my own age.

"It is very encouraging to see so many parents and students here to help raise money for the Warren McNeal High School arts program," Shannon says into the microphone. "Thank you for attending, for recognizing the importance of the arts just by being here, and for your generous donations tonight." As she introduces herself and talks about the silent auction and other ways that people can donate to keep the arts program thriving, I take in the smell of the gym, hear the occasional sneaker squeak as people move around in the back, and worry about the acoustics.

"Well, I am thrilled to introduce our first act tonight," Shannon says, indicating that it's almost my cue.

I shake out my arms, bend my knees, and stretch my neck. I clutch Maybelle in one hand and my lucky rock pendant in the other. I close my eyes and whisper a quick pre-show prayer.

"I'm sad to say that our original opener came down with a bad case of the flu and had to cancel at the last minute," Shannon announces. "We all hope she feels better real soon, but in the meantime, a good friend of mine offered to step in. Have any of you out there heard the song 'Notice Me'?" The gym gets a jolt as people in the crowd murmur to each other excitedly.

"This young new artist is as sweet as she is talented, and I feel very honored to call her both a colleague and a friend. Without further ado, allow me to introduce Bird Barrett!"

She leads the applause as she exits, and I race up the small stairs, walking purposefully across the stage, excited and intimidated, eager and scared. I take a deep breath and smile out at the audience.

"Everybody doing all right tonight?" I ask. The response is surprisingly raucous: applause from the bleachers, hooting from the students. "This is a song I wrote last year about, well, a boy." I grin, feeling myself blush. "I doubt any of you out there can relate." The crowd laughs. "If you've heard this song, then sing along. If you haven't, I hope you enjoy it. It's called 'Notice Me.'"

A few people woo-hoo, and I spot Stella in the front row smiling encouragingly. I turn back toward the band, take a deep breath, and count us in. The only other time I've sung this number live was at the release party for my single, and I played guitar then. As the drummer picks up the beat and the guitarist comes in with the melody, I feel my whole body melt into the sound, like a long burning wick falling into warm wax:

"Maybe you like me, or do you like me not?
May be wishful thinking, but wishin's all I got."

I know this song like the back of my hand, but when I look out into the crowd, especially at the kids standing and swaying next to Stella, it startles me that they do, too. We sing through the first verse, and when I get to the chorus, I smile as the entire female population of Stella's high school pleads with their crushes to just notice them already.

After the chorus, I step away from the standing mic and set to work on Maybelle for a quick eight measures. I wonder if any of the people out there knew I actually played the fiddle or if they thought it was somebody else on the recording. I grin to myself, relishing the experience of letting everybody see the real me.

The second verse comes around quick, and I settle in once more behind the mic, singing like I never want to stop. As I draw out the last word of the verse, I lift my arms out to my sides. Then the chorus starts and I jump up and down, singing as if my life depends on it. Heads are bobbing up and down in the crowd; the students are on their feet.

And as I belt out those two words, those beseeching two words that gave this song its name, I stomp the custom cowboy boots Amanda let me keep from my first photo shoot, and the crowd knows something is coming.

I toss my long red tresses over my shoulder and bring Maybelle up to my neck again for the big fiddling pass. As I play, my hair falls in waves around my right shoulder, and my elbow knocks it back as I saw across my fiddle with fervor. I play for the past four months in the studio, for the tour dates the BFB had to cancel, for the nightly jam sessions I didn't even realize I missed.

The crowd goes bananas. I see cell phones in the air and hear someone shout, "I love you, Bird!" They feed me. They push me.

"Sing with me!" I call into the mic.

And together, the students and parents of Warren McNeal High School sing along to my original song at the top of their lungs. I hadn't thought anything could top hearing my song on the radio, but hearing other people sing it? That takes my breath away.

"Yip!" I call, indicating to the band that we're wrapping up. I throw my bow across the fiddle and cut the song, tossing my head back and actually laughing out loud.

"Thank you!" I call to the crowd, waving. "Thank you," I repeat, bowing to the band. I look over at Shannon, who is smiling proudly at me from the wings. "Support the arts!" I call into the mic, but when I start to exit, she hustles across the stage and stops me. Linking an arm through mine, she steps up to the microphone.

"What do you think, everybody?" Shannon says mischievously. "Should Miss Bird give us another couple of songs?"

The crowd erupts with encouraging applause, and I look wide-eyed at Shannon. "What should I sing?" I ask quietly.

"Anything," she says. "You've got everybody on their feet already. Keep 'em there."

She waves as she exits again, and I turn around to the band leader. I give him a key and together we play a couple of bluegrass standards that I haven't played since my days in Winnie. Then on a whim, I call Shannon back onstage and put her on the spot the same way she did to me, asking if the crowd wants us to play her famous *American Idol* song. The response is deafening.

When I finally take my bow, I feel like I'm under a magic spell. Backstage, I immediately put Maybelle in her case and grab a bottle of water, downing half of it all at once. My body is still buzzing from the thrill of playing a live venue. Before making my way out to the crowd to join Stella, I take a minute—just a minute—and lean against the padding on the gym wall to let the moment sink in. I want to remember this feeling, this energy, this connection to the music. I feel like I've come home.

"Excuse me," I say, making my way through the crowd.

"OMG, you were amazing," a girl gushes.

"Thanks," I say, smiling and squeezing by.

"I love your song," another girl says. She holds up her cell phone. "I just put it as my ring tone."

"That's awesome," I say, flashing her a big smile, too. "Thank you."

I look for pockets of space in the crowd and try to get to Stella quickly, but it's hard to keep a low profile when you're six feet tall.

"Will you sign my program?" another girl asks shyly. Her friends roll their eyes, but she thanks me profusely as I scrawl my name across the front.

"Bird! You were so good!" Stella calls, holding her arms out as I get close. Her friends scoot over so she can bring me in, hugging me tight. "You guys, this is Bird."

"She's told us all about you," a pretty girl says.

"Yeah, 'Bird this, Bird that,' but we thought you were her imaginary friend," a short guy next to her adds. "Nice to see she hasn't completely gone crazy."

Stella swats him. "This is Erie, and this dork is Ty."

"Hi," I say, giving a small wave.

"Seriously, Bird," Stella gushes, her hands clasping both of my shoulders. "You killed it," she says. "Murdered it. Destroyed it!" She hugs me again, clearly excited by musical homicide. I laugh, hugging her back.

"I liked your song when I heard it on the radio," Erie says, "but you are really good live."

Before I can thank her, Ty jumps in. "Dudes, check out Clay. His fake boob just fell down to his belly button."

We all crack up as the guys onstage dance shamelessly in leotards and black high heels, flipping their palms back and forth with intense attitude, working the famous Beyoncé dance from her hit "Single Ladies." I have to admit, it's pretty entertaining. When they finish, the crowd goes berserk. Sweaty and muscle-bound Clay of the wandering fake breast hollers into the mic, "My girlfriend is doing a monologue next. She's going to be so famous one day. Support the arts!"

Stella rolls her eyes. "Now you know why the jocks are here."

I smile. "I think it's sweet."

"Bird! Bird, honey, that was terrific!" my dad calls. "Bird!" I turn and see my dad waving at me as he weaves through the crowd in his big tan Carhartt jacket, a huge smile on his face. When he reaches me, he grips my shoulders with both hands. "That is the best I've ever heard you on the fiddle, sweetie, and your voice! Wow. You just...that was a remarkable performance. Could you *feel* the crowd?"

"Thanks, Dad," I say, keenly aware of the looks some of Stella's classmates are giving us. I pull away slightly, as if interested in the next act.

"Shoo-wee!" He smiles and shakes his shaggy blond head. "Made me miss it, I'll tell ya that. But oh, honey, that was something else. Your mother is going to be so upset that she missed this," he says. He looks down at his wristwatch. "Speaking of, I need to swing by the store and get her some more cold medicine after I drop you off at Adam's show. Remind me, okay?"

Adam's show.

I can't believe I forgot about that...again. I pull my phone out of my jeans pocket and light up the screen. I've got two texts from Jacob. One from Anita, and one from Adam. I get really anxious when I see that his show started over half an hour ago. "Um, I've really got to go," I tell Stella.

"Oh my God, yes," she says, grabbing her big purse off the ground.

"You don't have to leave, Stella," my dad says, throwing his arm around me. I don't mean to, but I cringe. "I'll take her."

Stella looks at me, not sure how to respond.

"Um, Dad?" I ask. "I'd really like to ride over with Stella if that's okay." He looks slightly taken aback, but I wriggle out from under his arm and continue. "I mean, Mom sounded pretty sick on the phone earlier, and Stella is going to Adam's show, anyway, so you go ahead and get the medicine, and we'll just ride over on our own."

"It's no problem, Mr. Barrett," Stella adds.

"Oh," Dad says, nodding slowly. "Okay, if that's what you want to do."

"It is," I say, smiling up at him. "Thank you so much for coming, Dad. I'll see you tonight?"

"Sure, hon," he says. He squeezes my hand. "You made me one proud papa tonight."

I blush. "Thanks."

"Guys, I'll catch up with you later," Stella tells her friends. She leads us through the crowd, much better at navigating the bodies than I was. Plus, the act onstage now is a fifty-year-old harmonica player, so things have calmed considerably.

As we make it to the back of the gym, I read the text from Adam:

Can't wait to see you.

There are now three messages from Jacob, asking where I am. But it's two voice mails from Dan I just noticed and the text from Anita that stop me in my tracks:

I'm at the school with Dan. Where are you? We need to talk ASAP.

I swallow hard.

"Bird," Stella says, doubling back when she realizes I've stopped following. "What's wrong? You're white as a ghost."

I never do push PLAY to listen to Dan's voice mails, but his voice suddenly booms in my ear all the same. "Bird! What the hell was that?" I turn around and see him stomping toward me, a murderous look on his face and Anita right on his heels. "Did you seriously just give your first public performance as a solo artist without consulting, oh, I don't know, the president of your label?" he roars, his face redder than usual.

"Dan, not here," Anita snaps, flashing a fake smile at the few people in the lobby whose heads have turned at his shouting. She makes a beeline for me, her high heels like bullets across the tile floor. "Bird," she says when she reaches me. "A word?"

I glance over at Stella. "You mind waiting?"

"Not at all," she says. "I'll be by the doors."

Anita links her arm through mine as if we're the best of pals and forcefully leads me to a bench beside the school's trophy case. Only when we're out of earshot of the people getting popcorn or going to the bathroom does she speak.

"Bird, would you care to explain this little stunt?"

I blink. "Stunt?"

"Well, what would you call sneaking around and giving your first performance at a high school gym on a Thursday night to a couple hundred people without any sort of publicity plan whatsoever?" she asks, furious.

"I wasn't sneaking around," I say defensively. "Shannon's opening act got the flu and canceled at the last minute, and I was over at their house songwriting when it all went down and...I don't know. I offered to sing my song. It's no big deal."

"It is most certainly a big deal!" Dan yells, his hands on his head as he stares at me in disbelief.

"Dan," Anita says in a warning voice.

He fumes but takes a deep breath before continuing. "You didn't even think about the two people who are trying to build your career and turn you into a household name. No phone call. No heads-up. You did whatever you wanted and probably just jeopardized everything."

"And did you *fiddle*?" Anita asks, incredulous.

"I—" I stammer, clutching Maybelle's case to my chest. Before I can stop it, there are tears in my eyes. "I just wanted to help Shannon," I explain. "And I really miss performing live."

"That's what a tour is for!" Dan explodes.

I flinch. "I'm sorry," I say truthfully. "I thought that since the song was on the radio and I'd already had my release party, it would be okay."

Anita sighs, pinching the bridge of her nose as if she's got a headache. "Open Highway is a small company, and we had a small release party just to introduce you *and ourselves* to some industry people. What we were planning for your first performance was much bigger."

I look over at the doors to the gym and catch Stella's eye. Her face is full of concern. She gives me a thumbs-up, her eyebrows raised. I nod and she turns back around as another act takes the stage.

At this point, I really don't know what to say. Dan is pacing in front of us, and Anita is glued to her phone. My own buzzes in my pocket, but I don't dare check it.

"Excuse me." A timid voice comes from behind Dan. He nearly jumps out of his skin, but when he turns around, there are two little girls standing there with pens and programs in hand. "Could we please have your autograph?" they ask me.

I sniffle and dab my fingers under my eyes fast before pasting a quick smile on my face. "Sure," I say, scooting off the bench and bending down to their level. "What are your names?"

"I'm Mira, and she's Isla," one of the girls says. "She's shy."

This causes me to smile for real. "Well, you want to know a secret?" The girls nod, so I lean in close and whisper, "The first time I sang lead for my family band, I got a little shy onstage."

Isla's eyes widen. "You did?" she asks softly.

"Oh yes," I say. "My fiddle got me through, though."

The two girls look at each other in wonderment. "I want to play the fiddle," Mira says.

"No, I do," Isla says as if it's a competition. Then she surprises me by giving me a hug, and Mira does the same when it's her turn.

"Okay, girls," their mother says. I hadn't even seen her; she was hanging back. "Let's go."

270

"Mommy, take our picture!" Mira shouts.

Their mother opens her flip phone. "Do you mind?"

"Not at all," I say, still kneeling. I drape an arm around the shoulders of each girl and smile when they shout, "Cheeeeeeese!"

When they walk away, I notice that a small gathering has formed, and more people are waiting for an autograph or picture. As a person who has always learned her lessons quickly, I stand up and address Anita quietly. "So can I talk to these fans, or should we go?"

Dan glances over at the crowd, still seething.

"What's done is done," Anita says, waving me off. "Damage control dictates that you milk it now for all it's worth."

I wait to roll my eyes until after I've turned away, then I step toward the group with a big fake smile.

Over the next hour, it seems like I meet everyone that Stella goes to school with *and* their parents *and* their younger siblings. My cheeks are sore from smiling, and my signature has turned into two large Bs followed by squiggly lines. Anita and Dan sit together on the bench behind me, strategizing and frequently checking their phones, and I hope to God that they've cooled down a little. Finally, Vince Gill takes the stage with his wife, Amy Grant, and everybody runs to the gym, completely forgetting about me.

"What are they doing here?" Dan ponders aloud.

I shrug, searching in my bag for the rest of my water. "Shannon's friends."

"Maybe we can use this," he suggests to Anita. "Say it was Nashville's big artists coming together for community—oh, I don't know. Can you spin this?"

Anita looks at her phone, almost as if unable to believe her eyes. "Maybe I won't have to."

As the two country music legends sing from the gym, Anita says, "You're all over Twitter."

Bird Barrett rocked the house tonight at WMHS! #noticeme

BB surprise performance. Am DYING. #bucketlist #notevenjoking

Bird Barrett is my new fave singer y'all. #noticeme

She scrolls, her eyes skimming as if she's picking and choosing what to read. "And there are all kinds of hash tags: HelloBirdie, BB4Real, NoticeMe."

They both look up at me, wide-eyed. I am just as shocked.

"I knew you were here because a few kids were tagging you," she explains, "but now..." She pauses, disbelieving. "Bird, you're *trending*."

I grab her phone and scroll down the screen. What started as a great night turned into a bit of a nightmare and now seems to have spun around again, as a news reporter approaches me.

"Hello, Bird? I'm Yvonne Moore with NewsChannel 5," an attractive woman says, offering me a well-manicured hand to shake. "Do you think I could ask you a few questions?"

And although I still haven't left the school, it feels like I've finally arrived.

22

"I CAN'T BELIEVE you're a freaking online trending topic!" Stella shouts as we race through the parking lot. "Can you even comprehend that?"

"No," I reply truthfully. It feels like I'm running through fog.

"Nobody trends," she calls, her arms out to her sides. "I mean, natural disasters or politics or super famous people—those are trending topics. And now, you!"

When we reach Stella's car, she blasts the radio and the heaters, and I try to grasp the magnitude of tonight's performance. Anita spun it as "grassroots" and "a way to reach target fans." I think back to my mom and the flyers she made me pass out after every BFB show. I was so stoked each time our band got one new online follower. Now, as

I check to see if I have any new texts, my screen is covered with alert banners showing that the number of my Twitter followers has gone from sixty thousand to almost half a million tonight alone.

"Stella, I'm shaking," I say, holding up my hand as she pulls out of the parking lot. "Listen to this. Top Web searches are WHERE IS BIRD BARRETT FROM?, HOW OLD IS BIRD BARRETT?, and WHERE WAS JASON SAMUELS?, which is ridiculous."

"Can you imagine if he came and I had to give him a ride, too?" Stella asks, starry-eyed.

I roll my eyes.

"Anything from Adam?" she asks as we pull up to a red light. I started texting my brothers and Adam like crazy the minute my Open Highway parents decided not to ground me after all.

"No." I sigh, my leg bouncing up and down nervously. "Dylan and Jacob already left, but Adam hasn't texted me back."

"Maybe he's still there," she says as the light turns green. She punches the gas. "Just explain what happened. He's a musician. He'll get it."

I nod.

"It's not your fault you missed it," she adds.

"I know," I agree, nodding again. "You're right."

I just wish that made me feel better.

"Text me when you find him, and I'll come in," she says, pulling up in front of the bar.

I get out of the car, and she drives off to look for parking. There is a small line, but I am desperate to see Adam, so I walk right to the front and address the guy with the list. "Hi, I'm Bird Barrett. I'm here to see Adam Dean. I should be on the list."

"His set is over," the guy answers gruffly. "You got ID?"

I stifle a groan and open my purse, knowing that every second counts. Obviously, this bar is twenty-one and over and I don't look anything close to that, but I know how these places work: There's a list and my name should be on it. Now, whether he has to let me in if I'm late is another question.

"Oh my gosh, that's Bird Barrett," a girl in line squeals. "I love your song!"

I smile and wave. "Thank you!"

"What song?" the guy with her asks.

Clearly a little drunk already, she starts to sing "Notice Me" while holding up an air mic and closing her eyes.

"OMG, you sing that?" another girl asks. "I freakin' love that song."

"Go on in," the bouncer says, his attitude changing as he holds the door open for me. If I see those girls later, I totally owe them a hug.

Inside, another band is playing an original alt-country piece that makes my head hurt. I look around the dark bar, scanning the crowd for Adam's lean figure, but I don't see him anywhere.

My phone beeps, and I look at the screen hopefully, but it's just Stella:

????

I respond in kind:

☹

Still nothing from Adam.

"Excuse me," I say, leaning up to the bar. I wave at the bartender, who nods my way as he finishes mixing a drink.

"What'll it be?" he asks.

"Um, well, I was wondering if you know if Adam Dean is still here," I say. "He played earlier. About my height, kind of low voice—"

"He left a few minutes ago," the guy says. "Are you 'Lady Bird'?"

Shocked, I blink a couple of times before answering, "Um, yes. How'd you—"

"Adam ordered a drink for you before the show," he says, walking toward the end of the bar closest to the stage and motioning for me to follow. "Let me know if you want a fresh one."

There, sitting on the stool closest to the wall, is a small sign that says: RESERVED: LADY BIRD.

Next to it is a tall glass of Coke, watered down to an almost see-through consistency, the glass dripping onto the seat and drenching the little beverage napkin.

"No," I manage to say, swallowing an enormous lump in my throat. "This is perfect."

"Hello?" I call out as I enter our house late that night. Everything is dark and quiet. "Anybody home?"

"Bird, honey, we're in the living room," my mom calls, her voice scratchy.

I kick off my boots and hang my coat up in the front closet, exhausted from a day that felt like it would never end. The tabloids, work, the performance, the scolding from my label, and missing Adam. I shake my head. It's a miracle I haven't spontaneously combusted.

"How was the show?" my mom asks, meeting me in the kitchen. Her nose is red, her eyes are puffy, her auburn hair is in a messy ponytail, and she's got a large patchwork quilt around her shoulders.

"Aw, Mom," I say, pouting a little. "Are you okay?"

She holds out her arms to me. "I will be once I get a hug from my star."

Even though she's got a cold, I don't hesitate to fall into her arms. I close my eyes and let my mom embrace me, inhaling her honeysuckle-and-VapoRub scent. "I was about to make some more Theraflu," she says. "Do you want some hot cocoa?"

"You read my mind," I say, pulling out a bar stool and patting it. "But you sit. I'll make it."

She smiles at me gratefully and shuffles over. "So how was your show?" she asks again.

"I really don't want to talk about it," I answer.

"I already told you, Aileen," my dad says, entering the kitchen. "She was dynamite. But listen, Bird, honey, Dan called asking me about the performance. Did you forget to tell him?"

I shake my head, annoyed. "I already handled it, Dad," I snap.

"Okay, okay. Just checking," he says, holding his hands up defensively.

"Sorry," I say, sighing. "I'm just tired."

"I bet you are," my mom sympathizes. "You've been working around the clock this month. You almost done with the album?"

"Yeah," I say, grabbing two mugs from above the stove. "Just have to get Dan's approval. And Jack always seems to want to tweak something here or there, but at least we've finally recorded eleven songs and only have to do the one more that I worked on today with Shannon."

"I can't wait to hear it," my dad says.

I pour a package of hot chocolate powder into my mug, medicine powder into my mom's, add water from the tap, and pop them in the microwave. I lose myself in thought as the mugs spin, watch them circle, think about my day, about how the good and bad danced around each other.

"Bird?" my mother asks softly. "Are you okay?"

I inhale deeply, then turn around to face my parents on the loud exhale, leaning against the counter and crossing my arms.

"I'm just exhausted, Mom," I answer truthfully. "It's, like, I always thought to lay down an album you showed up and sang the songs and that was that. But it's all the publicity stuff on top of that, and the interviews, and singing every song until you hate it, and then hearing it back in a whole different way from what you expected, but loving it again, too." Without warning, I've got a lump in my throat.

"And I feel like I mess up when I try to do something nice." I swallow. "And I feel like I have to ask permission to even breathe." I look up, wiping my lower lashes with my knuckle. I turn toward the microwave.

"And then this stuff with Jason..." I say, trailing off. *And Adam*, I think.

My mom walks over, shooing my obviously uncomfortable father out of the room, and grabs a fresh tissue from the wad she has tucked in her robe pocket.

280

"Sorry," I say, dabbing at the corners of my now-wet eyes. "I don't know why I'm crying. I'm not sad. I'm happy. I'm just—"

The microwave beeps, and my mom grabs a bag of mini marshmallows from the cabinet as I bring our mugs over to the bar. The steam rises up and licks at my cheeks.

"You're just plum worn out," she says, placing her hand on mine and squeezing before taking that same hand and brushing the hair off my forehead. We each take a stool and blow on our hot drinks. My mom runs her fingers through my hair, lulling me into a wide-awake sleep.

"You know who I think about when I get so tired or frustrated that I just want to quit?" I ask, staring into my chocolate drink. "Caleb."

I glance up at her, and she smiles back sadly. "Me too."

"I keep thinking about what Brother James always said about the music—"

"Let it bring you together," we say simultaneously.

I nod. "But these days it feels like it's tearing me away from all of you." My voice cracks and a tiny tear escapes, sliding down my cheek and plopping right smack into my hot chocolate.

My mom rubs my back. We sit together, in silence, letting the night settle in around us. It's almost as if time stands still, as if we're both gripped by a profound need to do nothing more than exist in this moment. She rubs my back, around and around, and I sink into myself, feel the hot cocoa coat my throat and heat my chest, finally able to just stop—to just *be*.

"Honey, we're home!" Dylan calls from the entryway.

And like that, the spell is broken. I give my mother a small smile, and she lifts her hand from my back, turning toward the door and the sounds of my brothers. I hear them wiping off their boots on the mat and laughing about a well-endowed lady snowman someone built out front.

"Hey, fellas," my dad says, coming back in. I wonder if he's been hovering. I look over at him and smile. My dad has no clue what to do in emotional situations, but he never entirely checks out, either. "How was the show?"

The little kitchen feels even smaller when the guys walk in, but it also feels nice. As soon as they see my hot chocolate, they help themselves to some as well, my dad getting in on the action this time. I smile, watching their clumsy dance around each other. As one grabs a pack of cocoa, the other reaches across someone's shoulder for a mug, then somebody's filling up a cup with water. This is a typical scene from my childhood, except the kitchen would be rolling down the highway.

"The show was awesome," Dylan answers enthusiastically. "Adam's got some really good new stuff. He was supposed to eat with us afterward, but he ended up getting approached by this guy from ASCAP, so he stayed and talked to him. Hopefully that'll go somewhere." He looks over at me, and smiles. "We missed you, though, Bird. You should've told us about your show. Stella texted that you signed, like, a million autographs. You must have been a rock star."

Jacob snorts. "I'll say. Have you guys been online?" He holds up his phone.

"Let me see that," my mom says, holding out her hand. My dad leans over her shoulder as she scrolls through Jacob's Twitter feed. "Bird, honey, this is unbelievable."

"It really is," I say. I get up and put my mug in the sink before excusing myself. "I think I'm going to call it a night, y'all."

My mom gives me one more hug, and we all filter out of the kitchen, Jacob on my heels as I walk down the hall to my room.

"Good night, Bird," he says, passing me.

I can't help myself. "So does Adam hate me now?"

The question seems to take him off guard. "Hate you?" he hedges, turning slightly toward me. "No. No way. I think he was just a little disappointed, you know?"

"Yeah," I say glumly, leaning against my bedroom door frame. "I knew I'd be late, but I definitely thought I would make it at least for a few songs. But then Dan and Anita showed up at the school and they were pretty mad and—" I sigh. "The time just got away from me."

"Yeah, we figured," he says, nodding. I can tell he really wants to get to his own room. "He sounded great, though. His new stuff is really good. And when the show was over, he just seemed bummed that you weren't there. That's it."

"Well, did he say anything?" I press.

"Nope," Jacob replies. He's a terrible liar.

"Tell me."

He pauses. "Well, he asked me if you're really going out with Jason Samuels."

I lunge forward. "What'd you say? What'd you tell him?"

Jacob shrugs. "I told him, yeah, you went out with him," he says, as if the answer is evident.

A panic rises in my chest. No. No, no, no, no, no. This was not supposed to happen. It was just business!

"I *went* out with him," I say, "but I'm not *going* out with him. He knows that, right?"

"I don't know," he says. "Is there a difference?"

My brain nearly explodes. "Yes, there's a difference!" I yell, squeezing my head with both hands. "God, Jacob! There's a huge difference!"

He throws his hands up, suddenly every bit as exasperated as I am. "Look, 'Song Bird,' it's not my job to keep track of my little sister's celebrity love life."

"Agh!" I shout, turning on my heel. I shut my door firmly and throw myself across my bed, physically and emotionally exhausted. The tabloid lies, the great song-writing session, the awesome live performance, the horrific scolding about said performance, trending on Twitter, and then blowing any chance I ever had with Adam. This was the best worst day of my life.

And I think there might be a song there, but right now I don't have it in me to write it.

23

"So not a word from Adam?" Stella asks me. "Nada?"

"Nothing," I say forlornly. "I texted him yesterday and haven't heard back."

"Yeah, he's mad," she confirms as she browses the boots at this cute little shop over in East Nashville. "Do you like these?"

"They're okay," I say distractedly.

She looks at me as if I've hurt her soul.

"I don't know," I whisper to her as we move away from the owner. "They look old. Worn down."

"They're vintage," she says, rolling her eyes.

I glance at the turquoise low-cut boots she's holding up, but it's hard for me to focus on shopping right now. I missed Adam's show, and then he played for Kayelee last night (and, as her website showed, he looked adorable). I blew it.

Stella puts the boots down and turns her attention toward a rack of purses. "You know you've got to call him, right?"

"I don't know," I say, checking my phone for the gazillionth time. Now I'm afraid to let it out of my sight. "We usually text."

"Yeah, but you've kissed," she says, unsnapping a beaded clutch. "And after you kissed, you started flexting."

I look at her inquisitively.

"Flirting over text," she explains. "But then you went out with Jason Samuels—"

"It wasn't like that!"

She looks at me and says, "*I* know that. But *he* doesn't. And then you missed his show. So for all he knows, you're not interested anymore."

"What?" I whisper fiercely.

"Well, I mean, those pictures were pretty cozy," she says.

"Don't say 'cozy,'" I warn her.

She arches her eyebrows and backs away, perusing the handbags again. "So that's why you need to call him," she says simply, picking up a cute black clutch and posing with it in front of a full-length mirror. "I think I'm going to get this."

I nod absentmindedly and pull up his number on my phone as she pays, determined to call him and set everything straight. The minute our shoes hit the sidewalk, I push CALL.

287

"What am I even supposed to say if he answers?" I ask Stella as it rings.

"Just tell him what happened," she says.

"Right. I'll just explain it. Anita set up the Jason thing. I should have told him about it, but it was just business and no big deal. And I should have texted him about his show, but I really did think I could make it. And work has to come first, right? And—"

"Hey." His voice comes over the line.

"Adam! Hi!" I say, ecstatic that he answered. But then his voice drones on, and I realize that it's his voice mail. I hate when people pause at the beginning of their messages. The beep comes before I know it, and unfortunately, I hadn't prepared a monologue.

"Adam, hey, it's me. Um, Bird. Anyway, I'm so sorry I missed your show Thursday. I heard it was great. I mean, I was, um, working, and you won't even believe how that whole thing got off track, but um, Jacob and Dylan said you were great, well, of course you were great, I mean, I love your music, and, you know, I really hate that I couldn't be there. I should've texted you. I—"

I feel like I'm drowning here. Nothing is coming out right. I look up at Stella for support, but her expression is pained and she shakes her head. So I plow on.

"So, yeah. Call me back. Or text me. Or e-mail. Or

whatever." I want to explain everything, but the voice mail is not going great as it is, so I doubt I'll be able to articulate what really happened, anyway. "So okay, cool. Talk to you later. Call me back. If you want. Okay, bye."

I pull the phone from my ear and push END. Then I stare at it, feeling a little queasy. "Did I just make things worse?"

"No," Stella lies. I bury my face in my hands, and she rubs my back as we walk toward her car. "But maybe you should stick to saying it in a song."

Dad says grace and then we load up our plates. This is the first Sunday in a while that I haven't had to work. I went to church with my family and helped Mom make lunch when we got home. No recording, no publicity, just an almost eerie silence from Open Highway. I laid down the final track Friday, so now Dan is listening to the album and deciding with Anita what the best next step will be.

Meanwhile, I get an honest-to-goodness real weekend with my family. Yesterday I slept in, hung out in the afternoon with Stella, and then caught up on a little homework, which almost made my mom pass out since it was my idea. I was so far ahead in my course work before being discovered, and now Jacob's almost finished, leaving me in his dust. With all the attention I've gotten since the Jason Samuels gossip and the fund-raiser, it's actually been pretty nice to have a normal weekend.

"I was thinking we could all go down to the Station Inn tonight," Dylan says.

"I'm game," I say. "I'll bring Maybelle."

"Cool," he says, twisting his napkin. "Um, also, I have something else to say. It's sort of an announcement." He pauses. "I've been applying to colleges. Real colleges, with campuses, not just the online thing."

I freeze, my glass halfway to my mouth. "What?" I look to my folks for their reaction, but it's obvious that they already know about it and approve. "Where?"

He shrugs. "Somewhere with a good music program. I've talked to a guy over at Belmont, but I'm also looking beyond Nashville. Maybe New York, Boston, I don't know."

"Me too, actually," Jacob adds, wiping his mouth with his napkin. He completely misses a smudge of sauce on his cheek. "I'm almost done with my high school courses, so I'll enroll in the fall. Somewhere warm all year long. Probably Cali. I can't stand winter."

"So, everyone's just going to leave?" I ask quietly.

"Well," Dylan says, his eyes not unkind, "we can't really wait around here. I mean, I'm pretty sure the Barrett Family Band is over."

I nod, knowing in my heart that he's right. Maybe I've known it for a while. But now that it's been said out loud, I feel a deep sadness, a loud *thud* as if a very important chapter of my life has just closed.

And I know that it's all because of me.

My eyes blur a little, but I blink back my tears. My brothers have stood behind me for the past five months, putting their lives on hold and my schedule before their own, even though they would gladly change places with me in a heartbeat. They've never made me feel guilty and never treated me with resentment, so now that they want to follow their own paths, it's only right that I support them, too.

"Well, I know you'll both get in wherever you apply," I say with a small smile. "But what about this: Instead of the Station Inn tonight, we stay home. Dad can get the fireplace going later on, we'll make s'mores in the living room, and we play, just us. Just the BFB."

Jacob nods and Dylan visibly relaxes. I know it helped them that I didn't make it about me, so I act like everything is normal, but to be honest, I'm a little sad at the reality that nothing will ever be normal again. Or rather, that the Barrett family's idea of "normal" has once again changed so much.

Against Anita's advice, I do a Web search of my name later. Nobody had heard of Bird Barrett a few months ago, but now the search returns pages of hits. Blog posts, my You-Tube video, lyrics to "Notice Me," bootlegs of the fund-raiser, and lots of images. I try to stay off my fan forum, but it's impossible. And I know it's ridiculous, but for every twenty nice things people write, there is a negative comment that will overshadow them all and totally bum me out. At the present, a fashion blogger has posted a picture of me next to Dakota Fanning and, apparently, the voters think she wore it best.

"Some fans," I grumble, clicking off the page.

My cell phone rings, and I reach for it, expecting it to be Stella, but my heart skips a beat when Adam's name appears.

"Hello?" I say, answering immediately. I stand up and walk over to the mirror, running my hand through my hair as if he can see me.

"Hey, Bird. It's Adam, returning your call," he says, a little too formally.

"Yeah, I know. Hey," I say, clutching my lucky rock pendant and plowing ahead with my apology. "Adam, I am so sorry that I missed your show the other night."

"Yeah," he says, softening. "I missed you. But it looks like that fund-raiser was a big success."

"Yeah," I say, "bigger than I'd expected actually. We

raised lots of money for Stella's school, but also, it was really great being onstage again, you know? I've been in the studio so long that I didn't realize how much I missed an audience. It was amazing to share my music and actually see people enjoy it."

"I definitely get that," Adam says. I can picture him nodding. "And that's exactly where your focus should be: your music. The iron is hot, you know what I mean? You've got to take every opportunity and really make a name for yourself."

"Totally," I say, relieved that he's being so cool about it all. That's what would be so wonderful about dating Adam: He's a serious, talented musician who gets me, but he gets the business, too. "I think we've finally finished the album now, though, and I *have* to hear your new stuff. My brothers said it's really good."

"Aw, that's cool," he says. "I'm going to upload a new song to my website today, so maybe you can check it out."

"Oh," I say. Then I take a deep breath and go for it, flirting. "I was kind of hoping for a private performance."

"Bird," he says softly. "I don't think we—" He stops himself. "I'm in Austin, actually. I know a guy out here who wants to help me make a demo, so I left right after the gig with Kayelee."

"Really?" I ask, hollowly. "That's great."

The line goes quiet. Adam and I have always been able to joke around, even when I was totally crushing on him. It was always easy. But as the seconds tick by in silence, it's like we're out of sync for the first time.

"So you know that stuff with Jason Samuels?" I say quickly, the words spilling out on top of each other. I really need Adam to know the truth about that. "My publicist set that up. It was some crazy PR strategy to get my song in his movie. We're just friends. I couldn't believe how it got blown up like that, and I just wanted you to know."

"Oh yeah, I think I saw something about that," Adam says nonchalantly. I wish he sounded a little more relieved. "I didn't peg a guy like that as your type."

"Right," I say, my stomach in knots. I feel like this conversation is going downhill fast, and I need Adam to know that I want to take this thing with him somewhere real. "Listen, about that day in the car . . . after the Pancake Pantry—"

"Yeah," Adam interrupts. He takes a deep breath. "About that . . ."

I don't like his tone. I want to tell him to stop right there, not to say anything more.

"I shouldn't have done that," he continues, his voice apologetic, regretful.

"No!" I nearly shout. "I'm glad you did. Adam, I'm really glad you did."

The line goes quiet again. I can hear his breath; I hold mine. My pulse is racing, my mind, too. I feel like I'm teetering on a ledge. His next sentence will have the power to pull me back or push me over.

"It's just—" he starts in that same tone. He takes a big breath. "Okay, to be honest, Bird? You're blowing up. You're on the verge of something so major that it needs one hundred percent of your energy and your time and your commitment. You missed my show for work, not because you didn't want to be there, and that was the right thing. You'd hate me if you looked back at it all one day and thought you missed out on something big because you put a guy ahead of yourself. I just think . . ."

His voice trails off, and I feel myself start to fall. I know if I say anything, I might start to cry.

"I mean, you've got this album you're about to promote, you'll be touring I'm sure, and it feels like, I don't know, it was probably a bad time for— " He stops abruptly. "Hang on."

I hear him turn away and talk to somebody in the background about rehearsal.

"Hey, sorry about that," he says, finally coming back on the line. "Anyway, I've got to get going."

"Oh, okay."

"Adam!" a girl's voice calls in the background. I bolt upright on the bed, my spine like a lightning rod, her voice the jolt.

"I'm coming!" he calls back. "Hey, I've got to go."

"Okay," I manage to say. I'm sure he can hear my disappointment. I don't know how anybody with an ear as good as his could miss it.

He sighs. "Good luck on the album, Lady Bird," he says quietly. "You know I'm a huge fan, right?"

A lump the size of Texas forms in my throat, and the tears fall fat and fast so that I can barely eke out my reply. "Uh-huh."

"Good. Okay, then. Take care."

"Bye, Adam," I finally say, my voice cracking.

But no need to worry about my pride, because the line has already gone dead on his end.

"Bird?" my dad calls a couple of hours later, knocking at my door.

"Not now!" I yell back, lying sprawled out under my comforter, staring at my ceiling, exhausted and completely cried out.

He cracks my door anyway. "I built the fire—" he starts, but then he sees my swollen, red face, and his own crumples. "Hey, sweetheart," he says, walking over slowly and sitting awkwardly on the edge of my bed. "What's wrong?"

Right when I thought I'd finally gotten my emotions under control, my dad walks in and treats me like he did when I was a little girl, back when he could kiss the scrape on my knee and make it all better. My eyes well up again, and I pull the comforter over my head.

"Hon," he says softly. I feel the mattress dip as he reaches over me for the box of tissues that I've nearly emptied. He takes one and gently pulls the comforter down, handing it to me. I take a deep breath and sit up against my pillow, deciding that it might be quicker to hear him out than wait him out.

"I know there was some part in all of us that wished we could go on forever as the Barrett Family Band," he says tenderly. A small sob escapes. He has no idea why I'm really crying.

"But, sweetie, there's no going backward in life," he says, smiling sadly. "Even if you hadn't signed with Open Highway, the band would have run its course. It did its job." He takes my hand and squeezes. "It brought us together in a way that honored Caleb. But, Bird, if we stop being a band, it doesn't mean that we'll stop being a family. Right?"

I blow my nose and nod. *Sure, Dad.*

"I'm proud of you, Bird. It brings your mom and me so much joy, watching you spread your wings and fly."

My dad is doing his best here, so I fight the impulse to roll my eyes at the awful play on words.

297

"Dad," I say, looking at him through blurry eyes, "I love you, but I just want to be alone right now."

He nods sagely and kisses my forehead before heading into the living room, where I hear my family tuning their instruments. I know I promised them that I'd play tonight, but the BFB days only remind me of Adam, which makes me start crying all over again.

24

"It's me," I say into the intercom outside Shannon's building. Dan decided my album needed a "big-hit ballad," so here we go again, back to the grind.

Shannon buzzes me in, and I make my way across the lobby to the elevator, surprised when it opens and I see Stella, Ty, and Erie.

"Oh, hey, y'all," I say, wondering where they're going and wishing I could go with. Stella came over for a while last night—she's really been there for me with all of this Adam stuff—but seeing the sympathy on her face again now isn't helping.

"You okay?" she asks, stopping me.

"No," I answer honestly.

She pulls me aside and gives me a giant hug. "Stop torturing yourself, Bird. This really will get better."

I don't want to lose it in the lobby of her building, especially not with her friends watching, so I pull away and move toward the elevator.

"And use it," she says, pointing to my heart and then upstairs. "You need another song, so use it."

I wipe my nose and nod, waving to the group as they head out into the cold. I consider Stella's advice. It's not like Adam hasn't been my muse before.

But an hour later, after thumbing through my songwriting journal over and over, trying to piece together scraps of different songs while adding verses that don't really fit, I throw up my hands in frustration. Everything I've come up with has been total crap.

"You want to take a break?" Shannon asks.

"Yeah, sure," I say, setting down my guitar.

I follow her into the kitchen, where she pours us both a cup of chamomile tea with honey. We sit together, neither saying a word, listening as the neighbors' kids race across their floor upstairs.

"Is everything okay, Bird?" she finally asks, genuinely concerned. "You seem...distracted today."

I take a sip of tea and finger the bamboo place mats. "I'm a little down, I guess. My brothers are moving away so that means, you know, the family band is officially split-ting up."

Shannon nods knowingly. "That's tough."

"Yeah." I take another drink, follow its warmth to my belly, and sigh heavily. Everything feels fuzzy, out of con-trol, wrong.

"Can I do anything to help?" she asks.

I smile at her. My relationship with the Crossleys is one of the best parts about landing my record deal. "It just feels like everything in my life is going wrong except for the music, you know? And now, I can't even get that right."

I grab my lucky rock, rolling the pendant between my thumb and index finger, but I don't feel any better.

"Bird, has there ever been a day, through all of this, when you've gone to the studio or come over here and haven't felt like singing?" Shannon asks.

"Yeah," I admit.

"And what did you do?" she asks.

"I sang anyway."

Shannon smiles. "Exactly."

I feel a spark. My mind clears. I get up from the counter and walk briskly into the living room. I grab my guitar and my journal, scribbling across the page and picking out a few chords. The chorus writes itself before Shannon can even get back into her chair. I sing, I play, and my world regains clarity—thanks to the music. Always thanks to the music.

"You ready, Bird?" Jack calls from the booth.

I pull on my headphones in the live room and give him a thumbs-up. Dan and Anita are here today, along with my dad and Shannon. Usually, I would be nervous about the crowd, about the fact that the president of my label is itching for another hit to finish my album, but I'm not nervous. I'm confident.

We're calling the album *Wildflower*. It was my idea. A nod to my mom, who loves wildflowers so much that she named me after a random president's wife, but also a nod to Adam, who saw the sweetness in that, even if it makes me heartbroken now.

I don't know what this year will hold, I don't know how *Wildflower* will sell, and I don't know when my heart will mend. But I do know now that through it all, I'll "Sing Anyway."

The music flows through my headphones, and I step up to the mic. I close my eyes and sing:

"I shake the sleep from my head,
I drag myself out of bed,

You're still gone.
My heart can't handle this pain,
How do I sing in the rain?
The mic's on."

Jack doesn't stop me, so I keep going. I sing for what I almost had with Adam but lost. I sing for the years when I lived on the road with my family and for the months to come, on the road with a whole new family of sorts. And for once, instead of worrying about what the label will think, I sing for me.

"All right," Jack says as the last notes of the song fade out. I open my eyes and look at him through the glass, waiting for direction. "That's a wrap."

Confused, I ask, "That's it?" There are usually so many more takes.

"You nailed it," he answers simply. "Sometimes it happens that way."

Anita and Dan are talking enthusiastically behind him, already plotting the next steps for the rise of Bird Barrett, I'm sure. Jack grins up at me and plays my song back over the speakers, nodding along as if it were his baby. My dad and Shannon smile proudly at me from behind the glass and gesture for me to join them.

I take off my headphones and hook them over the music stand for the last time for a while, a bittersweet feeling as I prepare to leave the studio. Such a short time ago, this was all new to me: the fancy mic, the booth, the mixing, all the opinions. Now the studio feels like a refuge, and if what Anita tells me is true, things are about to get a whole lot crazier: sold-out arenas, screaming fans. It sounds intense, but I'm excited about sharing my music with the world.

And as much as I love Nashville, it's time to get back on the road.

ACKNOWLEDGMENTS

I must begin this page by thanking my youngest son, Rhett. When you were only three weeks old, I started writing this book. We didn't have the luxury of lounging around the house snuggling or taking naps together like I was able to do with your big brother, but you have always been a go-along guy and you were (literally) right by my side as I typed quietly next to you.

And to my two-year-old son, Knox, I have to thank you as well, because when a new baby and a new book came into our lives at the same time demanding your momma's attention, you adapted so easily it was as if our lives hadn't changed at all.

And to my husband, Jerrod, thank you for encouraging me to take this project and for believing that I could manage it all when I really didn't think I could. I thought I'd miss every baby milestone, every manuscript deadline. I thought I would let everyone down.

Which leads me to my agent, Alyssa Reuben at Paradigm, who has faith in me when I don't always have it in myself. Thank you for believing in me and having my back always. You are the best in the biz.

To my friends Pam Gruber and Elizabeth Bewley at Poppy, thank you for being my champions on this project. You were right—it was the perfect fit. And, Pam, your editorial instincts are spot-on.

And to my new friends, Kathryn Williams and Dan Tucker at Aerial, thank you for late-night phone convos and data-loss-recovery assistance. But mostly, thank you for trusting me with your concept. I love this book, these characters, this story—our team. And I'm so glad that Alissa Moreno lent her songwriting expertise to Bird's big hit, "Notice Me." I love that song!

There are few people I trust to care for my children, and I am so blessed to have had you in our lives as I wrote this novel. Glen and Vicki Whitaker, Kim Pace, the Rodie family, Jesse Szombathy, Jeanne Kullas, Lacy Bove, Miss Barbara, Melissa Mott, and the Mendez family—you are all very special to us.

There are few people I trust to care for my novel, but I have also been blessed in this area. To Bobbie Jo Whitaker, to whom I must give credit for the killer "Bon Jovi" line, thank you for your insight and honest yet tactful feedback.

To Becky Bennett, Vicki Whitaker, and Cindy Johnson, thank you for saying, "Keep writing! We want more!"

To the insanely attentive copy editors at Little, Brown, Wendy Dopkin and Chandra Wohleber, thank you for being rock stars at your jobs. The "lol" comments and smiley face emoticons went above and beyond.

And to my own personal copy editor, Loretta Fryman, thank you. And, yes, we are still on speaking terms.

And to my fellow writers Micol Ostow, Melissa Walker, and Katie Sise, I can't tell you how much I treasure breaks between deadlines with y'all, talking Books 'N Babies. And shout-out to my Bestie from the Westie, Cat Patrick.

Every good piece of contemporary fiction requires authentic details to ground it in this world. I must give Research Thanks to my Facebook friends for commenting on everything from colloquialisms to bluegrass bands.

Thanks to my Nashville tour guides Gary Dempsey, Annie Johnson, and Victoria Schwab.

Thanks to Darla Maguet for knowledge on all things home-schooling.

Thanks to David Hansen at McMahon RV in Irvine, CA, and to Jim Knestrick of Knestrick by Design and Karen Rippy of Zia Florist in Nashville, TN.

And thanks to Mamaw and Papaw for being my #1 Fans since the day I was born. This book is for you.

Big Props to my Pop Culture Peeps: Chad Schwalbach, Matt and Katherine Whitaker, Whitney Grannis, Liss Marie Mendez, Becky Bennett, Lisa Mantineo, and especially to my niece, Haleigh Maguet, and nephews Zach, Camron, Kaleb, Ethan, and Seth Maguet.

And to my readers, I hope you enjoy this series. Thank you for supporting me. Bird has great fans, but I have the best in the world.

Jeremiah 29:11

TURN THE PAGE FOR
THE COMPLETE LYRICS
AND SHEET MUSIC FOR
BIRD'S HIT SINGLE,
"NOTICE ME."

NOTICE ME

VERSE

Maybe you like me, or do you like me not?
May be wishful thinking, but wishin's all I've got.
Time to hit the pavement, on the road again.
Have you ever dreamed of being more than friends?

PRE-CHORUS

Oh, maybe it's insane.
We've got so much that's changing,
And nobody knows where this could go.

CHORUS

If I'm a wildflower,
Then you're the blowin' breeze.
I could get swept away,
Don't know where you'd take me.
And maybe we could shine
So bright in the sunlight.
Is it real? Do you see?
Say you notice me.

VERSE

You're shooting for the stars, I'm over the moon.
Life takes us in circles, and we're always on the move.
There's so much to say here, so much more to do.
I don't even really know if it's about me and you.

PRE-CHORUS

Oh, I wanna try it.
Maybe shouldn't fight it.
Who knows where this thing could go?

CHORUS

If I'm a wildflower,
Then you're the blowin' breeze.
I could get swept away,
Don't know where you'd take me.
And maybe we could shine
So bright in the sunlight.
Is it real? Do you see?
Say you notice me.

BRIDGE

[FIDDLE SOLO]

CHORUS

If I'm a wildflower,
Then you're the blowin' breeze.
I could get swept away,
Don't know where you'd take me.
And maybe we could shine
So bright in the sunlight.
Is it real? Do you see?
Say you notice me.
Notice me. Say you notice me.

Notice Me